The Dirty Players

PHILIP FIELDING

Copyright © 2016 Philip Fielding
All rights reserved.

To Mum, Dad, Paul and Pete

CHRISTMAS, MANCHESTER, 1989

CONTENTS

SATURDAY	11
SUNDAY	41
MONDAY	67
CHRISTMAS EVE	113
CHRISTMAS DAY	167
BOXING DAY	201
FRIDAY	217
SATURDAY	251
APRIL FOOLS' DAY, 1990	315

He who makes a beast of himself
gets rid of the pain of being a man.

   Hunter S Thompson

SATURDAY

THE Belle Vue centre forward had become immune to the thrill of football fans chanting his name. He bent his left knee, put his hands on his hips and dropped into a groin stretch, oblivious to the supporters who had got up early and made the journey down from Manchester to watch him and his teammates perform.

Over twenty thousand people were at Upton Park in east London and the atmosphere was crackling with static. West Ham were one of the biggest clubs in the division. Meat pies were being washed down with pints of Carling Black Label by men in festive mood. *I Wish It Could Be Christmas Everyday* was booming out of tannoy speakers and ringing around the stadium.

It was just before three o'clock and the groundsmen had done their job well considering the overnight blizzards. Piled-up snow obscured the advertising boards and while the best pitch in the division felt soggy underfoot, there was plenty of grass on it.

The centre forward was Callum Murphy. He was twenty-five and should have been playing for Manchester United, not Belle Vue. That wasn't just his opinion; everyone said so. He'd done all the right training, played for the right junior teams, got through the right trials and become a United apprentice. He was playing well in the reserves and thought he was getting a first team call-up when the manager told him he wasn't in his plans.

Cal tucked the yellow and black-striped number ten shirt into the back of his shorts and bent down to touch the toes of his New Balance boots. As he held the stretch he felt a deep, intense burn in his cold hamstrings. The West Ham players were warming up by doing practice drills at the other end of the ground. He rubbed his crew cut as he wondered which of his opponents would be marking him. The uncompromising defender all the papers were talking about, Julian Dicks, probably.

His first touch would be vital. If he miscontrolled the ball and Dicks nipped in and took it away, doubt might creep into his game. He couldn't afford for that to happen. He needed to be in control from the first whistle.

The Belle Vue manager George McNeill, a sixty-seven-year-old who had led five clubs in the lower divisions, was on the pitch near the South Bank goal. He was talking to his captain Jed Brennan, who had won the coin toss. Jed was two years older than Cal. He had dark blonde hair tied at the back in a pony tail and a wispy beard that didn't join up with his sideburns. What he lacked in skill, he made up for with arse-kissing. Cal thought he was a weapon.

The whistle went. Cal took the kick off but had to wait a few minutes for his next touch. He liked to play down the middle of the pitch, rarely going wider than the edges of the penalty areas. Dicks was marking him closely and let him know he was in for a tussle by giving him a swift dig in the ribs with his fist. Cal pretended he hadn't felt it, quickly trapped a pass and nudged the ball to his teammate Edo De Haan.

The Dutchman's dreadlocks swished from side to side as he surged forward, but his attempted through-ball for Cal was hit too hard and rolled into the arms of West Ham's goalkeeper Phil Parkes.

Dicks put his arm around Cal's waist as they got their breath back. "Fuck me Callum, you're like a blue-arsed fly today," he said. He pronounced fuck as fark because he was from the West Country. "Are you on whizz or something?"

"You've got me there," Cal grinned. "I nicked a bag of it off your sister when I fucked her last week."

Dicks sniggered. "Of course. You're the one with the tiny cock she was telling me about."

Everyone in football swore. Shit, fuck, bastard, cunt, arsehole and bollocks. Even Doris in the canteen asked if you wanted fucking gravy on your steak and kidney pie.

With twenty minutes gone, the game had taken its shape. David Kelly, a bustling striker who had recently joined the Hammers from Walsall, was causing problems for Belle Vue's centre-back Mark Shaw. Shaw was not taking being schooled well and muttering to himself. This worried Cal.

A long ball was hoofed diagonally across the pitch. Shaw turned quickly and tried to get in a defensive position goalside of his tormentor, but slipped. Kelly pounced on the loose ball and cut inside towards the penalty area. The striker's balance was amazing and the crowd buzzed in appreciation. Shaw regained his footing and lunged in. Kelly saw the tackle coming and hurdled Shaw's legs. Dropping a shoulder to wrong-foot goalkeeper Nigel Hornby, he shifted the ball onto his left foot and drilled a low shot into the far corner of the net. Goal! The roar that went up was so loud it rattled the corrugated iron on the Upton Park stands.

Nigel was a giant of a man. Cal had been the Best Man at his wedding. The giant spat a large ball of snot on the pitch and glared at Shaw. "Mark!" he snarled. "What the fuck are you doing? Sort your fucking head out!"

Shaw's sweaty face was bright red. "That were Edo's fucking fault, not mine," spat the Yorkshireman, pointing out his teammate like an IRA supergrass at the Old Bailey. "He left me wide open. I'm marking two players here."

Shaw turned and ran away to get in position for the re-start, shaking his head and muttering again. Cal shouted to him to calm down, but Shaw ignored him.

When the game got going again West Ham kept attempting attacks but the Belle Vue defenders had finally settled into the rhythm of the game. Well-timed tackles were keeping their opponents at bay.

Two minutes before half-time, Edo picked up a loose ball inside the centre circle and chipped a crisp pass sideways towards the winger Simon Cosgrove, or Cozzer as he was nicknamed. He was only twenty and though Cal ripped the piss out of him any chance he got, he looked after him like a little brother. Kelly tried to intercept the ball before it reached Simon, but Cal stepped between them and sneakily let his elbow connect with Kelly's jaw. He fell to the ground as if gunned down by a sniper. He was clutching his face. A painful shockwave ran along Cal's funny bone so he knew Kelly had felt the blow.

"Play on," shouted the referee as several West Ham players yelled for a free kick. Cal drove forward with the ball at his feet. As he pulled his leg back, Dicks threw his body forward to block the shot. Instead of shooting, Cal calmly rolled the ball sideways into Edo's stride. He had the goal at his mercy... but his shot pinged off the outside of the left post and spun safely wide.

The referee blew his whistle for half time. As Cal made his way to the tunnel, Dicks jogged past him and threatened: "Any more elbows and I'll break your fucking legs." Cal, who had heard it all before, jettisoned a large ball of snot of his own to the turf.

>>>

THE first snowflakes of the city's winter melted on the windows of the black taxi as it grumbled along Wilmslow Road in Rusholme. Neon signs from outside lit up the passenger's face, which was heavy with makeup and surveyed her surroundings with familiarity.

It was Christmas but the lights of Manchester's Curry Mile shone all year round. Indian Cuisine, Halal, Karahi, Shish, they proclaimed in red, green and yellow neon. The wipers swiped crescent-shaped arcs on the windscreen as they passed Spice of Life, where she had once eaten a Madras so hot that it virtually burned through her. The brake lights of the car in front kept flashing on and off, making her squint involuntarily.

The passenger's name was Victoria Heath and she was also twenty-five. Under the trenchcoat she was wearing was cheap lingerie and nothing else. Her black lace knickers made her thighs itch. The purple underwired basque, from the same market stall, nipped the tender skin under her arms. Her blonde wig from a fancy dress shop on Oldham Street itched her scalp. She wanted to scratch herself all over.

She uncrossed and re-crossed her legs, trying to get comfy, but exposed her stocking tops and suspenders just as the driver looked in his rear view mirror. Their eyes met and he blushed. She hadn't meant to give him an eyeful but supposed she should be pleased her appearance was having the desired effect as the BBC commentator Stuart Hall's voice crackled from the speaker beside her.

Here we are at the Coliseum of East London where a match of titanic proportions is taking place. West Ham lead Belle Vue by a goal to nothing at the interval but the gulf in class is as wide as the Thames. The Irons' lead was provided by fleet-footed Kelly after twenty two minutes. Taking advantage of a pantomime slip by Shaw, he danced into the area, floodlit as if by Jehovah, his shot angled into the corner, a thing of beauty, swerving, dipping, a fearsome parabola, unstoppable! Meanwhile, Belle Vue were cruel. Rustic, rumbustious, raucous, they appear rumbled. Murphy, fortunate not to get his marching orders after leading with an elbow. Forget fantasy football from them, it's back to the coal face with sweat and guts... otherwise, it's tears!

The green digits of the clock set in the dashboard blinked from 15:57 to 15:58 as the cab reached Platt Fields Park and turned right into Brighton Grove. The cabbie pulled up at the kerb, pressed a button on the meter on the dash and slid open the glass partition between them. "Here you are, love... number nineteen. That'll be three quid please."

She smiled. "Any chance you could hang about for an hour for twenty quid? I'll need a ride back into town."

He smiled back. He was about sixty and three stone overweight with a blotchy, unshaven face. Twenty quid was more than he'd taken since he clocked on at noon. "Course I will, love. I'll just park up the road on the right there and wait." He nodded where he meant.

"Great. See you in a bit, then."

She got out, opened the gate of number nineteen and walked up the path, her stiletto heels clattering on an intricate black and white mosaic of tiles. The garden was tidy and the house looked well-maintained. Three stone steps led up to a large, wide front door with stained glass panels. Rusholme was an old part of the city where wealthy fabric traders once lived. She rang the bell and waited. She could feel the cold wetness of the sleet hitting her ankles through her fishnets.

Eventually a teenager opened the door. He was tall for his age, about fifteen she reckoned, pushing six foot, and wearing a tidy suit and a skull cap.

"Yes?" he said, immediately suspicious of her.

She employed her sexy smile again, but nervously this time. "I'm Scarlett," she said.

"Scarlett?"

"That's my name. Don't wear it out." What the hell was she saying? This was no primary school playground. She took a deep breath and composed herself. "Are you gonna invite me in or what? It's... fucking freezing out here."

"What do you want?"

She could hear classical music coming from inside. Bach perhaps. She looked at her watch. "Darren from Sensations sent me. This is 19 Brighton Grove, innit?" She was trying to sound common.

"You've got the right address but..." his jaw dropped as she unbuttoned her trenchcoat and opened it. Her long, slim legs were clad in sheer black stockings. The basque gave her a deep cleavage which snow melted into. The outlines of her nipples were visible, and the wig was now wet.

"Do you think I'm tidy?" She nibbled her lip.

The boy, speechless, took an involuntary breath of freezing air.

"So d'ya want me to stay or not?"

"You can come in," he said, unsure. "But if David says you've got to go, you've got to go, my hands are tied."

She smiled. "I don't do bondage."

"Eh?"

"Never mind," she said, biting her lip. Here we go, she thought as she followed him inside. No turning back now.

>>>

VICTORIA was led into a big lounge at the back of the house. It was gloomy and dingy, lit only by a standard lamp with a dim bulb standing in the corner. A plastic litter bin overflowed with Regal packets. On Edwardian tables and shelves and on the floor were numerous unwashed cups, plates and glasses. The room was a stark contrast to the house's tidy exterior. The music was coming from an old record player on a teak sideboard next to it. Three young women sat shoulder to shoulder on a leather Chesterfield settee, all smoking cigarettes. Their lingerie looked even cheaper that Victoria's. The youngest girl was about eighteen. She gawped at the new arrival and absent-mindedly scratched her forearm with the hand holding the cig. Heroin addict, assumed Victoria, unfairly. The second hooker had squinty brown eyes and big breasts and the third was a slim, hard-faced blonde who looked Swedish or Norwegian. They nodded at her, not smiling.

A fat man with a bushy, wispy grey beard was kneeling in front of them at an oval teak wood table, sniffing a line of cocaine that looked big enough to get a horse high. A cigarette burned in an ashtray beside his face. His name was Rabbi David Yehudi and he looked much older than his forty three years, a walking heart attack with a sweaty brow and greasy curls of hair which seemed to grow like Japanese knotweed out of his blue and gold embroidered kippah. He raised his head abruptly and coughed, his eyes big and red.

"Fuck's sake, Samuel! We threw away the wrong bit when we circumcised you. I thought I said don't let anyone else in."

He looked at his drugs. There was enough white powder in front of him to fill a salt shaker and several more large lines were set out, ready to be sniffed. It wasn't exactly *Scarface*, and Yehudi was certainly no Tony Montana, but it was a lot of cocaine.

"Her name's Scarlett." Samuel shrugged. "She reckons you sent for her."

Yehudi exhaled sharply and then sniffed up the contents of his nose. "I didn't order anyone called Scarlett!"

Yehudi picked up the cigarette and greedily dragged on it. He was clearly wasted. She'd seen plenty of people off their heads on coke and knew what it looked like. He took a large swig of whisky from a cut-glass tumbler. He sniffed up and examined her from head to toe, in a way that made her feel deeply uncomfortable.

"Who sent you?"

Victoria answered quickly. "Darren. From Sensations."

Yehudi stared at her. "Sensations? Never heard of it."

Victoria put her hand on her hip as she stared back, assertively. She took a deep breath.

"It's in Chinatown. Listen, all I know is I was told to come here. Whoever you are, my time is valuable. Do you want me to stay or not?"

Yehudi took two puffs of the cigarette, which had burned down to the filter and was very close to his knuckles, and thought for a moment. He came to a decision.

"Sorry, my manners are atrocious. Give us a twirl, please."

The idea of showing off her body to him made her nauseous but it was work. She turned around, slowly.

The rabbi grinned, revealing nicotine-stained teeth. "Nice. Take your coat off."

Her heart thudded as she let the Burberry coat drop to the floor. He inadvertently licked his lips as he stared at her chest. The basque was very low-cut and there was plenty of skin on display.

"Very nice. Very nice indeed. So, Scarlett, you want to party, do you?"

She didn't at all, but she needed to stay in character. "Only if I get to suck off cheeky boy there," She said, looking at Samuel and smiling. Blood rushed to the youth's hairless face. The buxom brunette laughed a croaky laugh and drew hard on her cigarette.

Yehudi laughed. "I think he'd like that. You can stick around. What would a hundred pounds get us?"

She paused, teasing, keeping him waiting. "I make fifty quid an hour," she said, hoping the quote was realistic.

"I think I can stretch to that. You're on."

Yehudi took another pull on the cigarette and a plastic smell filled the room. It had burned down to the filter. He looked at it and stubbed it out. "Can I pour you something?"

"I'll have a glass of that wine, but I can't stay all night, you know." Victoria wondered if she had been too generous with her rate. "I've got other jobs on."

He poured her a glass of red and handed it to her. "Well, you're here now. Relax. Let's hear your story."

"What story?"

"You interrupted a little game we were playing. The girls here were telling us why they love cock. Melanie went first and Rosie was going to go next, but I think I'd like to hear what you've got to say." He grinned.

It was a tight squeeze on the settee but Victoria managed to slide her slim frame in the gap between Melanie and Rosie, the heroin addict. She wondered if the others could feel her heart hammering. She hadn't prepared for sexual *Jackanory*. She fluttered her eyelashes, which were heavy with mascara, as she pretended to rack her brains, and decided to just start talking and see what happened.

"Well..." she said after a few moments, "me and some friends used to hang around in town on Saturdays and one day we went into this sex shop on Shudehill for a laugh. It was mostly magazines, pornos, and crotchless knickers and that, but in the back they had all these vibrators on display. There were pink ones, purple ones, flesh-coloured ones... but the one that caught my eye was the Black Mamba. It must have been a foot long and two inches wide. It had all these, sort of, veins running down the shaft."

"Go on." She had rabbi's attention, which made her feel back in control. He was sweating and there was a vinegary smell in the air. It was disgusting.

Victoria began the next part of the story, which was partly true. "My mate Sharon took the Black Mamba down off the shelf and started jabbing us in the ribs with it. Eventually the fella who owned the shop got pissed off and told us to do one and we went off to McDonalds. Everyone seemed to forget about what had happened but I couldn't stop daydreaming about that dildo. I decided then and there, as I ate a cheeseburger, that I had to have one."

She had the room in the palm of her hand. They all appeared utterly transfixed. Samuel wiped saliva from his chin. The girls on the couch were smiling.

"Go on," said Yehudi, lighting another cigarette.

"All right. I saved up for a couple of weeks and bought one. I think it cost me fifteen quid.

It was so big I had to hide it under my bed. I used it every night, spending a small fortune on batteries. I hardly saw my mates for months."

She paused. The rabbi leaned forward, gripped. She continued. "My nan came to stay one weekend. She's not with us anymore, God bless her. She was senile. I got home and walked in the kitchen and she was making a cake and she was whisking the mixture with the fucking Black Mamba! She said it was the best invention ever and asked what it was doing in my bedroom. I was mortified but I managed to get it back without my mum finding out. Anyway, that's how I came to like sex." Everyone laughed except Samuel, who was looking at the rabbi's drug pile longingly.

"Brilliant," said Yehudi, again wiping sweat from his brow with his sleeve. "So glad you joined us, Scarlett."

>>>

THE snack bar area under the South Stand was packed with Belle Vue supporters and most of the talk was about how David Kelly was running Mark Shaw ragged.

Tom Semple, aged nine, wasn't worried though. He knew Cozzer would save the day.

Going to the match with his dad was Tom's favourite thing in the whole world. Away games were most exciting because they travelled by coach. Sometimes the coaches had a TV on them, and he had seen *Herbie Goes Bananas* for the first time that morning. Tom's mum hardly ever came to the match because she had to look after his little sister, Cathy.

Tom wanted to be a winger when he grew up, like Cozzer. He stood up to bullies. Some of the bigger lads at school tried to push Tom around, but he wouldn't stand for it, like Cozzer.

He had spent hours practising the flashy lightning bolt Z that Cozzer used in his autograph. Then, when Tom was a footballer he could sign autographs too. His exercise books were covered with his efforts. Mrs Green had told him off for that. He saw Mick and his dad holding their pints of beer, shuffled through the crowd and gave his dad the pie he had bought him. Mick, who went to every match with them, was flicking through the programme and shaking his head.

"Your pal Cosgrove's been garbage as usual," he grumbled, mockingly, knowing he was Tom's hero. "Says here he might get called up for England under twenty-ones. I wouldn't pick him for the girls' team."

Tom liked Mick because he took him to Blackpool Pleasure Beach once and let him sit on his lap and steer his Capri on the motorway but he didn't half talk some rubbish sometimes.

"He's gonna score a hat-trick today," Tom told him, confidently. Cozzer wouldn't let him down.

"You reckon? I'll give you three quid if he does," grinned Mick.

Big Tom had nearly finished his pie in three bites. Little Tom had bitten straight through the middle of his and it was now U-shaped and floppy. The sides had brushed his cheeks, leaving brown gravy marks. Big Tom stuffed the last of the pastry in his mouth and said: "He's been rubbish this season. Shite."

"He's not shite dad, he's mint!" A chunk of meat and potato fell on the ground with a splat.

Big Tom smiled and ruffled his son's hair. "Did you just say 'shite'?"

Mick laughed at the boy and looked at his watch. "Come on or we'll miss the kick off."

Tom grabbed his son's free hand. "Hang on, son," he said as they pushed through the crowd. "Watch you don't drop any more of that pie. And don't tell your mum about the fuckin' swearing." He grinned and rubbed his son's hair.

Butterflies fluttered around the chewed up morsels of meat and potato pie in young Tom's stomach. He was certain he was going to be three pounds richer by the end of the game. He was saving up for a Lego fire station. Cozzer wouldn't let him down.

MARK Shaw jogged to the edge of the penalty area, still in a sweaty, and started doing stretches alone. The West Ham fans were singing *I'm Forever Blowing Bubbles.* Cal, who was twenty yards away, saw steam coming out of the defender's nostrils as he bent down to touch his toes and spat on the grass. "That cunt's a prick," Simon shouted, not giving a shit if Shaw heard him or not. "What's up with him? He's getting on my fucking tits."

Cal shook his head. "I dunno, but he better not get himself sent off... if he does we're fucked."

The second half commenced. Kelly was soon causing problems for Shaw again. He managed to get past him twice with the ball in just a few minutes. Something had to be done about it. It was war. The next time Kelly was in possession, Cal sprinted over and smashed his right hip into his side. Kelly fell on the turf and shouted loudly as he rolled along. He wasn't hurt this time, but he wanted the referee to think he was. There was uproar from the home team's dugout and the referee put his whistle in his mouth and blew it loudly.

The West Ham manager Lou Macari stood up and started ranting from the touchline. "That's twice the dirty bastard has done him," he yelled at the ref. "Are you going to have a word or what?"

Cal stood over Kelly as he lay on the turf. "Sorry pal, it was an accident." As he helped him get up he grabbed a handful of armpit hair through his shirt and yanked it.

"Argh... you cunt!" shouted Kelly, shoving him off.

The referee was right beside them. "Sorry ref," said Cal, putting his arm around him. "I was a bit late. He did me for skill."

"I'm watching you Cal," said the referee. "One more foul and it's a card."

Cal jogged away, looking over at the gaffer to gauge his reaction. McNeill pulled hard on a Rothmans and a cloud of smoke billowed from the dugout. Cal took it as a smoke signal that his game plan was acceptable.

He kept making dangerous runs into the West Ham half but the ball wasn't getting through to him. A long ball over the top was too long and went out for a goal kick. Dicks was staying close to him. Kelly was standing by Shaw, who had hold of his shirt. He saw Kelly saying something and Shaw trying to elbow him. The gaffer needed to substitute him before he got himself sent off. Cal waved at the bench but couldn't get his attention.

With only ten minutes left, the ball landed at Cal's feet and he trapped it. He managed to hold off Dicks and play a quick one-two with Edo. He knew he had to score now, there would be no more chances. He dribbled quickly forward, avoiding a sliding tackle. He hit a perfect cross-field pass to Simon, who barely had to adjust his feet to trap the ball. Simon passed to Edo and sprinted off down the wing. His run was perfectly timed to collect Edo's return pass.

Cal lurked in the box, ready for his mate's cross. Simon chipped in a beauty towards the near post. Dicks dashed over to clear the ball to safety, but Cal was already airborne and felt leather thudding off the middle of his forehead. The ball flew under the crossbar and slid down the net with a reassuring swish. Goal! One-one! Cal got up and punched the air. Edo hooked his muscular arm around his neck and pulled him in to his chest. "Fucking sweet header, man," he roared, slapping his cheek several times.

The West Ham players were desperate to get the game started again. They were top of the league and were desperate to keep up a winning run. It was rare for a team to take points off them at Upton Park.

They kicked off again. Kelly punted the ball forward but it went straight to Shaw. He chested it down and laid it off out wide to Simon, who dribbled it into the corner of the pitch, a common technique to run down the clock. No one could score if the ball was in the corner. He held out his arms as two defenders kicked him repeatedly in the back of the legs trying to get their feet on the ball. A West Ham fan screamed: "You fackin time-wastin cahnt!"

A defender's toe eventually poked through Simon's legs and connected with the ball. It hit the corner flag, bounced back onto Simon and rolled over the dead ball line for what should have been a goal kick. But the linesman gave Belle Vue a corner. Dicks was furious and was shown a yellow card for calling him a "blind cunt". Cal couldn't believe it either. He looked up at the clock mounted on the East Stand. It was gone quarter to five... they were into stoppage time now. If everything stayed as it was, all would be well.

Simon placed the ball down ready to take the corner. A badly-taken, scuffed one that swung or bobbled out of play would do, Cal thought. There was some pushing and shoving in the box as he ran up to the ball and punted in an in-swinging cross with very little power behind it. Parkes, the Hammers' goalkeeper, should have caught it easily. For some reason, he stood rooted to the spot. Shaw was inexplicably tussling with Kelly at the far post. He knew it was supposed to finish one-one but appeared to be in some sort of detached state, trying to be first to the ball. He powered a header downwards. It bounced on the goal line before bulging the net. Goal. The Belle Vue fans erupted with joy in their small corner of the ground. Shaw spun away, arms in the air in jubilation. Jed grabbed him and kissed him. Cal couldn't believe what had just happened. He looked down the pitch to

Nigel, who was at the edge of his penalty area. Nigel had his huge, gloved fists raised in the air, but he wasn't smiling, he was angrily shaking his head.

>>>

YEHUDI'S gaze was fixed on Victoria's chest again. She folded her arms to cover her cleavage but he frowned so she unfolded them again and let him stare. She felt dirty but forced a smile.

The Scandinavian stretched and yawned. As her chest expanded, the top of her left breast lifted briefly out of her red lace bra, exposing a gold nipple ring. "Nice piece of jewellery you have there, Melanie." He scratched his head. "Give Scarlett a kiss, will you?"

It was all in a night's work for Melanie. She shrugged, and turned to Victoria. Her lips were moist and red, bright red like a fire engine. She put her hand on Victoria's hip and closed her eyes. Victoria's pulse started racing again. She could feel the heat of her breath. She had once necked with a girl at college for a bet. How different could this be? She was about to find out. She put her hand on Melanie's hip and closed her eyes too. Their lips met, softly. Melanie seemed to drink her in. Their tongues touched and Victoria was no longer afraid. It felt much nicer than one of Miles' snogs, which often left stubble rash around her mouth. She could vaguely taste cigarettes on Melanie but even that didn't bother her. She kissed back, enjoying the tiny thrill each time their tongues met again. Melanie's felt like smooth, hot, moist velvet in her mouth. She was lost.

Melanie ended the kiss abruptly and there was a tense moment of silence. It was broken by Yehudi, who was still sweating profusely. Victoria hoped he didn't keel over. "Well congratulations you dirty little minxes," he said, very pleased with himself. He snorted another line of cocaine, tipped his head back, wiped his nose with the back of his hand and licked it. "You've got me hard." He looked at Melanie. "Here, have a line of this for your trouble."

She shook her head.

"I mean it," he insisted. "It's the good stuff."

"I can see that, and I mean it too." Victoria was surprised to hear Melanie was Scouse, not Swedish or Norwegian.

"Come on, this is the best coke you'll ever taste. I thought you came here to party?"

"I said no, all right?"

"All right. Fucking hell! I try and do someone a favour..." He turned her nose up so he turned his attention to Victoria. He offered her the rolled up-tenner. "What about you then Scarlett? I bet you'll have a sniff."

"Nah, it makes me go weird, that stuff." She kept a close eye on the rabbi. People on coke could be unpredictable.

He shook his head and finished the cigarette. "Your loss. Daft whores. Oh well, all the more for me and Samuel." He held the note out to the boy.

Victoria suddenly sprung to her feet, reached down the back of her knickers and pulled out a camera the size of a matchbox. It had cost her two ninety-nine from a stall called Fags and Poppers at Affleck's Palace. She had tested it on her pet Jack Russell, John, and the photos had turned out fine.

She aimed the camera at the rabbi. He lifted his head in surprise, white powder all around his nostrils and beard. Perfect. Click. Wind. Click. Wind. Click. The fat line of cocaine was right in the middle of the frame with Yehudi's bearded face behind it. She had just managed to get a third shot off when Samuel dived at her midriff and they fell to the floor, a tangle of arms and legs. Victoria's blonde wig flew off, revealing she was really a brunette.

"Get your hands off me," she grunted as they rolled around on the floor. "I'm Victoria Heath of the *Evening Chronicle*."

Samuel tightened his grip on her, trying to get her in a headlock. She bucked like a donkey before a flailing elbow caught him on the temple. His body went limp. She wriggled out from underneath his prone body, holding the camera tightly, and crawled to the corner of the room. She ripped the cheap stilettos off her feet, snapping the straps, and shuffled backwards along the carpet. Yehudi towered over her like a fat, sweaty Goliath. He was over six feet tall and his belly hung over his trousers. She could see the whites of his eyes and smelt the vinegary odour again as he swung his giant right fist at her head. He missed her eye by less than an inch. A left hook brushed her forehead. She rolled out of the way, sprung to her feet, grabbed a glass of red wine and threw its contents in his face. He recoiled, rubbing his eyes. She then hurled the glass at him but it missed and smashed against the wall. She kneed him in the bollocks with all she had left.

Yehudi groaned and doubled over in agony. "Muuuurgh," he wheezed.

The heroin addict and the brunette made a run for it. The door slammed shut behind them. Melanie, who Victoria thought looked a bit like the singer of Roxette, launched herself at the back of Yehudi's legs. The room shook. He went down hard, banging his head on the floor. As he lay groaning, she quickly removed one of her fishnet stockings and hog-tied him with it.

Then she took off the other stocking and trussed Samuel up the same way. It obviously wasn't the first time she had restrained a man.

Victoria was impressed. Melanie looked at her and burst out laughing. "Black Mamba... Fuck me."

"It was the first thing that came into my head." Victoria was shaking, exhausted but exhilarated.

"Not bad, but I could tell you were fake. You're too clean to be on the game."

Victoria put her coat back on gingerly, her back sore. She took a roll of banknotes out the pocket, thought about peeling a couple off, then handed the whole thing over. "That fat bastard might have killed me. There's two hundred quid there. Courtesy of the *Chron*."

Melanie looked very pleased. "You sure? That is a serious amount of dosh."

Victoria nodded and smiled. "For a job well done."

"Well... cheers. My dad would have been proud of that tackle. He was a big Warrington fan. You don't remember me, do you?"

"Should I?"

"You interviewed me in the red light district last summer about that kerb crawler who was picking up girls and beating the shit out of them. You quoted me in the paper."

"Did I? Sorry. I meet a lot of people. Melanie, is it?"

She smiled. "It is this week. Don't worry. I had brown hair then. Like yours."

"Fucking slags," the hog-tied rabbi growled. "I'll fucking have you both killed."

Melanie, or whatever her real name was, kicked him in the ribs and there was a dull thud. She grabbed a filthy handkerchief and stuffed it deep into his mouth to gag him. "What happens now?"

"I'll go back to the paper and ring the police and tell them I was at this party, saw him giving cocaine to that kid, tried to stop it and got assaulted. They'll send a car over with two coppers in it. They'll come up here, find these two and all that coke and, hopefully, arrest them."

"Do us a favour?"

"Name it."

"Give it half an hour before you ring the filth. I'm having that charlie."

Victoria scratched her chin. Maybe she'd been too hasty giving away her cash. You give an inch, they take a yard. "Okay. But you do me a favour too."

"What can I do for you?"

"Leave a bit behind, or the coppers won't have any evidence to nick that... piece of shit."

Yehudi tried to shout out again but his words were muffled. "I will... trust me." She then surprised Victoria with a tight hug, which she held for several seconds.

They parted and stood looking at each other for a moment. "Thanks," said Victoria, feeling ten times calmer. "I needed that. Have a nice Christmas."

Her new friend looked at the cash in her hand. "I fucking will do now. Thank you."

Victoria buttoned up her coat, slipped the camera into the inside pocket and left the house. She was excited. This could be her ticket to Fleet Street and the big time. She would have to pay the taxi driver when they got to the *Chron*. There was a twenty pound note in her desk drawer.

SUNDAY

IT was just after eight in the morning and forty or so men were kicking footballs around on a training pitch covered by a silver sheet of morning frost. Clouds of steam rose from their heads and torsos as they ran around, the imprints of their football boots leaving tracks behind them.

Belle Vue's training ground was situated on the edge of Saddleworth Moor. Next to the pitch was a large, ramshackle, weather-beaten wooden building which housed the changing rooms, showers, boot room, gym and the canteen. The gaffer was in his private office, literally a garden shed tacked on to the end, working on tactics. His side had a busy festive fixtures schedule with away games against Coventry City and Leeds United coming up in quick succession.

"Make sure you're all warmed up lads," shouted Jed Brennan, who was in charge of the training session. He was taking the UEFA coaching exams in his spare time. "We don't want anyone getting injured."

Shaw was holding a younger player in a headlock, laughing as he tightened his grip. The lad was struggling to breathe. He was full of himself after scoring the winner in London and this was his idea of friendly banter. Anger was twisted up in a knot in Cal's stomach. He booted away a ball that someone passed to him and spat on the ground. He'd hardly slept a wink thanks to that cunt.

Cal was tough, born in Wythenshawe, Manchester, and brought up by his uncle, Billy, and his auntie, Carol. He was captain of South Manchester Boys by the time he was fifteen. They won the 1981 North West Schoolboys cup final four-one and he scored a hat-trick. A United scout at the game invited him for trials and a month later he signed a two-year contract with his favourite club. "Good luck son," the manager, Ron Atkinson, told him at the time. "It's all up to you now."

But it wasn't up to him. The Red Devils hadn't won a cup since the seventies but Cal never got a run in the first team. Atkinson wanted a big name striker, not some skinny kid from the reserves. Cal turned professional after the two years but a chance to show what he could do never came. He started coasting through training, making sure he scored often enough for the second string to justify his wages – two hundred quid a week was a lot more than any of his mates earned. It didn't take him long to work out that he could get off with almost any bird he wanted. He bought a Brutus shirt and a Baracuta jacket from a boutique in King Street and got a mod haircut like Paul Weller's. He treated his mates to nights out at Athenaeum. He drank imported Stella Artois, not the piss brewed by Scottish and Newcastle, and found it easy to run off a hangover.

Carol convinced him to get on the property ladder. He bought the second floor of a former spoon factory near Stevenson Square for twenty grand. It had a high ceiling crisscrossed with pipes and massive windows that looked over the square and to Oldham Street at the side. He had the concrete floor painted white and bought a red velvet three-piece suite from Habitat and a waterbed which swished when he fucked birds on it. Mates from school in Wythenshawe would turn up in the evenings with beer and weed. Annoyingly, records would sometimes go missing, but he didn't make a fuss. Not everyone was rich like him. He hung a punchbag from a joist and bought a set of old-school iron dumbbells and spent hours putting in extra training until he was lean like Bruce Lee.

Atkinson told him he was being sold on in the summer of eighty-six, a year before his contract was due to expire. The manager said it was nothing personal. Belle Vue had offered twenty five grand, with a full professional's contract worth a grand a week and a five grand signing-on bonus. It was a good deal, he should take it. Cal, twenty-one, didn't know what to say.

Uncle Billy reacted with fury and threatened to go and have a word with Atkinson, but Cal convinced him it would do no good. Billy had dedicated his life to making Cal a better footballer and driving him to matches and training and schools of excellence all over Manchester.

He put some of the blame on Cal's mates, saying they were "knobheads" who had led him astray and should be "bombed off". Cal didn't need to bomb anyone off after United because they stopped coming round.

Billy advised him to invest the bonus and another ten grand he'd saved by buying a pub. Billy would run it for him and take a wage out of the profits. When Cal told him he'd he bought an empty cellar in a building at the back of the Kendal Milne department store to turn into a bar, he looked like he was going to puke. Billy fancied himself as landlord of a nice local boozer in Chorlton or somewhere with a big telly that showed *Final Score* on a Saturday, not some dingy dive bar in the city centre. The cellar stood empty for nearly two years before Cal could afford to turn it into his pride and joy, Reds.

Jed whistled loudly, bringing Cal's mind back to training. It was attackers versus defenders. His mate Simon was out by the right corner flag preparing to put in some crosses. Footballs spilled out of a net bag beside him. He nudged a Mitre Multiplex into position and took five paces backwards. Cal positioned himself on the edge of the box. Nigel clanked his studs against the back post. Shaw went to mark Cal and put his hand on his shoulder. Cal jerked it off and snarled: "Fuck off, Mark."

Simon crossed the ball into the penalty area. Shaw stuck his arm out to block Cal's run. Cal adjusted by moving his weight forward but lost his balance and fell over. His training shorts and his top were covered in mud as Nigel took two steps forward and caught the ball.

Jed roared with laughter. "Got your granny's slippers on, have you?" He blew his whistle to stop the drill.

Shaw stood over him, offering him a hand. "You all right?"

Cal sprung to his feet and squared up to him. "Course I'm fucking alright, you fucking cum stain."

Shaw stepped back looking surprised and he muttered: "Wanker. Just cos of yesterday..."

Cal's face suddenly felt hot. He found himself landing a punch on Shaw's nose. Shaw staggered backwards a couple of steps but didn't fall. Flecks of spit flew out of Cal's mouth as he got right in his face and raged: "I'll put you on your fucking arse next time."

A trickle of blood ran down Shaw's top lip and he had a confused look on his face. He touched the blood and looked at the tip his finger. "Jesus Christ... Touchy cunt. I'm sorry about yesterday and that, but..."

Cal grabbed Shaw's training top so roughly that the stitching around the neck groaned. His eyes were wide open as he growled: "Shut your fucking mouth Mark... I'm telling you."

A strong arm suddenly hooked around Cal's neck, pulling him away. "Easy now Cal. Chill." It was Edo. His deep voice was soothing but Cal stared right through him.

Jed, not laughing now, tromped over, his boots squelching in what was now mud. "What the fuck's all this about? Lovers' tiff? Calm down Cal, for fuck's sake. I'm the captain. Got a problem, you talk to me. Got it?"

Cal, still seething, said nothing so he said: "Right. Everyone. Tea break."

The players trudged back towards the training hut, gossiping about what they had just witnessed. Cal hung near the back, silently fuming.

Nigel caught up with him. "Cal... y'alright or what?"

"I swear it, man. That cunt's gotta go."

"Shh. You've got to relax, Cal. You'll make every cunt suspicious."

"He's a fucking liability. He's gonna fucking blab, I can feel it. He can't keep his fucking trap shut. You've got to sort him out."

Nigel shrugged. "What do you want me to do about it?"

"Dunno mate. Get him to go AWOL or summat. You know where he lives, you bring him to training every day... You're the one he sees as a mate. Have a word with him."

"The cunt can't drive, that's why I pick him up..."

"He trusts you though."

Nigel scratched his head. "S'pose," he said. "Leave it with me. But do us all a favour and chill out, man."

"Sorry mate. I'm knackered, I've barely slept. The pimp's gonna go bananas about that fuck up yesterday."

\>\>\>

THE tyres of a taxi lost their grip before the pedestrian crossing outside Piccadilly station and the bumper nearly clipped Billy's leg. He made angry eye contact with the driver, who had finally come to a halt, but decided it was no time for a bust up, pulled up the collar of his sheepskin coat and continued down the hill. *Granada Reports* said the night before that the council had already run out of grit, so he put it down to that.

Billy Baldwin was the closest thing Callum Murphy had to a father. Cal was his younger sister Cath's child. The midwife had barely wiped the afterbirth off the bastard before she disappeared to Spain. Billy suggested taking him to Barnardos, but they were both knocking on a bit and Carol wanted a child, so it was decided. They were keeping him. At least it was a boy he could teach football to. They had a garden where he could play, the garden where Billy and his mates sat around boasting about their motorbike adventures. Billy had a Norton which he kept in order himself, and he saw himself as Manchester's answer to Dennis Hopper. Baby Callum was good natured and always smiling, and Carol literally gave him everything. Her soothing voice singing Bowie's *Space Oddity* was Cal's earliest memory.

Carol died in nineteen seventy-nine. Cal, then fourteen, was doing keepie-ups as they walked to the shops but lost control of the ball and ran in the road after it. Carol saw the Austin Allegro coming but still stepped out in front of it to shove the boy to safety. The driver had no chance of stopping. He looked in his mirror and saw her lying in the road, her leg right sickeningly crooked and a pool of blood forming around her head. She had been on life support for a few hours when the doctor came to the waiting room. Cal saw Billy's shoulders drop and just knew. Billy confirmed the news, roughly ruffled his hair and said: "It's not your fault, son." Then he started sobbing. Of course it was Cal's fault.

Billy continued down Canal Street into the Gay Village, taking care not to slip. It was starting to snow again, not that he would ever take refuge around here. Someone had chalked on an A-board outside a pub: Smokers Welcome. Come In From The Cold And Suck On A Fag. Freaks. He walked around the corner and crossed over Portland Street.

Sensations occupied the top floor of a Georgian building in Chinatown stained charcoal grey by traffic fumes. There was no sign outside. Only matchbooks passed between men in pubs carried the name. Billy was a regular. He and the owner, Harry O'Donnell, went back a long way. He walked up the front steps and pushed open the heavy, bright red door. It took ages for the lift to arrive. When it finally did he opened the concertina doors, stepped inside, removed his gloves and pressed number three. He heard the familiar sound of metal grinding as the car ascended and beads of sweat formed on his brow. It always sounded like the fucking cables were going to snap. The elevator finally came to a halt and Billy, relieved to survive yet another trip, let himself out and pressed a buzzer in the centre of a heavy door. A slot opened and a pair of grey, steely eyes with bushy brows appeared.

"Mr Baldwin... noice to see you," said an Irish voice. It wasn't the pimp, it was Hugh, his thug. "Ten o'clock. Bang on time."

Billy nodded as he opened the door. The bar area had ornate ceiling cornices, oak-panelled walls and heavy velvet curtains covering the windows. Five men sat around a table in upright leather armchairs, holding playing cards, some smiling, some grimacing, all smoking. O'Donnell called it a gentlemen's club, not a brothel. Hugh was a six foot five slab of Irish beef who towered over Billy. His long brown hair was shaved away above the ears in a mullet style. His index finger was jammed in the middle of the copy of Stephen

King's novel *Misery*. "He told me to send you straight in. Can I take your coat?"

Billy took off the heavy brown sheepskin and handed it over.

"Wanna drink?"

"A large gin and tonic, cheers," said Billy.

"No problem. I'll bring it in. Oice and a sloice?"

"Eh?"

"Oi said oice and a fucking sloice."

Ice and a slice. "Oh right... yep," Billy said. "Please Hugh."

O'Donnell quickly slammed his desk drawer shut as Billy entered his office. He looked shifty behind the huge teak piece of furniture, which was topped in gilt-edged green leather. Two huge grey boxes with individual screens and a black monitor took up most of it. He liked to keep an eye on his shares. Beside the screens was a human skull with the lower jaw and the strip of bone under the nasal cavity missing.

The pimp wore a pink and white striped shirt with the sleeves rolled up. A navy blue paisley cravat was tucked up under his wrinkled chin. A big gold Rolex Oyster decorated his hairy wrist. He was slim, fit for a man of fifty nine, and had a mahogany tan from hours by the pool at his Costa Del Sol villa. His hair was long at the sides but he was bald on top, a bit like the light entertainer Mick Miller.

In contrast, Billy was overweight, pale, wore a ten pound Casio and hadn't had a holiday since well before Carol snuffed it. His hair was still quite thick and dark though.

"Billy," said O'Donnell sharply. "Don't bother fucking knocking, will you?"

He nodded at a wooden chair in front of his desk that was painted gold and upholstered in red velvet. Billy took a seat. Hugh came in with a tray, placed a silver coaster in front of him and put the gin and tonic down. He went and stood in the corner of the room, arms folded.

O'Donnell placed his hands on the desk and sighed. "I know we go back a long way but this thing with Cal is like a fucking bad joke."

Billy thought back to the old days, the seventies, the parties. The weed, the acid. And that was just what they sold. O'Donnell sorted out the ones who didn't pay. Billy still couldn't believe Carol had chosen him over the Irishman, a burly, handsome devil in the old days. Perhaps his paramilitary links put her off. O'Donnell's cousin was said to be big in the IRA.

"He asked me to tell you he's very sorry," he said.

"I had a lot of money riding on that West Ham game being a draw. So did a lot of my associates. He's made me look a right cunt."

Billy nodded, knowing what O'Donnell meant. "One of the players didn't get the message, apparently. Mark Shaw. Cal assures me he is going to sort it out."

Harry breathed out slowly and picked up a gold pen. He took a deep breath. "How's business?"

"Business?"

"Yeah. That fucking nightclub, Reds."

"It's busy most nights... especially before the Hacienda gets going. Cal's got some promising DJs in. They bring in all their mates. Word's getting around about the place."

"Yeah but... I know for a fact that I sell more beer in here than you do there. Most of those kids neck disco biscuits, sip tap water and hug each other all night. That can't be paying the bills. Can it?"

Billy was staring out of the sash window behind Harry. O'Donnell was right. He could see the Pennine hills in the distance, despite a concrete office block built across the road in the seventies ruining the vista. "A few of 'em still get pissed, even if they are on the pills, but things could be better, I s'pose," he conceded.

Harry sighed grumpily. "Cal got lucky there. Fucking prime location now. I hear they want to build a great big office complex near there. Bank headquarters, offices, entertainment quarter, you name it. It's going to be massive."

"What are you saying, Harry?"

Harry continued. "We both know young Callum should be playing for United, or someone in the First Division at least. And I should be getting ten per cent of his earnings."

"You do get ten per cent."

"I do... but I should be getting a thousand quid a week, not a hundred. Ten per cent of fuck all is fuck all."

Harry picked up the skull, poked the gold pen in its eye socket.

He said: "About two years ago this skull was on a man's shoulders and had a fully functioning brain inside. I say fully functioning..." He then turned the skull around, revealing a small hole in the back.

"I did that with my dad's pistol from the war. Nasty cunt. This fella, not my dad." A devilish smile appeared on his face.

Billy nervously took a sip of his drink. "I didn't know your dad was in the war? What regiment was he in?"

O'Donnell tapped the pen against the chipped bone. "Don't take the piss, Billy. Do you know why the mouth is missing? Hugh bashed it in... with a hammer. After he was dead, of course. We're not animals. Do you know what he did to have his head end up here?"

Of course Billy knew. But he knew better than to interrupt the pimp when he was making a point. His temper was legendary.

"This cunt did me out of twenty grand," said O'Donnell. "And young Callum's already cost me nearly fifty..." He tapped the skull again.

"He's lucky we're old mates then."

Harry took another deep breath. "Us being mates only goes so far, Billy. So here's what I propose. I'm going to give young Callum one more chance. I want a two-all draw at Coventry. If he fucks it up, Reds is mine."

"Two-all? Do you know how hard it is to score two goals on command? Coventry are a good side. They've got Steve Ogrizovich, one of the best keepers in the..."

"Shuddup Billy. I want it to be a two-all draw. And I want the deeds to Reds, signed over to me, as security in the meantime. All goes well, I give 'em back. He fucks up again, his club is mine."

"He won't agree to that... no way."

"Well you'd better fucking convince him," said the pimp, tapping his pen on the skull again. "Now get out, will you? I've got some other business to take care of."

>>>

THE Majestic Hotel's giant Christmas tree dominated the lobby where Callum Murphy was having a brew before going to meet Billy for nine holes. Hundreds of gift wrapped boxes were stacked under the tree. The light from the huge chandelier made the baubles sparkle. A man of sixty-odd was playing *Santa Claus is Coming To Town* at a slow, relaxing tempo on a grand piano. Oak tables and armchairs bound in dark green leather were thoughtfully positioned around the massive room.

Cal had lived at the Majestic for four months. It wasn't cheap, but it was conveniently located in the heart of the city and it was nice not having to do his own cooking, washing and ironing. He had developed a liking for sipping Earl Grey tea out of bone China cups, which he did as he picked up a copy of the *Manchester Evening Chronicle* from the chair beside him.

RESPECTED RABBI'S 'DRUGS AND VICE' ROMP By Victoria Heath, special affairs reporter

A respected rabbi who influenced thousands of children is today in disgrace after being exposed as a drug-abusing pervert.

Jewish scholar David Yehudi, 45, was photographed inhaling a suspicious white powder believed to be cocaine during a wild party at his home.

Children were at the bash in Fallowfield and at least one woman who attended was a prostitute, a neighbour claimed.

Sources said the sordid gathering was one of a number hosted by Yehudi over the last six months.

Evening Chronicle reporter Victoria Heath, who infiltrated the party in disguise, said today: "Rabbi

David should be setting a much better example to younger members of the Jewish community.

"His behaviour was nothing short of shocking in front of an impressionable boy who looked up to him."

Neighbour Maureen Daniels, 66, said she was looking out of her window at teatime when she saw a "scantily-clad" woman on Yehudi's property.

"The lass was brass," she added. "I was disgusted. This is a respectable area."

She said many people had been "coming and going" from the house in the evenings in recent weeks.

Yehudi admitted to having "personal problems" when confronted with Miss Heath's notes and photographs. The Chronicle has decided not to publish any images which might identify minors at the scene.

Worried friends and relatives today escorted the rabbi to Ringway Airport, where he was due to be put on a flight to the Isle of Man. He is going to spend a month in a rehabilitation facility on the island, a source from the Jewish community confirmed.

Miss Heath has personally passed the Chronicle's dossier of evidence to detectives. She went on: "I hope the treatment is a success so Rabbi David can begin to rebuild his life."

A 15-year-old youth who suffered a head injury at the party spent the night under observation at Manchester Royal Infirmary. A spokesman said he recovered and was discharged to his parents' care.

Det Insp Gerald Maxwell, of Greater Manchester Police, said: "The lad is going to be okay, thankfully. He has been reunited with his parents, who had no idea where he was and were very worried."

Officers found traces of white powder on a table at Yehudi's house, which is being tested by scientists at UMIST. Investigations are continuing.

Hello, a fucking rabbi, thought Cal. Caught red-handed by the sound of it. Or white-nosed, more like. By special affairs reporter Victoria Heath. There was a little picture of her beside her name. She was pretty. No wonder the dirty bastard let her in. He folded the newspaper gingerly, his right hand swollen and aching after lamping Shaw, and placed it on the table beside him.

"Mr Murphy..." The hotel manager, James Kidd, had sidled over. A snivelling little shit, but in Cal's opinion it was important to keep a manager onside when living at their hotel.

"Ayup Kiddo!" He said, in pally fashion, and forced a smile. "What can I do you for?"

Kidd crouched down beside him and kept his voice low, conscious that other guests were sitting nearby. "I'm very sorry to have to bring this up here, Mr Murphy, but I've been knocking on your door and I can't seem to catch you in. It's just... your bill for last month is overdue. I've told head office you are a footballer and not to worry about getting the money, but they are on my case every day it's not paid. You know how it is with these pen-pushers."

"Oh right, yeah, er... I do apologise. I'll sort it out tomorrow. How much did you say it was?"

"It's seven eight six, including VAT. I did push an invoice under your door."

Cal's earlobes felt hot. He had found an envelope on his bedroom floor but thought it was junk mail and put it in the bin. Seven eight six. He didn't even have five hundred in his bank account. Being the owner of Reds was skinting him.

"We do take Access and Visa, you know. If you give us your credit card number now, we can simply charge you automatically. I don't wanna keep having to pester you like this..."

"Did I not just say I'll fucking pay you tomorrow?" Cal shot back.

Kidd didn't want a scene taking place in the lobby of his exclusive hotel. "Okay Mr Murphy... tomorrow will be fine."

"Good. I'll come straight to the desk. And you can tell head office I'm not happy about being pestered all the time. There are other hotels in this city, you know."

He quickly stood up and charged off towards the lifts with his head down. Jesus, he couldn't ask Nigel for more help, he was already into him for three grand. He realised he might have to pawn his Rolex. There was an electricity bill for Reds that also needed paying, and Manweb had sent out a disconnection notice. The watch money should cover that too. His Cosworth's ten thousand-mile service would have to wait. Merry fucking Christmas.

>>>

CAL walked past a sand bunker which had a puddle of rainwater frozen in the middle of it, scratching his head. How the hell he was going to engineer a two-all draw against Coventry? It was a cold grey afternoon in New Mills, in the hills south of Manchester. He teed up his ball as the wind swirled around him. He wore a navy blue Seve Ballesteros Slazenger V-neck, a white Ping golf cap, light grey stay-pressed Farah trousers and black FootJoys. No windcheater despite the cold.

Even with a sore hand he was confident about beating Billy. The old man wore a battered flat cap over his grey hair and golf attire that looked like it had been handed down to him by Jack Nicklaus' grandad. His tweed trousers were held up at the waist by a length of twine. His paunch hung over the knot at the front. He reached into his pocket and handed Cal a folded sheet of thick pink paper and a Biro. "Sign this, will ya?"

"What is it?"

"Nowt. Tommy Norlington's granddaughter is a fan of yours, for some reason. I think she's tapped. Anyway, he asked me to get her your autograph."

"On an old bit of paper?"

"It's all I've got on me. Don't you worry. She can cut it out and stick it in her autograph book."

Cal shrugged, signed his name with a flourish and handed the sheet of paper back. Billy quickly folded it and stuffed it in his back pocket.

The tee-off area was on top of a cliff about fifty feet higher than the green. On a clear day the CIS Tower was visible to the north, but this wasn't one. To do well on this hole, you had to hit the ball over a tree-lined gully and hope for a good lie. Cal focused and drove his ball with his five wood. It flew through the air straight and true and landed just in front of the green.

Billy set himself for his turn. He was employing his six iron. Cal had seen him shank his ball into the bushes in front of them and lose his rag many times. If that happened, the iron would get bent over his knee. This time, however, he cleared the gully and his ball stopped not far from Cal's. He grinned and winked. Cal checked his wrist for the time, forgetting that his Rolex was no longer there. He heaved his golf bag onto his shoulder and said: "Why the fuck does it have to be two-all?"

"Fuck knows. It's just what he wants."

"How the fuck does he expect us to do it with no defender?"

Billy was ready for the question. "You can do it," he said. "You can afford to let two in... you've just got to make sure you score two."

"Well that'll be a piece of piss won't it, with Brian 'Killer' Kilcline breathing down my fucking neck."

"Maybe a more experienced negotiator could've got you a better deal after your last fuck-up. What's happening with Shaw, anyway?"

"Nigel's going to get rid of him."

"Get rid of him? Fucking hell Cal. You sound like a fucking nutcase. You should be playing centre-forward for United, not acting like some kind of a gangster."

"Yeah well... it didn't work out though, did it?" replied Cal, petulantly.

"You're only twenty-five. It's not too late. You could be playing for England at USA 94 if you sort yourself out. All that hard work we put in..."

"Leave it, will ya? I'm sick to the back teeth of hearing about it. I gave it everything and they fucked me off. Football's just a fucking job now. A way of making money for Reds. It's gonna take off man, I'm telling ya."

Billy shook his head. "Fancy calling a fucking bar in Manchester Reds. We should have called it Soviet."

"I like Reds. What?"

"We live in a city of over a million people and only half of 'em are reds. City fans avoid it like a kick in the cunt. You're alienating half the fucking city."

"What if I don't want fucking City fans coming in?"

"Then it's no wonder we're fucking going bust, is it?"

"I'm kidding. City fans are welcome. I've got loads of mates who're blues. Anyway we can't change the name now, we can't afford it. Everyone knows it. And I'm happy."

"You don't seem that happy."

"Well I'm fucking skint, aren't I? I've had to pawn my fucking Rolex. The tight cunt would only give me a monkey for it."

Billy spoke in a baby voice. "Ahh, poor little Cal had to pawn his expensive watch... My fucking heart bleeds. Still living at that fucking posh hotel though."

Cal realised he couldn't win the argument so he turned away and took out his pitching wedge. He walked to his ball, which was a yard off the fairway and half-buried in the grass, and slyly kicked it into a better position. Billy was looking away, shielding a fag from the wind as he lit it. Bad luck, old man. Cal set his feet and dinked the ball onto the green. It stopped rolling about four feet from the flag, an easy putt.

"You fucking jammy cunt."

"The more I practice, the luckier I get," Cal replied, nicking the legendary Gary Player's famous line.

Billy also had his wedge out. "Watch and learn."

Despite hundreds of lessons and years of practice, Billy's swing was far from a thing of beauty. The club head collided with the middle of the ball instead of getting underneath it – and it flew off over the back of the green, finishing up further from the hole than where it started. "Fuck!" He took the iron in both hands and snapped the shaft over his right knee. "Cunt!"

Cal shook his head. "Careful. You'll give yourself a fucking heart attack."

"Fucking thing." Billy threw the pieces of club on the ground and stomped off into the woods. After a few minutes stamping around in the bushes he accepted a one-shot penalty and dropped a new ball on the fairway. He chipped onto the green and both walked onto the smooth, damp surface.

"Me again," said Billy. He knocked a difficult one straight into the middle of the hole from about eighteen feet. "Fucking typical."

Cal tapped his ball in easily. "That's a hundred and twenty quid you owe me."

"Hang on, there's two holes to play yet."

"I'm three up. It's over. Come on, it's freezing. I'll buy you a pint in the clubhouse."

Billy scratched his head. "I'm fucking barred."

"What've you done now?"

"I had a hundred-and-four-shot round last week and Barry was taking the piss. So I said 'Well I can get lessons, but you'll always be a fat cunt...' I got barred for two weeks."

Cal frowned and scratched his head. "He could go on a diet if he's fat."

"I know, but I'd had about eight pints when I said it."

MONDAY

ANGRY-looking dark grey swirls filled the sky over Stalybridge. It was early. Nigel Hornby looked out of the window of his dark grey Range Rover. The snow on the bungalows seemed to illuminate the atmosphere around him. Mark Shaw's two-up two-down semi was part of a Barratt development a bit further up on the left. It was one of several houses that the club rented out to the younger players.

There was not much Nigel wouldn't do for Callum Murphy. Cal was his Best Man when he married Carla, with good reason. Nigel never wanted to be a footballer. He wanted to be a fireman like his brother. He started training with a non-league team only to get him fit for the physical. One night, the goalie didn't turn up for training so Nigel volunteered to go in nets. He'd always been a decent stopper but the teacher who ran the school team wouldn't pick him because he smoked. Nigel saved every shot that night and commanded the penalty box like a pro. A few weeks later, he failed the fireman's test. The bit where you are locked in a tiny, pitch-black room full of smoke wearing full breathing apparatus got too much for him. He didn't know he was claustrophobic. He carried on playing and made the evening paper after keeping eight clean sheets in a row. A Belle Vue scout approached him after the eighth game and he was signed up by the gaffer within weeks.

Jed Brennan thought it was a joke that the club had bought a non-league goalie and relentlessly took the piss out of any minor slip-up. Cal never joined in though and made an effort to get to know him. This touched Nigel, who wasn't used to having people trying to make friends with him, and they started going out for pints together. Cal helped him settle in to this weird new life. That was three years ago.

The Shaw situation was Nigel's responsibility. Shaw came from Leeds with a bad reputation and was cocky and brash. When he asked Nigel to pick him up for training because he was banned from driving, he did it in front of the gaffer, so he couldn't really say no. Shaw's constant chatter got on his tits early in the mornings. It was like having a bird in the car. But he sometimes brought coffee and bacon barms out. That was welcome because the canteen only did poached eggs and cereal. Nigel warmed to him further when he said he'd been to borstal when he was fourteen for hitting a teacher. Nigel had too, for attacking a bloke who caught him nicking a copy of *Razzle* from Lavells. When Cal told him they needed a defender in their gang, Nigel suggested Shaw might fit the bill.

Nigel turned onto the driveway of Shaw's house, fresh snow creaking under his tyres.

He got out of the car and walked up to the front door, his Adidas Stan Smiths taking on water through the little holes in the sides. He rang the doorbell and didn't hear anything. Fucking doorbells you can't hear from outside. He waited ten seconds before rapping loudly on the front door.

"Hang on," he heard Shaw grumble. "Give us a chance, for fuck's sake."

The door opened and the defender looked half asleep. He was wearing a white towelling dressing gown open at the front revealing black and white striped cotton pyjamas. The head of the colourful snake tattooed from his ribs to his neck was visible below his left ear.

"Nigel. What you doing here? We've got the day off, haven't we?"

"Having a tug were ya?

"No. Why?"

Nigel pointed at his groin. "Your fucking cock's hanging out... and you've got a fucking semi."

Shaw looked down. "Fuck," he said, quickly tucking away his half-erect penis. "You've got me. Come in, quick."

"Dunno if I should now," said Nigel, following him in. His eyes panned around the messy room. In the corner by the window was a tatty silver Christmas tree with gaudy blinking fairy lights. It was like a relic from the seventies. Most of the branches were crooked and bent. An Anglepoise lamp with a dust-covered head looked like it had been on all night. A living flame gas fire flickered in the hearth. A video game was paused on the screen of a large Sony Trinitron telly in the corner. Black wires led from the giant box to a Nintendo console.

"What's up then, mate?" Shaw rubbed his eyes.

"Jesus," groaned Nigel, creasing up his face. "Smells like you've been having a fisting competition in here."

Shaw laughed. "Fancy a game?"

"Fisting?"

"No... *Street Fighter*."

"I'm taking the piss. Computer games are for kids. Are you brewing up, or what?"

"Go on then." Shaw pointed at a grubby futon. "Sit there. Nescafe?"

"Tea. Two sugars."

Shaw went to the kitchen. He was twenty-two and had a reputation as a tough, uncompromising defender with discipline issues. A month before he joined Belle Vue, he headbutted a lad outside a pub, breaking his nose and fracturing his jaw. One of the papers was campaigning against thuggery in football and Shaw was a sitting duck. The victim posed for a photo with his purple nose splattered across his face. An Elastoplast was stretched across the mess. The headline screamed MARK OF A THUG.

"I was gonna ring you anyway," he shouted. "What's up with Cal? He was being a right wanker yesterday."

Nigel said nothing. Shaw must have switched a radio on because Nigel could hear The Pogues' *Fairytale in New York* playing. Carla loved that song. They sang it together in a bar in New York on their honeymoon. She blew a small fortune on Fifth Avenue that trip.

"You agreed to help us make sure it ended one-all, Mark. For twenty grand. We trusted you. I trusted you."

"I know but... that Kelly was getting right on my tits. He kept saying I was toss. Teckin' the piss. I played with him at Walsall, you know?"

Nigel said nothing.

"Anyway, with Simon setting me up I just thought it was okay to head it in... I mean, West Ham are top of the league. I've got my career to think about. But if Cal wants to do another one, the next game. I'm up for it... you know?"

Nigel calmly picked up his tea and took a sip. "You seem to have got the wrong end of the stick. Saturday was just a one-off. A bit of Christmas fun between the lads. Nothing more."

Shaw snorted. "It didn't seem like it was just a bit of fun when the cunt gobbed me for mentioning it yesterday..."

"Well never you mind that. I've come to tell you we want you out. Out of Belle Vue, out of Manchester."

"Out?"

"Say you're homesick or summat. No one will be surprised, not with your background."

Shaw was taken aback.

"I'm not leaving," he said. "I like it. And the fans like me. So does the manager."

"Tough shit. If Cal wants you out, you are out. That's that."

Shaw couldn't believe what he was hearing. "Tell you what... if Cal gives me my twenty grand, I'll go," he replied defiantly. "If not, he can get fucked."

Nigel suddenly sprung to his feet and grabbed him by the throat. There was a dull thud as his head bashed against the plasterboard wall behind him. "No, you can get fucked," he snarled.

Shaw tried to shout but his air supply was cut off and he could only gasp. After a few seconds, his eyes clouded over and he slid down the wall.

His vision was blurred when came to. He was tied to one of his dining chairs with his washing line. His left leg was fastened against the leg of the chair but his right leg was stuck out in front of him, with his foot resting on his coffee table. His groin area was wet.

"Alright, Mark?" he heard Nigel ask. "Looks like you've pissed yourself."

"Mung..." Shaw couldn't speak. "Masur..." He noticed his pyjama leg was rolled up and tried to wiggle his toes. Nothing happened. He struggled in his seat.

"There's no point struggling, Mark," Nigel said, matter-of-factly. "I've given you a little injection to dull the pain. Handy if you know where Tommy the physio keeps his supplies."

Cold fear gave Shaw his voice back. "What the fuck Nigel...? You can't do this. I'll go to the press." It felt like someone else was talking as the drug clouded his thoughts. "I'll tell them you were trying to fix the match..."

Nigel laughed, his eyes wide open. "You're not in a position to make threats, Mark. You're part of the conspiracy. Now shut the fuck up."

"You cunt," he whined.

"I said shup." Nigel stuffed a sweaty sock he'd found on the couch into Shaw's mouth and wrapped Sellotape around his head several times. The taste of his own sweat made Shaw gag. Nigel took hold of the leg resting on the coffee table and stroked it in a disturbingly gentle manner. "This won't hurt me as much as it will you," he said, menacingly.

Shaw's eyes were full of terror as Nigel took a couple of long, deep breaths. It was like he was in some kind of trance. Suddenly he dropped all fourteen stone of his body weight on his knee in an American wrestling-style elbow drop that the Ultimate Warrior would have been proud of. There was a sickening crunch of bone and sinew, like a tree's branch snapping. Shaw tried to scream but only a blood-curdling squeal came out. Snot dribbled from his left nostril. As it rolled down his top lip, he passed out again, this time into a world of nightmares. Nigel untied him, removed the gag and lifted him to his feet. He was heavy so it was no easy task. He came to again. Nigel set him to stand but he immediately buckled and flopped onto the carpet. His knee had already swollen to the size of a grapefruit in the leg of his pyjama pants.

Nigel was satisfied. He kicked Shaw in the ribs. "If anyone asks, you fell over jogging. I don't want to see you at the club again. Do not fuck with us, I'm warning you."

Shaw lay groaning on the carpet as Nigel left the house. He must have rolled on top of his Nintendo control pad and un-paused the game because on the TV screen his character Ryu was taking a heavy battering from his American rival, Ken.

>>>

VICTORIA'S eighteen-year-old MGB had stubbornly refused to start and she had been lucky to get a seat on the packed bus travelling up Wilmslow Road. The festive spirit of her fellow passengers, or looking at it another way, the whiff of stale booze, still clung to her clothes as she walked across Piccadilly Gardens under her pink umbrella. A twenty-foot-tall Christmas tree covered in thousands of lights twinkled in the morning gloom beside the Queen Victoria statue. The tramps who usually dossed there had been moved on by the police. Two stern-looking cops hovered, talking amongst themselves and smoking.

Victoria hurried down Market Street, lifting up her handbag so it too benefited from the shelter her brolly provided. The windows of the HMV were full of posters for Simply Red's latest album *A New Flame*. The drizzle continued to fall as she passed the Royal Exchange in St Ann's Square.

The Chronicle Building was an ugly, grey office block on Deansgate just a hundred yards along from the stunning Victorian neo-Gothic John Rylands Library. Victoria nipped into the revolving doors ahead of a sub editor she vaguely knew. He looked hung over. Christmas provided good cover for alcoholics like him. She stuck her hand between the doors of a lift as they closed. It was packed but she pushed her way inside, leaned across a red-headed man in a jumper with a reindeer on the front and hit the door-close button before the drunken sub could try to squeeze in too.

On level two, she walked through the double doors into the newsroom and sat down at her desk. A scrap of paper lying on top of her keyboard read: "Victoria. Granada Dave has a story for you. Kerry."

"Heath!" shouted The *Chron*'s editor John Waters through the open door of his office. "Get in here, now!"

Victoria did as she was told and the venetian blind on the back of the door swished as she pushed it closed. "Sit," Waters ordered, pointing at the orange plastic chair in front of his Formica desk.

Around the walls were framed copies of various important front pages from over the years. There was a drinks cabinet in the corner. Waters was slumped in a tatty leather armchair under a portrait of the Queen. He had a red, puffy face from thousands of long boozy lunches with contacts, sycophants and hangers-on. He had been married four times, the women who became his wives eventually learning that he cared for nothing as much as newspapers. Trivial mistakes such as an apostrophe in the wrong place in a story about a school fête at the bottom of a column on page thirty-nine enraged him. The *Chronicle* was Newspaper of the Year and he was proud of it.

He began what he had to say with a hacking cough. "The rabbi story," he continued, eyes watering. "Incredibly brave, Heath. Incredibly brave. Nasty bugger, by all accounts. Could have turned violent."

"He could, John," she replied, full of herself. "He was a big man, fat... very sweaty. Gross."

"Yes," said the editor, tapping his index fingers together in front of his double chin. "That little stunt put on nearly nine thousand extra sales. The printers had to stay on for two hours to get them all off the presses. Double time. They were chuffed, I can tell you. Merry Christmases and doubles all round. I was summoned to the boardroom today. The directors asked me to pass on to you their thanks."

Victoria smiled. "It was nothing," she said. "I was just doing my job."

He nodded at her so she nodded back.

"Guess what else," he said.

"They want me to put your name forward for Group Reporter of the Year. And if I'm being honest, I'd say you were a dead cert to win it."

Victoria couldn't help but blush. "Thank you, John."

He suddenly slammed his fist hard on his desk, causing his most recent wedding photo to topple over. "Don't you fucking thank me, Heath... because I'm not thanking you for going undercover without my permission. What did you think you were playing at, going into a brothel, alone, dressed as a prostitute, and jumping up to take pictures? How do you think it would look for this newspaper, or for me, if one of my reporters got stabbed or shot or... raped, while working undercover. Who do you think the police would want to speak to first?"

Victoria scratched her head. "Er... me, hopefully? If I'd been raped, that is. Anyway, it wasn't a brothel. It was his house."

Waters' face was deep scarlet now. "Watch it, Heath. The board might think the sun shines out of your arse, but I don't. Your ego worries me. Your attitude worries me. We're not insured for those kind of tricks. There should have been someone there with you. You should have at least taken a snapper along."

"A man, you mean?"

"Wipe that smile off your face." He pointed at her. "Listen here. If you ever keep me in the dark about a story again, I'll sack you on the spot. I don't care how many fucking sales your stories put on."

>>>

EDO strode down King Street holding Christina's hand tightly. The Dutch midfielder had joined Belle Vue from Ajax before the start of the previous season. Edo loved his girlfriend very much. His family had moved to Amsterdam from Aruba before he was born. His father found a job at the Heineken brouwerij and they moved into a block of flats in Haarlem, where Edo spent his childhood. Christina was eighteen when they met at a fashion show. She had smiled at him as she walked down the catwalk and he waited until she was about to leave before he went to say hi. She ended up staying at his flat near the Vondelpark that night. His timing had always been impeccable. In Holland, Christina had appeared in fashion magazines and adverts and a facsimile of her face appeared on a Time

Bandits single sleeve. In Manchester, Factory Records had cast her as the love interest in the video for a song that went nowhere, and that was all. The local girls got all the work. She missed Amsterdam and they had argued that morning about moving back. Edo hoped this shopping trip would cheer her up.

King Street was busy with Manchester's wealthiest Christmas shoppers. Snowflake-shaped Christmas lights twinkled above them suspended on wires crossing the street. Edo and Christina reached Chanel, where a black sequinned cocktail dress caught her eye.

"Edo, look," she said. "It's so beautiful, don't you think?" She moved in close enough for him to smell of her No.5. Christina was six feet tall and slim with coffee-coloured skin and big brown eyes. Plump lips framed a brilliant white smile. Edo imagined the dress shimmering on her hips as she sat sipping a Cosmopolitan in a New York City bar.

"It's not as beautiful as you, baby, but you should definitely try it on," he replied. "It would be perfect for tonight."

She giggled and put her hand to her cheek. Compliments never got old on the likes of Christina. "Let's go inside, they have many nice dresses here."

Edo had ventured out in a chunky jumper but no jacket and was glad for a bit of time indoors. The boutique was decked out with gold rails that each displayed just a few pricy garments. The polished tile floor made the retail area appear bigger than it really was.

A blonde assistant approached.

"Hey Christina," said the girl. "Nice to see you again. How did those boots work out for you?"

Christina's grin showed off perfect teeth. "Cheryl! Nice to see you. Ah, the boots. I've only worn them once but Edo thinks they are very sexy. Don't you honey?"

Edo didn't have a clue which boots they were talking about but said: "Yes, very sexy. Especially without clothes."

"Edo! Shush." Christina put her hand over her mouth this time, and blushed.

Cheryl smiled. She had a nice smile. She was about nineteen. Edo wondered what it would be like to fuck her. Maybe she went to Reds. He would keep an eye out for her.

"Are you looking for anything in particular today?"

"Yes, I think I like this dress," said Christina. She took Cheryl's hand and led her across the shop.

Edo was browsing at a flashy leather jacket with gold trim when he heard Cheryl tell Christina: "A City player's girlfriend bought that one earlier. You don't want to be seen in the same dress as someone else."

Christina sounded disappointed but relieved. "What would I do without you, Cheryl? Why don't you show me what else you have? Edo!"

Edo had put the coat on and was admiring himself in a full-length mirror. He took it off and handed it back to a sales assistant.

"I might be a while here, baby," she told him. "Do you need anything for yourself?"

Edo stared at the big square face of his watch, a Tag Heuer Monaco. "Yeah, I could do with some new jeans. And maybe a jacket. I might as well head over to... one of the other shops... to have a look. Back in half an hour?" He smiled.

"Okay baby," she said. "Half an hour should be fine."

>>>

THE denim selection at French Connection was at the rear of the narrow shop. Two female assistants wearing similar tight black and white striped tops and baggy jeans stood chatting behind the counter. One was filing her red nails. Edo pretended to be interested in a pair of flared jeans on a peg. He scanned around the store and saw Rebecca helping another customer. When she became free, he took down a black pair of jeans he liked the feel of and moved over to the coats. A distressed black leather bomber jacket caught his eye, much more Manchester than the Chanel number. He took it off the rail and saw it was his size. He was about to slip it on when Rebecca tapped him on the shoulder.

"Er, who said you could try that on?" She grinned, playing with her hair.

"Rebecca." he smiled. "How are you? This jacket is mint." He found it amused girls when he used Mancunian phrases.

It worked and she smiled back. "Well we'd better get you into a cubicle," she said, holding eye contact.

She was about twenty-two, Edo reckoned. She had a pretty freckled face and wore a faded denim skirt and a white cotton blouse knotted at the front. "There's no one in the far one. Try it on and you can model it for me."

"You're coming in the changing room with me?"

Rebecca punched him on the arm. "No... you put it on, then come out, I meant." She opened the door of the far cubicle and showed him inside. "There you go, cheeky," she grinned.

Inside was a padded bench, a full-length mirror and three pegs on the side wall. Edo reckoned he had twenty minutes. He got naked and sat down. "Rebecca. Are you there? I need an opinion."

"Come out, then, show me," she replied.

"No... You come in. In case I look like shit."

Rebecca took a deep breath and checked no-one was looking before opening the door. Edo was sitting on the bench wearing nothing but his watch. The clothes he had arrived in hung on the pegs alongside the new gear. He had a huge grin on his face and a hard-on. "What do you think, baby?"

She was speechless so he pulled her onto his knee. He leaned around her and kissed her softly on the mouth, sucking her top lip. He could tell she was nervous and it added to the thrill. The kiss lasted a minute or so, during which time he had skilfully unbuttoned her shirt. He scooped her breasts out of her bra and as he sucked a nipple there was an obvious smacking sound.

"Shush," she whispered. "I can't afford to get caught. It's more than my job's worth."

"Don't worry," he replied, "I know the manager and I'm a good customer."

Rebecca sighed, stood up and turned to face him. "Just be quiet," she whispered. She then hitched up her skirt, moved her baby-blue knickers to one side and lowered herself onto him. She gasped and had to bite her lip as he entered her. His eyes were closed and he had a big grin on his face. He enjoyed her wet warmth and her tightness as she jiggled up and down.

After a few minutes, he came, grinning. Rebecca eased herself off him, quickly got dressed and left the cubicle. She nonchalantly walked back over to the cash desk in the middle of the shop floor and took a swig from a can of Cherry Coke. About a minute later, Edo emerged, wearing his own clothes and also the bomber jacket. He went up to the counter where Rebecca was pretending to be busy, folding clothes.

"I think I'll leave the jeans," he said. "But I'll take the jacket. It's freezing out there."

"Good choice," she said, some buttons on the till beeping as she casually tapped them.

He handed over his Visa card. She laid it on the metal surface of the card imprinter and slid the chunky plastic bridge across with a clunk... and back with a click. She then pushed his card and the shiny paper card slip towards him. He signed it and put the card away.

"Thank you, Rebecca. Until next time, huh?"

She giggled. "Yes. Have a nice evening."

Edo left the shop, striding across King Street, relaxed and sated. Snow was coming down from the bruised sky in massive flakes. He looked at his watch and saw he had been gone nearly half an hour. He stepped up the pace back to Chanel, where he found Christina sitting on a chaise longue beside Cheryl. Both were sipping glasses of pink Champagne. Everything was fine.

>>>

THE neon red Granada TV sign on top of the eight-storey glass building shone out in Castlefield's darkening sky. Snow was falling in massive flakes and there was a thick white blanket settling on the pavement. Victoria was going to see David Ashton, or Granada Dave as he was known to her and Kerry. She introduced herself at reception and five minutes later, he appeared. He had a Manchester City club pin on his tie. Victoria had never seen him in anything smarter than a Fila polo shirt. She and Dave were roughly the same age but he seemed much older because his hairline was receding.

"Victoria. How are you?" he said, offering a hand.

"Very well thanks, Dave... good to see you. Nice tie." She laughed, ignoring the hand and kissing his cheek.

He frowned and pulled at the collar of his shirt. "New directive from upstairs. I feel a right knob in this noose. Cheers for coming."

"Good to see you." She gave him a hug.

They parted and he grinned. "You n'all," he said. "Come up to the shoe box."

The edit suites at Granada Studios were small, soundproof rooms with screens, control wheels and keyboards on a desk. The door to Dave's "shoe box" was the first in the corridor. A half-inflated lilo had been kicked under the desk. It was blue and covered in cartoon lobsters. He noticed her looking at it. "For when I need forty winks," he explained.

Victoria took off her coat and hung it up on the back of the door. She sat down and folded her arms. He was a nice guy but he had previous for ogling her boobs.

"I've got something to show you," he said.

"Does it come in a green glass bottle that pops when you open it?" She smiled. Dave had once put a hundred pound bottle of Moet on his Access card when he was drunk and it got mentioned every time they got together.

"Haha, no... you beat me to it. Work related, this. Check this out. I was editing a highlights package last night, and I spotted something fishy." He gestured at a screen.

Granada Dave could slow down the footage of games, images the public hadn't seen, to just a single frame at a time. Victoria thought he only covered United and City and was surprised to see a lower league match being played. One of the teams wore black and yellow.

"What's all this Dave?"

"It's a Division Two game from Saturday... West Ham against our very own Belle Vue down in London. Hold on a sec," he said, nodding as he rotated the dial. "Watch."

He hit the pause button to freeze one of the screens. He pointed at a player who was running away from goal with his fist in the air with two men also in yellow and black sprinting after him. "The lad who scored for Belle Vue is called Mark Shaw."

Victoria nodded.

"And that bloke there is Callum Murphy," he went on, tapping the screen where the striker was standing. "You might recognise him. He used to play for United."

"No."

The footballer had short cropped hair, a sunbed tan and muscular arms and shoulders. He was short but looked strong enough to throw Victoria over his shoulder if he wanted to. The camera zoomed in on his handsome face. He was grimacing. He certainly didn't look like a man whose team had just scored the winner.

The second screen was frozen on an image of another man. "This is Nigel Hornby, big pal of Murphy's," said Dave. She saw a gingerhaired giant and out-of-focus numbers on the scoreboard behind him. His arms were held high but the expression on his face was also one of intense disappointment.

"Is this what you do instead of watching porn?"

"No, I mean..." Granada Dave was shaking his head.

"I'm taking the piss. So why am I here, exactly?"

"I don't think either Callum Murphy or Nigel Hornby wanted that winner to go in," he said. "As for Shaw, who knows? I'm thinking it could be match fixing."

Victoria shrugged. It looked like Murphy needed a hug. "Maybe," she said. "I'll look into it when I get a chance but I've been spending a lot of time in the library lately. Maybe it's one for the sports desk."

Granada Dave shook his head. "I could have given it to your sports lads, Victoria. If this is match fixing it's a criminal matter. That's front page news, not sports news. Sports writers would just bury this, they don't want to upset the clubs."

He could not disguise his annoyance at her lack of enthusiasm. But he knew full well that Victoria hated football, she had told him many times. She thought the players were immature, self-centred and callous. "I'm not a fan of football," she said.

"I know, that's why I came to you," said Dave. "You're a terrier when you get going. You won't let chairmen and agents fob you off. But listen... if you're not interested I could always pass it on to McIlhenny."

Victoria hated Rob McIlhenny from the *Sunday Mail* more than she hated football, and Dave knew it. McIlhenny had tried to cop off with her one night at the Press Club and turned nasty when she knocked him back. "All right," she said. "Don't tell him. Give me a day or two. Now. Fancy a pint?"

Victoria was happy in the haze of a drunken hour, or two hours in fact, when she got back to the paper. She had polished off three large gin and tonics while Dave knocked back four pints of Boddingtons.

She dodged a couple of sports journalists kicking a ball around the newsroom on her way to cover the story. Dave had convinced her. The Belle Vue thing was potentially huge. Loads of people bought the paper just for the football coverage, wanting the latest news about United and City and the other clubs.

Millions thought there was nothing more important in life than football.

If Mark Shaw, Callum Murphy and Nigel Hornby were fixing matches, the public had a right to know.

\>\>\>

CAL sat up on his bed quickly, rubbing his eyes. His head felt hazy. He had fallen asleep immediately after Nigel had phoned to say the Shaw situation had been sorted. He could think about how to engineer the two-all scoreline O'Donnell had demanded later. He stretched, stood up and went in the bathroom. After ten big swigs of very cold water from the bathroom tap, he flexed his muscles in front of the mirror. His thick eyebrows stood out above his blue eyes. His cheeks and chin were covered in a three-day stubble growth.

Cal's burly chest was covered in dark curls. A thin line of hair ran down the centre of his abdominal muscles, which were sharply-defined in segments like a shield of muscle around his torso. His lower abdomen was shaped like a V that pointed down to his groin. His legs were strong and firm and marked with various scars from bad tackles and his arms were toned but not too muscular. He was an athlete, not a bodybuilder.

He lay down on the tiled floor and did five dozen sit-ups followed by five dozen press-ups. He got in the shower and turned the water as hot as he could stand it. After five minutes in the steam he was wide awake again. He had a wet shave and applied a palmful of Kouros which stung his skin. He stood in front of the mirror, naked, assessing his body. He was satisfied by what he saw. His crew cut needed doing again but it looked okay with a bit of wax on it. He brushed his teeth and remembered he had no clean underpants. "Fuck," he muttered. He retrieved the Calvin Kleins he'd been wearing all day from the laundry bag. They were a bit baggy but thankfully there were no skid marks.

He buttoned his wing-collar shirt, which was pressed to perfection by the hotel's laundry, and clipped his white silk bowtie around his neck. He put his Armani tuxedo and crocodile skin Patrick Cox loafers on, locked his room and headed downstairs to the hotel ballroom. It was party time.

>>>

INSTEAD of having their own Christmas party, Belle Vue Football Club had several tables at the Majestic Christmas charity ball. As one of the club's senior players, Cal was seated on the one with the gaffer and his pasty white wife Elsie; the chairman Dave Chandler, who had made a fortune from fireplaces, and his orange-tanned wife

Veronica; and the club captain Jed Brennan. Two other VIPs he had seen around the club on match days completed the circle. On the table beside them were another two sponsors and their partners along with Edo and Christina, Nigel and Carla, and Simon. Every now and then, Cal would hear Edo's booming laugh and wished he was sitting with his friends. At least his wages had gone into his bank account.

United had five tables at the ball, City had three or four, Granada TV had four and so did Factory records. The others had been booked by local businesses eager to tie their Christmas party in with a charity event and rub shoulders with the city's stars. Tony Wilson was on table five with some young lads in Top Man suits looking just scruffy enough to be in one of his Factory bands. Cal had also seen the *Coronation Street* actress Julie Goodyear in the lobby. All in all, about three hundred people were there getting pissed and shouting over each other.

Dean Martin's *Let It Snow* was playing as Jed asked Cal to pull his cracker with him. The gift fell on the table in front of Cal, a miniature deck of cards wrapped in cellophane. He put on the green paper party hat, had a gulp of his red wine and unfurled the little slip of paper that fell out of the cracker too. Tapping his fork on his glass, he said loudly in his best posh voice: "I say, I say, I say!"

One of the suits, a heavy woman of about thirty-five with the top two buttons of her blouse undone to reveal a freckled cleavage, said excitedly: "Oooh, joke!" The others on the table turned to look at Cal.

"Why did the man who ate Christmas decorations get taken to hospital?"

"I don't know," the woman said.

"He was suffering from tinsel-itis." Cal forced a fake grin.

The woman cackled and her chin wobbled. Cal had read in the paper that some women were fat because of water retention but surely she had a case of cake retention. That's cruel, he admonished himself. Christmas is no time to be an arsehole. He drank more wine.

Jed grabbed Cal's cracker, desperate to take the table's attention for himself. He gripped it in a way that he couldn't lose. His prize was a plastic bulldog clip.

"This one ain't bad," he said, as he read the joke to himself. "Why didn't Joseph throw the myrrh away? There was no room in the bin."

No one laughed.

Chandler was a fat man of about sixty who liked to smoke cigars before, during and after a meal. The female suit wasn't enjoying the smoke and kept coughing theatrically but he either didn't notice or didn't care. "Fantastic performance at the weekend, lads," he said. "What a result."

"Thanks very much," said Jed. "We're on a bit of a roll at the moment."

Like the chairman, the gaffer was also enjoying a smoke; one of his beloved Rothmans. His white hair was stained orange at the front thanks to his habit.

"So George, any good young 'uns coming through I should know about?" Chandler asked.

The gaffer took another drag as he had a think. "We've got a young coon called Anthony Butterworth who's very promising. A real prospect."

Chandler nodded. "Butterworth? I don't think I've seen him play."

"He can be a bit lazy at times but you expect that. I've managed a few darkies over the years so I know how to handle them. He's fast and tricky but a bit thin yet. He might give Simon a bit of competition on the right when he fills out."

"Good work. They seem to do very well over here. They're very athletic, aren't they?"

The gaffer nodded and it triggered a bout of coughing and spluttering.

Cal grabbed the opportunity to change the subject from Butterworth, who was a good kid. Over here? Fat prick. Young Tony was born in Oldham, for fuck's sake.

"Well, I'm looking forward to giving Coventry a good stuffing on Boxing Day," he put to the table.

"Haha, stuffing," Jed piped up, sniggering. "Like Christmas turkeys."

The chairman laughed and cigar smoke filled the air. A plate was placed in front of Cal. On it was two disks of overcooked white meat, a shrivelled sausage wrapped in streaky bacon, and a crispy ball of what was once stuffing. That was flanked by three dried-up roast potatoes and two boiled potatoes. Completing the medley was some wrinkled peas, rock hard carrot batons and a lump of cauliflower in a puddle of water. Poured on top of the so-called Christmas Dinner was some dark, lumpy gravy.

"Festive," said Cal to no-one in particular, and shrugged. He raised his glass. "Cheers everyone, a merry Christmas to you and yours!"

Everyone raised their wine glasses. "Cheers."

Suddenly, something slimy hit him on the cheek. It was a sausage wrapped in bacon and it had come from the next table. Simon was holding his fork like a catapult and grinning. Nigel and Carla, sitting to Simon's left wearing red and green party hats, were stifling laughter. Edo and Christina were having an animated conversation in Dutch, oblivious.

Cal shook his head and growled: "Grow up, Cozzer, you penis."

He was smiling though as he wiped gravy off his face with a napkin. Fuck me, I am actually enjoying myself here, he thought.

When everyone had done with their main course, waiters replaced the plates with bowls of Christmas pudding and custard. The pudding was like a giant brown boiled sweet and the custard was lumpy. Cal chipped away at it with his spoon and ate it quickly, hoping the taste wouldn't linger. He took off his bow tie and pocketed it, relaxing in his head as he did so. He found himself slightly drunk, slightly full and very much in the Christmas spirit.

\>\>\>

"BANG!" shouted Victoria.
Kerry Winters nearly jumped out of her skin. She spun around on the office chair in the basement library of the *Evening Chronicle* building clutching her hand to her heart.

"Fuck me Victoria! Jesus. I nearly shat myself."

Victoria grinned as she patted her on the shoulder. "You should have seen your face. Classic. What are you doing down here at this hour?"

Kerry was five foot tall and, as she would say, curvy because of all the canapes and cocktails she consumed in her job as a showbiz reporter. "I'm trying to dig out this fucking interview we ran last time Belinda Carlisle was in town. Some fuckwit's fucked up the order of the cuttings. I need some background info about her. Apparently she's just going to roll into Manchester on her tour bus, play her gig and then fuck off back down to London straight after. No interviews, no press conference, nothing. Fucking cow. Jesus, Victoria, my heart's still beating like fuck."

Victoria patted her friend's arm. "Sounds like a pain in the arse. Here, breathe. Relax. That's it."

Kerry wiped her brow and then her eyes. "You get used to these fucking divas in my line of work. Waters wants me to jump out as she gets off the coach but there's no chance she'll speak to me. I bet life's not such a load of shit on investigations. What are you doing down here?"

The library was gloomy and dank even on the brightest summer day. In the middle of winter it was probably warmer outside. The walls were plain grey concrete which no-one had ever painted. Bored journalists had scribbled intellectual graffiti on them. Fight apathy, or don't. The floor-to-ceiling banks of bookshelves were fixed to rails along which they moved back and forward to save space for all the old newspapers, periodicals, biographies and *Who's Who*s.

"I'm going to pull the cuttings out on these footballers, Callum Murphy and Nigel Hornby."

"Murphy? Where have I heard that name before?"

Victoria shrugged. "He plays for Belle Vue. Maybe you've read about him in the sports pages."

"I doubt it, I fucking hate football. Is that gin I can smell on your breath?"

Victoria laughed. "I've just had a drink with Dave Ashton."

"Granada Dave? I haven't seen him for fucking yonks. Tell me more!"

Victoria just smiled. "He's well."

"Well? I hope your novelist boyfriend doesn't find out you're having secret late-night trysts with other men. The boring bastard might cut you out of the royalties when he finally finishes that bestseller of his."

"Oi! I get to say that about him, not you."

"You're always saying he's a boring fucker."

"I don't always say that." Victoria scowled. She stared at the ceiling. It was painted white but condensation made it appear to be covered in scabs. "When are you going to get yourself a man anyway?"

"Men play far too big a role in my life as it is, Victoria. Editors, agents, managers. All fucking men. Men, men, fucking men. Coffee?"

"Please."

Victoria put her coat on the seat next to Kerry's, went to a filing cabinet and brought back a box of microfiche cards. She inserted one into the Kodak reader machine and a *Chronicle* front page appeared on the backlit screen. She started by searching for stories about Hornby, the goalkeeper. Dave's theory was that he was the most likely to be up to something. A keeper could let a goal in and make it look like a mistake.

"Here you go," said Kerry, passing her a small plastic cup from the drinks machine. She began reading over Victoria's shoulder. "What's this bloke's name again?"

"Nigel Hornby."

"Not him, the other one."

"Callum Murphy?"

Kerry cackled. "Why do you say his name in a funny way?"

"I don't. I just say it normally. Callum Murphy."

"You did it again. I heard it clearly. It's your tone. You want to fuck him."

"Not everyone has a one track mind like you, Kerry," said Victoria, taking a gulp of coffee. She winced. "Bloody hell. Good job I'm not driving."

"I made 'em Irish. There's a Jameson's miniature in each one. No denials then? He must be a looker. Budge over, let me see."

Kerry pushed in and began twiddling the knobs on the reader as Victoria sipped the most Irish coffee she had ever had. After a while, a headline: BELLE VUE STAR TIPPED FOR ENGLAND CALL UP.

"Here he is. I do know him, well of him anyway. They say he has the biggest knob in Manchester and likes to use it on reporters."

Kerry had a knack for making her blush. "Don't mess about... Who is he?"

"He owns Reds, this backstreet dive up near Deansgate. Last I heard he was living at the Majestic."

"What's this Reds place like?"

"It's a bit sweaty. Full of ravers and pill heads, that sort of place. Do you want to scope it out?"

"Now? How many of these coffees have you had?"

Kerry grinned. "A couple. I just thought you might want to go and talk to Callum Murphy. Since it's obvious you want to have his babies."

Victoria spat coffee over the desk. "Shut it! I don't even know the man."

"You're gonna hunt him down, aren't you? Femme fatale job. It'll end in tears."

"Shup! Look, I hate footballers and I love Miles and that's it."

"Whatever you say."

"Footballers are thick as pigshit and all think the sun shines out of their arse."

"I'm still not convinced."

"One of them treated a friend of mine like shit at university."

"What happened?"

"He got her pregnant and after she told him he told her to get an abortion and blanked her. Turned out he was married and had just been out pulling students with his mates. Arsehole.

"At least he didn't give her the virus."

"You're sick."

"Yeah I know. Why isn't Dave investigating it himself?"

"You know he never leaves his little box unless it's to go to the pub or his flat. He said the TV reporters would just bury it, not wanting to upset the clubs."

"Because he wants to shag you, more like."

Victoria sighed and tapped her Parker pen on the grainy image of the muscular footballer with the stubbly, angular jaw on the screen. "He lives at the Majestic?"

"Mad eh? I'd love to live in a posh hotel, me. Room service all the time, get all your washing done, never have to make your bed..."

"It must cost a bomb."

"He's a footballer and he owns a nightclub. Do the maths."

"I suppose so... Listen, what are you doing in the morning? Fancy breakfast at the Majestic? I can put it on my exes. I'll show you some real investigative journalism."

"Well I've got this Belinda Carlisle piece to write... but the Majestic does do a top full English. Fuck it, see you there at nine."

>>>

A TALL silver-haired gentleman in a silver suit with a silver pencil moustache walked up to the podium and tapped the silver microphone three times.

"Is this thing on? MAGIC! Good evening folks and a very Merry Christmas to one and all," the compère shouted. Feedback squealed out of the speakers.

"Oops, my apologies. Thank you all very, very much for coming tonight, ladies and gentlemen. We're very, very grateful that you are all here to help us celebrate the season of goodwill and to raise money for the most wonderful cause, Pendlebury Children's Hospital!"

He paused until the applause and whistles and whoops died down. "Allow me to introduce myself..." he continued. "I'm Michael Ramsdale and I am the head of publicity at the hospital and let me tell you, ladies and gentlemen, that there is nowhere those young boys and girls would rather be than at home celebrating Christmas with their mums and dads and their brothers and sisters. Unfortunately for some of the little tykes that won't be possible... but what we try and do, ladies and gentlemen, is make Pendlebury the second best place they will ever spend Christmas."

"Whoop!" called a woman. Applause rippled around the room again.

"Thank you. Thank you," said Ramsdale. "Now. Are there any Ebeneezer Scrooges here?"

The woman, clearly drunk, stood up and pointed down at the man sitting beside her.

There were chuckles on their table. Ramsdale cleared his throat.

"One there is there, love? Oh dear, never mind eh?... Now without further ado, it's time for our very popular bachelors' auction! We're hoping to raise ten grand tonight to kit out the hospital with loads of new toys. Now, I'd like all the eligible bachelors to come down to the front within the next five minutes. Remember, fellas, it's for a great cause, so no hiding in the lavvie!"

Jed elbowed Cal in the ribs. "Go on, get up there pal," he slurred, having nearly finished a bottle of Riesling. "It's about time you had a bird."

"I'd rather jam a red hot knitting needle in my Jap's eye."

"Come on Cal, don't be a spoilsport... It's for charity. I've got two hundred quid in my purse with your name on it." It was the woman who had taken a shine to him earlier. Her name was Trish and she was a big noise at Radio Rentals, the Belle Vue shirt sponsor. She had consumed a lot of booze. "Mr Murphy," said the chairman as smoke from another fat cigar billowed from his mouth. "You don't want to disappoint our Trish."

"All right. But first I need a triple whisky."

"No," said Trish, "you'll run off. Grab him, Jed!" There was a crazed look in her eye.

"I won't run off, I swear, not from a charity night," said Cal, pretending to be offended. "I just need some Dutch courage. Surely you wouldn't deny me a stiff drink before I stand up and make an arse of myself?"

"I s'pose not," she conceded.

Cal went to the bar. He muscled his way to the front by vaguely muttering "sorry, my mate's there," to no one in particular. He peeled a twenty pound note off his wad. The barmaid smiled. "Yes sir?" It was a very pretty smile. He smiled back.

"A massive whisky, please," he said, "and make it a Talisker."

After being served he turned around and literally bumped into Caroline Parker. Caroline, the one that got away. Her cocktail dress was black and lacy and low cut, putting her cleavage on display. She was tanned and wearing her light brown hair up. She wore white silk gloves that came up to her elbows, fishnet stockings and high heels. "Mind your Scotch," she said.

"What the fuck are you doing here?" He couldn't believe his eyes. Last he heard she was down in London, living with a lad from Sale called Gavin whose band had a record deal. Cal had heard a couple of their songs and had to admit Gavin was a fine guitarist. Caroline had a thing for famous or soon-to-be-famous people.

"Nice to see you too," she replied. His pulse raced. Her tone was sarcastic and her looks were sensational.

He composed himself. "I do not believe this. Someone is looking down on me. This is fate.

Look, our outfits even match." He straightened his jacket.

"Every man here is in black and white, Cal."

He sipped from the strong, smoky liquid in his glass and moved closer to her. "Oh fuck, I didn't notice that. Listen, you've got to help me."

She screwed up her face. "I don't have to do anything. That stuff reeks, by the way. You're not going to try and kiss me again are you?"

"No. It's not that. The chairman's making me go in this bachelor auction. I spose I don't mind, it's for Pendlebury and that, but will you bid two hundred quid for me? You don't have to actually come out with me."

She was softening. "I haven't got two hundred quid."

"I have. If you bid for me, I'll give you the dough."

She half-closed one eye as she considered for a second. Her hand went to her hair and she began playing with it. "I don't know, Cal. I'm here with some mates from Factory records. They might think it's weird."

The auction was about to start. Four men were already on stage, including one of the scruffs from Wilson's table. Ramsdale was tapping the microphone again, getting ready to start.

"Please... I'm begging you. One of the sponsors... she's been eyeing me up all night and I know she's going to bid for me and try and take me home and I don't fancy her and it'll be awkward as fuck when I turn her down."

Caroline thought about it for what seemed like ages before she caved in. "Oh fuck it... all right. But you'll owe me a massive favour, I mean it."

Two blokes beside them at the bar cheered sarcastically. One slapped him on the back.

"Thank you," said Cal, and knocked back the whisky. "I've got to go. Listen out for when they shout me up. Just keep bidding until you get me."

"Alright, I will. Go."

"Oh and Caz..."

"What?"

"Merry Christmas."

>>>

IT was gone two in the morning when Cal went back to his room. Caroline followed him in, tipsy and hiccupping. The drinks had been flowing on the Factory Records table, at which Cal had joined her after the auction debacle. She kicked off the shoes.

"Four hundred quid," he said, shaking his head as he locked the door. "Four hundred quid."

"Please stop going on about it. It's for charity, you can put it down as a tax write-off. You should be thanking me."

"Thanks," he said drily. He put his arms around her from behind and squeezed her tightly. He and Caroline had dated, as the Yanks would say, for three months over the sunny summer of eighty-seven. He was still at United then. She was a year younger than him and had introduced him to the joys of all-night raving instead of sitting drinking at parties at his flat. She always got them invited back for the after-party.

When pre-season training came around in August it was hell. He was exhausted before, during and after every session. He suggested that, now it was football season they could try out some country pubs or go for meals in town. She laughed. There were no rows or fallings-out. She just told him she was moving to London and the following week she was gone.

She turned around to face him. "What am I doing here? You're so bad."

"I asked if you wanted to come up to my suite... and you said yes."

"I thought you might have some whisky and ginger beer."

"I have. But you have to promise not to throw it up on me."

"When have you ever seen me puke? I can drink you under the table."

"Can't we just go to bed?"

"Is that you or your knob talking?"

They were standing in the middle of the living area. He was lightly feeling her arse. She broke the silence. "Ground rule. This is just a one-night stand. Got it?"

He didn't know what to say. He went over to the stereo, loaded Sade's *Stronger Than Pride* into the CD player and hit play as she kissed him lightly on the cheek.

"I own you," she whispered. "You have to do whatever I say."

"Since I gave you the dosh that's not strictly..." She silenced him with a kiss, holding it for a second before pulling back. Her soft lips felt as lovely as ever.

"Okay, you own me, but what about Gavin, your boyfriend?"

"Gav's not my boyfriend. We're just seeing each other."

"I get it," he said, not getting it at all.

He embraced her, taking in the smell of her hair as they looked out of the bay window and over St Peter's Square. A snowball fight was going on among men in suits. Caroline turned, stood on her tiptoes, took his cheeks in her hands and kissed him again. Their tongues met. Her hand brushed his groin and his cock stiffened.

"Mmm." She groaned. She pulled back and began unbuttoning his shirt to reveal his torso. She pushed the fabric back off his shoulders. He slowly unzipped her dress. It fell to the floor and she stepped out of it. He caressed her nipples through the pink satin of her bra as the song *Paradise* reached a crescendo.

He reached behind her and unfastened the clasp, one-handed. As the bra fell, he cupped her smooth, round tits. He pulled close again, skin touching skin and sending shivers down his spine. They took turns planting kisses on each other's upper bodies. He kissed her neck, arms and breasts, gently sucking her nips as his warm hands caressed her arse.

Caroline rubbed against him, kissing his neck and his chest and moving up to his earlobes and flicking her tongue in and out of his ears. She ran her hands over his firm biceps and his solid chest and stomach. Her touches gave him goose pimples and increased the pressure in his cock. She took a deep breath, unfastened his belt, pulled it from its loops and threw it away behind her. His trousers fell to his ankles. She pulled his Calvin Kleins down, got on her knees and took him in her mouth. He could feel the velvety insides of her cheeks on his cock; it felt amazing.

He ran his fingers through her hair, careful not to come, taking deep breaths trying to count the Christmas lights in the square whenever he was getting close. She came up to kiss him again. His hand fell to her pubic mound; below it, she felt wet and warm. His elbow quivered as he put two fingers inside her. It was time for her knickers to come down. She stepped out of them too. She grabbed his shoulders, hoisted herself up and slowly lowered herself onto him, enveloping him, her legs crossed behind him. He carried her to the bed. She gasped as he lowered her onto the Egyptian cotton bedsheet and eased his cock fully in. He kept his strokes long, slow and smooth, enjoying it so much that he was already about to come. She groaned as he pulled out, so far that he could feel cool air on his shaft. Only the tip was inside her now. Her juices glistened on his cock. He pushed back in and she moaned and he knew she was coming and he knew he was coming too. Every nerve in his body tingled as he erupted.

They had sex two more times. He was relieved that she hadn't noticed he'd gone out in dirty undies.

CHRISTMAS EVE

HE woke up at eight o'clock with a fat head and his arm under his pillow. Why did he mix his drinks? You always got punished for it the next day. A long, slow swim would clear his head. A couple of hundred lengths of Chorlton Baths would sort him out. Caroline lay next to him on her front, fast asleep. She was covered from the waist down by the bedsheet, her arm across his torso. He took her wrist and gently lifted her arm. She let out a quiet, low moan but didn't wake as he slipped out of bed. He put his Adidas tracksuit and trainers on quickly and ran her a glass of water. She looked so peaceful, he would leave her to sleep in. She could let herself out when she was ready. Her hair fanned across the pillow and the curve of her right tit was just visible in the gloom. He pulled the white duvet up over her and gently kissed her cheek. He stuffed a towel and his Speedos and goggles into a Head holdall and left the room, closing the door quietly behind him.

>>>

VICTORIA slid the heater switch across to full with a clunk as she pulled out of the public car park under the G-Mex centre. It was a beautiful morning and the sun was high and bright in a blue sky. She drove past the

Majestic and looked over at Kerry, who had the *A to Z* open. "Left... no right," she said.

"Make your mind up..."

"Right. I mean okay, it's on the right."

The Palace Theatre was on their left. "I'm overruling you. It's definitely left after the theatre..." She flicked on the indicator and made the turn.

"Straight on now," said Kerry. "Piece of piss this navigating lark."

"We've only gone around two corners."

Victoria accelerated and heard slush splashing in the wheel arches. The MGB was definitely a summer car. She kept driving. They passed Piccadilly Gardens. "Stevenson Square is third on the right," said Kerry. "Fresh is on the first corner, you can't miss it."

Many of the journalists at the *Chronicle* disliked Kerry. Victoria could see why. Their first meeting had been in the Press Club, when Victoria declared she had "read" English Literature and Kerry sniggered and replied: "What the fuck else do you do with it?"

Kerry had straight blonde hair and had never had a steady boyfriend. She had a steady stream of them. Kerry asked her out to lunch to show her what could and couldn't be claimed on expenses. It turned out there wasn't much that couldn't. And if you didn't play the game, everyone else would look bad. Kerry claimed George Michael had once invited her back to his hotel room after a gig at the Apollo but Victoria suspected she was lying. It was a known fact that George liked brunettes, not blondes.

The plan was to stake out the salon where Cal was getting his hair done. Good old-fashioned journalistic legwork had gleaned this information. After a hearty breakfast of fried egg, cured bacon, pork sausage, grilled tomato, mushroom, baked beans and toast at the Majestic, they had calmly strolled up to reception and asked for the manager. "Hello, er, James," Victoria had said, using her considerable powers of deduction. His name was on a gold badge on the lapel. "Victoria Heath and Kerry Winters. We're supposed to be meeting a friend here today. I don't know if he's come down yet. Can you help?"

James Kidd shook his head. "Sorry. We don't give out details of our guests' movements without permission, I'm afraid. The Majestic prides itself on discretion."

Victoria exhaled. "Damn," she said. "I'm late for a meeting with him, you see. I was meant to meet him in the lobby twenty minutes ago. Got stuck in a bloody traffic jam on the East Lancs Road."

"Sorry to hear that," he said, clearly not sorry at all, and looked away as if to suggest he had other things to get on with.

An idea came to her. "Are you sure you can't help me? It's a revenue matter. His name's Callum Murphy." She was hoping to convince him she was some sort of official.

Kidd's eyes lit up. Could this be his chance to get Murphy out of his hotel? Guest discretion suddenly meant a lot less to him.

He leant over the polished counter and whispered: "Are you investigating him? What's he done?"

"Well let's just say he shouldn't really be flashing his money around like he does."

Kidd nodded knowingly and took a deep breath. "You might find him at Fresh off Oldham Street. It's a hairdresser's. They rang up to confirm the appointment about an hour ago." He tapped the side of his nose. "You didn't get it from me though."

Victoria took the corner into Stevenson Square very slowly. They were off the gritted roads again and driving on compacted snow. There was a parking space across the road from Fresh between a Metro and a Ford Escort. Victoria pulled up next to the Escort. The gears crunched as she shifted into reverse and gently let out the clutch. She heaved the steering wheel into full lock position. Her back tyre bumped the kerb as she backed up.

There was silence as Victoria's face turned red.

"You have to turn the wheel back quicker or you won't get it in the space," advised Kerry.

"Shush... I'm doing it!" Victoria decided to pull out and start again. She drove out into the road and lined up parallel to the Escort again. She jammed the gear stick into reverse with another crunch and the MGB began to roll back as she released the clutch. Her heeled boot slipped and the car suddenly jerked and stalled. Kerry said nothing, just grinned. Victoria turned the ignition again, and moved back into position alongside to the Escort. There was now a knot in her stomach. Relax. You can do this. She let out the clutch even more slowly this time. She checked her mirror and the back of the car seemed to be too perpendicular to the Metro. Still edging back, she quickly turned the wheel back clockwise as far as it would go.

"Watch out!" shouted Kerry.

Victoria jammed on the brakes. Her bumper was an inch from the Metro, which she could now see had a couple inside both wearing colourful bobble hats. "Stop shouting, or you can bloody well get out and walk."

"Sorry," said Kerry, not meaning it. "I won't say another word."

The Metro suddenly pulled away, leaving her a huge space. She straightened the wheel, accelerated a bit and, to her surprise, ended up with both offside tyres nestling snugly against the kerb.

"Amazing driving," said Kerry, clapping sarcastically.

Cal suddenly emerged from the salon, hot air from inside turning to steam around him. His hair was freshly crew-cut and he was wearing aviator sunglasses. He looked like Tom Cruise in *Top Gun*. He walked towards a grey Ford Sierra across the street. The indicators flashed as he disarmed the alarm.

"I thought he'd have a nicer car," Victoria said.

"That is a nice car. It's a fucking RS Cosworth. It'll do a hundred and forty miles an hour, no problem. It's virtually a racing car."

"It looks like a Ford Sierra to me. What do you know about racing cars?"

"Victoria, he's backing up. If we're gonna follow him, I'd better drive."

"I don't think so. I've always wanted to follow someone. I'll just stay two cars behind him. I saw Jill Gascoine tailing a robber like that on *C.A.T.S. Eyes*."

Kerry sighed. "Fine, but could you turn the heater down a bit please? It's like a fucking sauna in here."

Victoria followed Cal down the A6, through Stockport and down lanes passing snow-covered fields until they reached Disley. Eventually Cal pulled into the driveway of a cottage five minutes from its closest neighbour. Snow-covered hills meandered off into the distance. Victoria carried on going for a hundred yards before stopping on the snow-covered verge.

"Could you not have parked any further away? I think I saw a space outside Kendal's," said Kerry, sarcastically.

Victoria got out and went round to the boot. She hadn't used her Olympus SLR since the summer but she knew there was a roll of film in it. She took it out, screwed her zoom lens on it and hung it around her neck.

"Follow me," she said, stamping her way towards the highest point of a high stone wall that ran alongside the cottage. "Right," I need a leg up."

"This'll be fun," Kerry replied, putting on a pair of sheepskin mittens. She stood by the wall and held her hands out around waist height.

"Hop aboard, Lady Victoria."

"I'd feel a lot safer if you could interlock your fingers. Are they your nan's mittens?"

"Just get your fat arse up there. It's fucking freezing out here."

"Shush," Victoria hissed. She hiked up her leg and placed the sole of her boot into the cradle Kerry was making with her hands and whispered "ready?"

Kerry nodded. Victoria gripped her shoulders and pulled herself up. Using her right hand she grabbed the top of the wall. She couldn't see over the top.

"Shit," she said. Kerry's foul language was rubbing off on her, she thought. "I still can't see. You'll have to give me a bunk-up."

"A what?"

"A bunk-up... you know. I need to get on top of the wall."

"Okay, brace yourself. How tall are you?"

"Five foot nine."

"And how heavy?"

"I'm not telling you."

"Fine. How do you want to do it?"

"I'll count to three, and you boost me up. Hopefully, I'll be able to climb on top from there."

"What if you get seen?"

"We jump in the car and do one."

"Okay. Turn around... and don't blame me if you fall... Let's go."

"Okay." Victoria moved her foot around in Kerry's hands, making sure she had a firm, two-handed grip on top of the wall. "Got me? Good. One, two..."

"Hang on, are we going on three? Or is it one, two, three, go?"

"I said on three, div head."

"Got it," said Kerry, grabbing Victoria's thighs at either side. "Jesus, your arse is massive..."

"Now, one, two, THREE!"

Kerry pushed up hard. Victoria managed to get her elbows on top of the wall and pulled herself up. She clambered up, lying on her belly. Her camera, dangling, knocked against the wall. She steadied herself.

"Okay? Comfy?"

"I wouldn't say comfy... but I'm up."

Her view was blocked by thorn bushes. That was fine as they were giving her cover. She freed her scarf from the prickles, the camera's weight pulling against the strap. She held it away from the wall and shuffled along until she had a decent view of the house. The daylight was fading and the lights were on inside. There was a picnic bench on the back patio. There were one, two... three, four men standing beside it, hot air coming from their mouths in the cold. She instantly recognised Cal. She got him in the crosshairs. Click, click. She focused on the man next to him, a shorter bloke of about the same age as Cal... Click. Then Nigel came into focus. "It's Hornby," she whispered to Kerry, excited. "The other one from Dave's video!"

Kerry was smoking a Marlboro Light. "Whoopee," she muttered as she gave a thumbs-up.

Got ya! Victoria snapped away excitedly. Click, click. another younger bloke was there, muscular black man in a white Gold's Gym vest. Click. Bit cold for a vest.

Nigel opened the patio door and they went inside. The house was built of brown stone and was hundreds of years old. Victoria could see herself living somewhere like that one day. She imagined sitting up in bed looking out of the window, drinking in the views of Peak District as she ate breakfast brought to her by a handsome man who respected her job and loved her for who she was. She zoomed in on the window. There was movement. As she adjusted the focus, she saw the black man throwing darts and the smaller man waiting for his turn. Click, click. She could see a weight bench set up and Cal bench-pressing what appeared to be an awful lot of weight. Nigel stood over him, spotting him. Click.

She trained her lens on the bedroom window above and saw a woman with red hair looking out towards her. Shit!

She dropped the camera and put her hand down on top of the wall to push herself backwards, but it slipped and she lost balance. Her ribcage hit against the cold stone. Suddenly, she was in mid air. Her back hit the snow-covered grass six feet below with a thud. It was sheer luck that she had fallen outside the garden.

"Classy," said Kerry, stubbing her cig out in the snow and going to help. She leaned down, and put her gloved hand on Victoria's forehead. "Are you okay?"

Victoria got up and hugged her. "Ha ha, got 'em all... Now this is investigative journalism!"

"What happened? I thought you'd broken your back."

"I'm fine... but this woman was looking right in my direction... I don't know if she saw me... fuck!"

Kerry grinned. "Chill out. If anyone comes we'll say we are... birdwatchers or something. Good job you had that big arse to break your fall."

Victoria slowly got to her feet. "I've got the perfect arse." Adrenaline was pumping through her body. Maybe Murphy and his mates were... what did they call them in the Westerns? A posse.

They got back in the MGB and Victoria started it up. A red Ford Fiesta sped past them. Driving it was the little bloke.

"I think we're in the clear," said Kerry. "If that woman had spotted you, he would have stopped and asked what the fuck we were up to."

>>>

SIMON Cosgrove was leaving Ladbrokes on Millgate in Stockport. In the afternoons after training, when he wasn't with Cal and the crew, he would be in a bookmakers somewhere. If there was no horse racing on, then he would bet on the dogs. There was always something to have a flutter on. Gambling was in his blood. His old man was known in every betting shop in Burnage. His mum nagged him about it all the time and sometimes she threatened to leave. She had to, or every Friday he would stop at a turf accountants on his way home from work at Boddingtons and blow half of his wages. Their three boys needed feeding. Once, his dad came home late, stinking of booze after a big win. He gave her a gold ring, thinking she would be happy. She made him pawn it for cash.

Simon stuck his head out of Ladbrokes and checked the coast was clear before stepping onto the street. It was dark and the street lights flooded the pavement with an orange hue.

A beautiful brunette suddenly jumped out of the shadows of a nearby doorway and threw her arms around him, kissing him on the cheek.

"Er, are you all right love?" he said, still being tightly hugged.

"You're that footballer aren't you?" Victoria gushed, their faces so close he could smell her Doublemint. "What's your name again? You're amazing! You must be so fit to play that game."

"Well, I er... It's Simon. Simon Cosgrove. Cozzer. I've..."

Victoria butted in as he stumbled over his words, his heart beating like a drum machine. He wasn't very good with women. His only recent girlfriends were ones he paid.

Victoria let him go and stood back a step. He was wearing blue stonewashed jeans, a Stone Roses T-shirt and a pair of blue and yellow Nike trainers. He noticed her nipples were poking out from her white shirt.

"Can I have your autograph?"

He was miles away.

"Simon?"

He came to his senses. "Ok... yeah, sure... got a pen?"

"I think so." Victoria snatched the betting slip out of his hand and quickly handed him a pen.

"Here's one," she said, her pulse racing. "Write it on this," she said, passing him back the betting slip reverse side up. "Can you put: 'To Victoria, my favourite supporter in the world. Love Simon.' Here... lean on my back."

Victoria bent over, sticking her bum out, the top of her French knickers visible over the waistband of her tight jeans. Simon put the betting slip on her back and scribbled, his hand shaking. When he stopped she turned around, smartly grabbed the pen and paper from him. He had written: "To sexy Victoria, you are a total darling. Simon Cosgrove."

She raised her eyebrows and kissed him sloppily on the lips. "Thanks so much, Simon, you've made my day." She had a brainwave. "Don't suppose you're going out tonight are you?"

Cosgrove felt like Christmas had come early. His knees were knocking and it wasn't solely because of the weather. He was getting a semi, and quickly thrust his hand into his pocket to cover it up. "Yeah, I'm going out in town," he stuttered. "I'll be at Reds with some mates. It's just near..."

"I know it," she smiled. "Might see you there."

She turned and walked away. She looked back and saw him stood there with his gob wide open and treated him to another smile.

She walked around the corner to where Kerry was waiting in the MGB. She got in and flipped over the betting slip. It read, in scribbled handwriting: Coventry 2-2 Belle Vue. Simon Cosgrove had bet three hundred quid on his own team's Boxing Day result.

"Put your jacket on before you take my eye out." Kerry had her camera on her lap. The lens cap was off.

Victoria pumped her fist. "Wanna know what the Belle Vue score's going to be on Boxing Day?"

"Fuck off."

"Serious. I've got his betting slip. And guess what? He's going to Reds tonight with his mates. I'm gonna go and introduce myself. Fancy it?"

"I would if I could... but I'm reviewing Meatloaf at the G-Mex. Anyway, Callum Murphy's bound to be there. I wouldn't want to be a gooseberry."

>>>

VICTORIA braked a little bit too hard as she pulled into the driveway of the Didsbury house she shared with Miles and the wheels briefly slid along the frozen, compacted snow. The car was diagonal on the drive when it came to a halt but Victoria didn't bother to straighten it up; she was off out again soon. She went inside and her boyfriend of five years was lying on the Laura Ashley settee in the living room, his hair greasy like he hadn't showered yet. He was reading *Brideshead*

Revisited. The carriage clock on the sideboard said it was six thirty.

Victoria had been with Miles since their Cambridge University days. His father, who was a QC, had bought him their four-bedroom semi-detached off Wilmslow Road. It was expected that they would settle down there and start a family. Instead they got John. She loved walking the Jack Russell around Fog Lane Park. Chasing him across the football pitches every time he smelled a bitch on heat was great exercise.

Victoria attended to Manchester High School for Girls, where her dad was an art teacher. She excelled in English and had read everything Jane Austen had written by the time she was twelve. She discovered *Lady Chatterley's Lover* by D.H. Lawrence at fifteen and loved that it contained the word fuck and that there was, in fact, fucking in it. Her education had given her a posh accent for a Mancunian but in Cambridge she was immediately singled out as a Northerner, the word usually used in a disparaging way. You're so Northern, Victoria. No need to be so Northern about everything. Typical Northerner. She decided the best way to impress her peers was to build up her tolerance to drink and she drank copious amounts of wine and spirits at every party and ball. She was lucky to be able to study with a hangover. None of the others seemed to be able to.

Miles was the Clifford to her Connie. They met at a Clare College black tie ball. He was full of himself but her experiences of men were limited and she was just pleased he was interested. A collegiate rower, he was muscular and toned. Victoria, a hockey player, didn't see the point in non-contact sports but had to admit rowing had given him a good body.

They made eye contact that night, both tipsy. Later, he removed his bow tie, undid the top three buttons of his wing-collar shirt and asked her to dance. He asked her name, made polite conversation and let her take the lead. She was a bit embarrassed when the slow songs began and he started snogging her in the middle of the dancefloor, but she didn't pull away; it turned her on.

They started going out together and after two months, he booked them a room at a Best Western in town. He took her out to dinner at a Michelin-starred restaurant and when the coffee came he said he thought it was time they did it. Victoria, tipsy on fine wine, was curious what his muscles would feel like when he was on top of her, taking her virginity, and agreed.

They were soon embracing in a soft, queen-size bed that smelled of Daz Automatic. Miles was already hard and Victoria tickled his testicles as they kissed. He put his fingers in her. Was it supposed to hurt? She didn't know so she went along with it. She had read a magazine article on how to give a great blow job so she did that for a bit. Then she lay back. The writer implied that a gentleman would return the favour. Apparently Miles wasn't one. He climbed on top of her, asked if she was ready for it and, without waiting for an answer, pushed it into her. She should have realised he was a selfish bastard then. He was shaking, nervous. It hurt at first, then it felt better. He came after about ten minutes. He had never lasted that long since.

"Good day? What have..." she began.

He jumped to his feet. "Thank Christ you're home. Where have you been? I was worried sick." He didn't look worried sick, he looked stoned. The whites of his eyes were pink.

"At work... obviously."

"I tried you there, several times. They said you were out... you promised to tell me where you were going when you went out drinking."

"I wasn't out drinking, I was out on a job." Victoria didn't like being given the third degree but tried to stay calm. "Look sorry. I should have checked in, but I was busy. What's the matter?"

"It's John. He threw up his breakfast, lunch and dinner. He's being weird."

Their beloved dog had been causing them headaches recently. The previous week, their neighbour Clive, a loner who lectured in engineering at UMIST, tried to stroke him. He knew John didn't like strangers and had been warned to stay away several times but he kept stroking him, insisting he was "good with dogs". She and Miles both agreed he was asking to get bitten.

John's razor sharp incisors had pierced the skin between Clive's thumb and first finger and left a bruise on his hand. He could have just put a Band-Aid on it and forgot about it but no, he went to Accident and Emergency. Two stitches and he was threatening to get the police involved. Victoria took him a box of Quality Street as a peace offering but he refused to take them, fuming: "I'm having that vicious little fucker put down."

Victoria went home and gave John some chocolates and a good stroke and a big hug. Having access to a newspaper's library could be very useful sometimes. She looked up Clive in the cuttings and... tut tut. When he was nineteen, he been cleared by Glossop magistrates of having inappropriate relations a fifteen-year-old boy. Cleared, but still. Smoke, fire, etc. She and Miles suspected he was gay but never imagined he was a paedophile. Victoria went round and told him she knew of his history and that if he didn't drop his complaint about John, she would post a note to every house in the street warning the neighbours he was a nonce. Clive went chalk white, said she would hear no more about it and added he hoped she had a nice Christmas.

"The vet reckons it's irritable bowel syndrome," said Miles. "She said to keep an eye on him and bring him back if it becomes persistent. Just what I needed on Christmas Eve, a trip to the vets."

"You took him to the vet because he threw up?"

"What else was I supposed to do? There was dog puke up the stairs, on the landing, in his basket, you name it. I was worried and you were nowhere to be found."

John was lying on his side in front of the open fire, which was popping and crackling. Victoria crouched down, feeling the warmth on her cheek as she gently stroked his side. "Poor John boy, don't worry, you'll feel better soon."

She thought it best to break the news to Miles sooner rather than later and took a deep breath. "I have to go back out. I'm working on a big story. We think some footballers are fixing matches."

Miles didn't take it well. "Footballers? You don't even like football. Couldn't they send someone else? What about a sports reporter?"

"I am sorry... I have to do it and I don't know when I'll be back. Probably not until late so you shouldn't wait up. I've got to get ready. I'm meeting Kerry at eight," she lied.

"It's Christmas Eve. I thought we could get a Chinese. Share a bottle of wine. I've been looking after your bloody dog all day instead of writing. Fuck."

"Oh, writing eh? Why didn't you say the muse had finally landed? I'd have dropped everything."

The writing charade had been going on for over a year. Victoria knew he sat watching television for most of the day, taking John for occasional walks in the park when he wanted a joint. His research trips to the library were actually a couple of hours doing the *Telegraph* crossword in The Dog and Partridge. His parents gave him an allowance of a grand a month which was plenty for him to live on. If he was writing, he wasn't doing much of it.

"I've told you. You can't force writing when you don't feel like it. And with the way you've been acting lately, I don't feel like it at all."

"I don't always feel like writing but when someone gives you a deadline, you get to work. Anyway, who wants to read an English person's perspective of a Miami private detective?" She was being cruel now. "The Americans have already done it a million times. And the dialogue... your main character could never be the womaniser you have written him as. People just don't speak like that!"

"Fuck you! You... bitch." She could tell he instantly regretted that. He groaned and walked out of the room towards the kitchen, where he would no doubt get a beer from the fridge.

Victoria went up to the bedroom and packed a bag. She looked in the mirror and began to well up. They were supposed to be spending Christmas at her mum and dad's. She would pick Miles up in the morning, if he was lucky. He would still be in a mood no doubt but bollocks to him. Their relationship was turning into a nightmare. She left the house without saying anything to him, slamming the door behind her. It felt good. She was going to check into a hotel room and stay out all night. She knew just the place. She climbed into her car and turned the stereo up to full blast before reversing out into the cul-de-sac and flooring it off up the road. Bernard Sumner's singing cheered her up. *Round and Round*, an amazing song. The lights changed and she merged on to Wilmslow Road, heading back towards the city centre. She was going to the Majestic and it was going on her expenses.

\>\>\>

SHE felt a thousand times better after a long, hot shower. She sat down in front of the dressing table mirror and set to work on her makeup. She wanted her eyes to smoulder sexily. She decided to give them a neon green and glitter look. That was how the *Pretty In Pink* actress Molly Ringwold did hers. She would wear a subtle pink lipstick; she wanted her lips to look full and inviting, but not steal attention from her eyes.

The Levi's she pulled from her overnight bag were tight-fitting. She wasn't a baggy sort of girl. They were bleach-rippled and had a small tear which showed off a bit of her naked thigh; perfect. They were low cut, so that when she was dancing her midriff, and maybe even the top of her black French knickers, would be on show. She last wore the shiny silver vest she put on at a science fiction-themed fancy dress party at Cambridge. It looked good over her black lace bra, which pushed her boobs together. She slipped on a pair of white Converse All Stars. Not ideal in the snow, but she didn't want to tower over Callum Murphy in stilettos. She tied her hair back in a pony tail with a white bobble and, for a laugh, slipped a chunky, fluorescent green plastic ring on her wedding finger. It was time to go to work.

>>>

SHE asked the cabbie to pull over outside the Kendal Milne department store and wished him a Merry Christmas. She decided she would go straight to the bar as soon as she got inside Reds. She wanted a drink to relax her before she approached Murphy. Two black men in long black coats stood either side of a rusty iron door under a red neon light. Reds was apparently so cool it didn't need a sign.

The shorter of the two bouncers looked her up and down and nodded before ushering her in. She went downstairs into the club, checking she looked okay in the mirrors on the walls.

It was nine o'clock and not very busy. A couple of girls were dancing in front of the DJ, who was stood behind a teak sixties sideboard with two turntables on top, holding a pair of headphones to his ear. She couldn't name the Happy Mondays tune but recognised the singer's dirty voice.

Reds had the feel of an abandoned abattoir. It was a long, narrow space with a small room to the side behind a corrugated iron wall. The floor was concrete; the dancefloor was simply the back third of the venue with no furniture in it. The bare brick walls were decorated with Communist propaganda posters in Athena-style frames. One depicted a smashed up tractor and people digging with shovels around it. A tall Christmas tree stood in a corner, metallic red and covered in red tinsel and glittering red baubles. Instead of an angel, a Santa sat on top of it. Yards and yards of the same red tinsel had been stapled around the walls and threaded in and out of a cargo net pinned to the ceiling. Four rusty desk lamps were screwed upside down to a thick wooden beam above the bar. What Victoria didn't know was that Cal had purposely left them outside for two weeks to corrode. In a small open-fronted room off the main bar, a couple were snogging enthusiastically on a tatty red sofa under a wall of flickering TV screens.

Victoria's eyes itched in the smoky atmosphere. She blinked several times as she made her way to the bar, determined not to let tears spoil her make-up. A gruff, sixty-year-old with a paunch finished serving a man and turned his attention to her. It was Billy.

"What can I get you love?"

"A martini please," she said.

"Does this look like a fucking cocktail bar?"

Victoria was taken by surprise but stayed calm and smiled at him. She hadn't got where she was by taking shit from barmen. "What sort of way is that to talk to a paying customer?"

"My way," he grunted.

She scanned the selection of booze bottles on the shelf behind him. "Everything you need is there."

Billy stood with his arms folded, hoping she would back down, but she didn't. "Okay," he said, exhaling. "Martini it is." He could hardly complain they weren't selling enough booze if he was refusing to mix drinks. He slugged roughly equal amounts of Tanqueray and Cinzano into a wine glass with a slice of lemon. "Ice?"

She preferred her martinis shaken, not stirred, but she couldn't see a cocktail shaker in the shelf behind him. She nodded and Billy chucked three ice cubes in the glass. "Two quid."

Victoria paid him. "Quiet tonight," she shouted and had a sip of the martini.

Billy just shrugged and walked away to serve another customer. She licked her lips and tasted gin. She looked around towards the door and in came Callum Murphy.

He swaggered across the club with his chest sticking out, with Hornby beside him and Cosgrove and the black man behind them. He wore a white Lacoste tennis shirt, baggy blue jeans and a pair of red square-toed Kickers. His chin was covered in stubble. His bright white teeth sparkled like stars in the darkened club. Kerry was right. He was fit.

>>>

HE strode towards the bar like a boxer heading for the ring before a big fight. Smoke from the dry ice machine surrounded him as *Shall We Take A Trip* by Northside made the floor vibrate.

He was swaying his shoulders to the music when he noticed Victoria standing next to him. He wasn't quite sure but she seemed to be checking him out.

He stood waiting for Billy to get around to serving him. He didn't take out his wallet. "Oi Bill. Beck's for the lads," he shouted.

Billy opened four bottles of beer and placed them on the bar. "Four quid."

"Comedian," replied Cal, taking a swig of beer. He licked his lips and looked around at the clientele. "How's it been tonight?"

"All right. Busier than usual for this time. The DJ seems all right. A few new faces about. I've just made a cocktail for fucking Martini Navratilova over there." He pointed at Victoria.

She turned and offered Murphy her right hand to shake. "Hello, I'm Victoria Heath. Pleased to meet you."

He took it and kissed it and she had to stifle the

urge to cringe as he said: "Callum Murphy. The pleasure's all mine."

"Hey, remember me?" Simon butted in. "Victoria, innit?"

"You two know each other?"

"Hi Simon." She gave Simon a hug and felt his hand touch her arse. "We just met today... in Stockport," she told Cal, as she extricated herself from Simon's clutches.

"I was hoping you'd come down tonight," said Simon, almost drooling as he looked at her.

She ignored him and turned to Cal. "So this is your club?"

Cal nodded, drinking her in. Mid-twenties with gorgeous, gorgeous eyes, a cute, cheeky look on her face. There was something familiar about her. Nice cleavage, great tits. She had jeans on but he imagined her legs were amazing. "Yep, this is Reds."

"It's nice."

"Much nicer with you in it though."

She smiled. He obviously thought this old-fashioned gent-style patter was charming.

Simon, not taking the hint, tried to butt in again. "Who are you out with, Victoria?"

"Thanks," she said to Cal. "You're not bad yourself."

"That's a bit forward from a married woman," he replied, pointing at her ring.

"My husband works for Kinder Surprise."

Simon stepped towards Cal and spoke in his ear. "You bastard. She asked for my autograph in Stockport before. She snogged me in the middle of the street. Tongue and everything. I virtually had to wrestle her off me."

"I'll make it up to you."

"You better had."

"I can hear you both, you know," said Victoria.

Cal turned to her and flashed a cheesy grin. She chewed her bottom lip. He couldn't tell if she was annoyed or not, but it caused a twitch in his Calvin Kleins.

Simon exhaled, defeated. "I'll leave you pair to it then...." He turned around, looking for Billy to serve him another drink.

Victoria sipped her cocktail. "You've got a good thing going here. The atmosphere is nice. And I like the Russian theme."

"Well I wanted it to look like an Emperor's palace in ancient Rome, you know, pillars, marble, toga dress policy. Topless women feeding grapes to punters... raw silk bog roll in the loos. But this was all I could afford."

Victoria screwed up her face.

"Kidding. It's just how I wanted it to be. Even down to the Russian maple bar. I was in Russia once, for football, and this place in Moscow had a bar like that. I swore then and there if I ever bought a club the bar would be propped up on breeze blocks."

She laughed. He was as full of himself as she expected, but she was enjoying his company. He was charming, not what she had expected at all.

"What do you think of the DJ?" He asked, finishing his beer.

Victoria recognised the song which was playing as *Never Too Late* by Kylie Minogue, even though it was a dance remix which was heavy on the piano.

"Unusual for a club like this," she said. "Pop music. He knows the idea is to get people dancing. I thought it would be a lot busier. Maybe you should get a sign. Most places that play this sort of music get packed out. Look at the Hacienda."

Everyone used the Hacienda as the benchmark when talking about Reds. No wonder; It was the most famous club in the city, probably the country, and possibly the world. Cal scratched his chin, irritated. "Give it an hour or so. It'll fill up. It's Christmas Eve. And this song was remixed by Paul Oakenfold. This DJ gets hold of tunes before the *NME*'s even heard them. Listen... you know who I am. Do I know you? Your face rings a bell."

"Don't think so."

Suddenly he placed her. She was the journalist who was on the front of the *Chronicle*. That was it. He placed his hand on her upper arm briefly, then took it away. He was about to say where he had seen her but stopped himself. "Do you want another drink?"

"That would be nice."

>>>

"CAN I ask your advice about something?" Finally, she thought. He'd been banging on about himself for half an hour.

"Sure," she said. "Ask away."

"Well it's for my brother really. He's got a bit of a whatsit... a conundrum."

He smiled, chuffed he had found the word he was looking for. She didn't know he had a brother and she felt pleased they had something in common. "Really? What is it?"

"Well, er, his name's... our Terry. I love him to bits. He's sound as a pound. Anyway he used to go out with this girl, Rebecca, she's Scouse, and they've kept in touch. They're still mates. His new girlfriend, er... Mandy, doesn't like it one bit, and wants him to stop seeing her."

"That seems a bit extreme."

"Yeah. And the plot thickens. His best mate is getting married this summer and Mandy doesn't like him either, so she won't go. It's going to be a lovely do. So Terry's thinking of asking Rebecca to go as his plus one. Mandy said 'no way' and they had a massive bust-up. He wants to know what I think. It's still all up in the air. I don't know what to suggest." Cal shook his head and looked right into her eyes, making her feel like the only woman in the world.

She enjoyed being in his gaze as she said: "It sounds like Mandy's jealous of his relationship with Rebecca. Is there any reason she should be?"

"No way man, they are over... definitely just mates these days."

"How much does Terry love this Mandy?"

"Loads." He held his arms wide, his shirt pulling tight against his muscular chest.

"I think he should go to the wedding by himself then. He could just get pissed with his mates. But he should still keep in touch with Rebecca if he wants. I think Mandy should agree to that."

"Why do you think that?"

"Well if I was going out with you and you said you were going to a wedding with an ex, I don't think I'd like it. But I suppose if you were mates with her I couldn't stop you keeping in touch." Had she really just said that? The martini must have been a strong one.

Cal grinned and swigged his beer. "If we were together I would definitely want you with me. I wouldn't go if you didn't want to come."

Victoria's pulse was racing. He was very nice but she was here to do a job. Thankfully, three young lads appeared on Cal's left hand side, giving her a time to compose herself.

The teenagers were far too smartly dressed for a place like Reds. In their white shirts with embroidered lapels, black pleated trousers and slip-on shoes, they looked like they had been on a shoplifting spree in Burtons. Two had very similar curly hairstyles, heavily gelled. The third lad was Belle Vue's most promising young talent, eighteen-year-old winger Tony Butterworth, who had a crew cut with a lightning bolt shaved into it above his left ear. He was of African descent and over six feet tall.

"Tone! What's up pal?" Cal offered up a high five which Tony took down with a loud slap. He looked like a young Luther Vandross and reeked of Calvin Klein's Obsession for Men.

"I didn't know you were coming in tonight. This is Victoria." He grinned. She held her hand out and Tony took it more gently than she expected. "Nice to meet you," he said, not letting go.

"Nice to meet you too," said Victoria.

"Oi, hands off the merchandise, pal," Cal laughed.

"Er, I'm nobody's... merchandise," Victoria informed him.

"I'm only messing." Cal waved Billy over from the end of the bar, where he was polishing a glass. "None of these lads pays for a drink tonight," he told him. He turned to Victoria. "Tony Butterworth. Remember the name. He'll be playing for England one day."

Tony smiled. "Thanks Cal. Just thought I'd come over and say hello."

"Nice one. Here, I'll shout you all a drink." He summoned Billy over. The old man was wiping a glass. "What do you fucking freeloaders want then?"

"Three JD and Cokes," said Butterworth.

Billy raised an eyebrow and shook his head all in one movement. "Straight to the top shelf, eh?" He scooped ice in three glasses, sloshed Jack Daniel's into them and topped them up from a bottle of Coca-Cola. "Here you go boys. No expense spared."

Cal put his arm around Tony and turned him around. "I'll come and have a chat a bit later. Make yourselves at home or whatever."

Tony took the not-so-subtle hint. "Cheers Cal. Let's, er... have a scout round lads. See you around, Victoria. Nice to meet you."

"Yeah cheers, merry Christmas," added one of his mates, raising his glass.

"Sound lads, them," Cal said, when they had gone.

Victoria had met much bigger arseholes than Callum Murphy. People seemed to like him.

The young lads were in awe of him. She would let him keep boasting, get him to open up, and then bring up Cosgrove. A big part of her job was the knowing when to shut your trap and just listen.

"What brings you here tonight, Victoria?" Cal asked, his fingertips lightly brushing her wrist. "Is it business or pleasure?" He was trying to tease her hand into his. It went on for a couple of seconds longer than it should have before she took it away.

>>>

CAL's posse had deserted him. Nigel had gone home after only one beer. Listening to Simon moaning about Cal nicking his bird had quickly got boring. He said his daughter would be up early, wanting to open the presents Santa had brought her, and he didn't want to be tired for that.

Edo had also left. He said he was getting up early to help Christina prepare Christmas dinner. Simon had gone to the casino in a bad mood, and would probably blow hundreds of pounds. With no wing men to bounce off, Cal was forced to improvise.

"Has anyone ever told you that you look like Leslie Ash?"

"No, that's a new one."

"Well, you do, especially with your eyes done like that."

Er, thanks, I suppose." She smiled bashfully at the comparison to the beautiful actress. *C.A.T.S. Eyes* was her favourite TV show.

Cal couldn't believe he was getting away with saying this stuff. They had fuck-all in common. She was into all these books he had heard about at school but never read. He threw in the odd "nice one" or "cool" or "sweet" but her words were going over his head. He was distracted by her moist red lips and her facial expressions. She was very passionate when she was banging on about literature.

The martini had given her a nice buzz. A young lad dressed in Army surplus gear reached behind them to collect her empty glass. She was impressed. It was her turn to pay him a compliment. "This place is very cool. I think you've got good taste. You're not as daft as you make out, are you?"

He raised his eyebrows.

"I didn't realise I made out I was daft," he said.

Victoria paused. "How old are you?"

"Twenty-five."

"All this at twenty-five," she said gesturing around. "Would you say you were lucky?"

"Lucky? How d'ya mean?"

"Lucky to lead such a rich and prosperous life?"

Cal took a deep breath. "I'm probably not as rich and prosperous as you reckon... but I suppose I am pretty lucky. I'd have liked to have been a musician or a DJ so this is the next best thing."

"You're a footballer though. A good one."

He liked being told that. "Yeah, that too. The wages help to pay for the... luxury... you see around you. But you make your own luck in this life." Bullseye, she thought. The headline could read MATCH-FIXER MURPHY: YOU MAKE YOUR OWN LUCK.

He decided to test her. "Are you a Belle Vue fan or summat? Simon said you asked him for his autograph. I thought that was why you were here. I thought you were some mad stalker."

She burst out laughing. "Is that what you thought? Really?"

"It does happen... you'd be surprised. One lass followed my mate Edo home and started turning up at his house with her mates at all hours and hanging around outside. His missus was not happy."

"I know you play for Belle Vue. I read a piece that said you were punching below your weight. That you should really be playing for England by now."

"Where did you read that?" he asked, genuinely interested.

"In the *Telegraph*. And one of my mates works as a sports editor at Granada TV. He says you're good."

Cal loved having his ego massaged. He was like a cat having his chin tickled. "Well, we're having a decent season..."

"Fookin hell, alright Cal."

A man with a big belly slapped him roughly on the shoulder. He was wearing black and gold British Knights basketball boots and baggy jeans. On his oversized T-shirt was the slogan And On the Sixth Day, God Created Manchester. He leaned his considerable weight against the bar and it moved slightly.

"Steady Dan... do us a favour, mate. Don't lean on the bar."

Danny White was a friend from his schooldays in Wythenshawe and could be a pain in the arse. "I'm fucking battered, Callum. I've got to lean somewhere, know what I mean? It's a bar for fuck's sake."

Cal prodded his belly. "Sound, but try not to put all your weight on it eh? It might fall over." He turned to another man stood with Danny. "Norm, you cunt. Y'alright?" Norman Groves took a drag on a joint. It was because of him that Reds smelled like an Amsterdam coffee shop.

Norm had the strongest constitution of anyone Cal knew and he never seemed wasted. "Top. We're on a Leo..." Norman said. "An all-dayer, man. Rhyming slang. You know that curly-haired twat?"

Victoria, whose father was a Leo Sayer fan, smiled. Norman gulped down half of what he was drinking. It might have been iced water but Cal's money was on vodka.

Norman, who was wearing a yellow Adidas tracksuit top, introduced himself to Victoria.

"Norman Groves. Me and Cal go way back. I learnt how to party all night at his old flat. Who's this then?"

"This is Victoria Heath," said Cal. "I'm keeping an eye on her."

"I bet you are," Norman laughed, shaking her hand. "Victoria. Let me buy you a drink."

Victoria smiled and pointed at Billy behind the bar. "He knows what I'm drinking."

Cal was chuffed that Victoria finally seemed to be enjoying herself. Accepting a drink was the first spontaneous thing she had done since they met.

He asked for a Beck's. "Put 'em on my tab," he said, knowing he would anyway.

Norman let go of Victoria's hand and offered Cal the joint. He shook his head. "That's just a roach, you tight bastard."

Norman grinned and chucked it on the floor. He nodded at Victoria. Thick, purple smoke billowed slowly out of his mouth as he pushed in at the bar. Reds had filled up as Cal predicted and they were pushed closer together. She shuffled around, put her arm around Cal's lower back. He was very muscular. He didn't seem to mind, but what was she doing?

After just a couple of minutes, Norman turned around with four drinks and handed them out. Danny spilled a bit of his down his top. Norman winked. "Cheers Cal," he said. "We'll leave you lovebirds to it." He grabbed Danny's sleeve.

"Merry Christmas," said Cal as they disappeared into the crowd. It felt amazing the way Victoria had wrapped herself around him. "Are they all right?"

"Yeah, they are sound. Danny can be a pain in the arse at times. I had to throw him out once for pestering a bird."

"No I mean, they seemed... wasted."

Cal laughed. "It's just a state of mind for them two. I've known them for donkeys' years. Ages. Danny's always fucked... wasted, I mean. Norman can handle double what he can."

New Order's *Round and Round* came on.

Victoria looked up and smiled. "I love this one."

He nodded, put his beer down, took her glass for her and put that down too. "Let's dance then."

He took her hand and they moved away from the bar. He put his hands on her waist and enjoyed watching her move as she enjoyed the song. She nodded and they moved in time together. Their eyes locked. It was probably only for a second but it seemed like ages. He ran his fingers through his hair and it tingled in a really pleasant way. It felt as if every single hair had a mind of its own and was rubbing itself up against his hand. Cal was struggling not to get lost in the music. He found himself licking his lips.

He stood behind Victoria and put his arms around her waist. She was the essence of beauty. The dancefloor was mobbed and they were pressed together and he could feel her arse touching him through his jeans as they swayed to the music. Her silver top felt so smooth. He was experiencing a feeling of the utmost euphoria. His legs tingled and the contents of his stomach tingled. Suddenly it dawned on him. Some cunt had spiked him. "Are you feeling... okay?" he asked.

Victoria turned around, her face inches from Cal's. Her pupils were massive. "I'm feeling nice but... strange," she said. Suddenly, she looked worried. "Your mate wouldn't have slipped us something, would he?"

Cal gazed into her big brown eyes and took her hand again. "Dunno, but I'm pretty sure someone has. How big are my pupils?"

"They're really, really big. Like saucers."

"I doubt it was Norman... he'd see spiking us as an act of generosity. And he's as tight as two coats of paint."

"Maybe." She had a look of concern on her face. "Promise me you've had nothing to do with this?"

He would normally have got the hump and said that spiking people was a cunt's trick. But he felt so mellow and happy. "I promise you... It wasn't me, so thrive my soul."

"Pardon?"

"It wasn't me."

"No, the last bit."

"So thrive my soul?"

"So thrive my soul. Where did you hear that?"

"My auntie used to say it."

She took a deep breath. "It's from *Romeo and Juliet*."

"I never knew that."

She put her arms around his neck. It was as if he had earned her trust. Her face was just inches from his and they were rocking from side to side, not dancing, just rocking. Their upper legs were touching and it felt like electric currents were passing between them. It was as if they had been programmed to work together as one. They were in their own tingly world. They weren't the only ones. People around them were hugging, swaying and smiling as they moved to the rhythm.

"Promise you'll look after me? This is all new to me."

"Course I will."

"Promise properly."

He looked right into her eyes as another wave of euphoria swept through his body. "I promise. Properly."

>>>

MARK Shaw sat alone in The Old Wellington with his leg up on a stool. It had been a busy night in the Shambles. He took a swig from a bottle of Budweiser. An open fire was roaring nearby but his toes had a purple hue as they protruded from his cast. White plaster went all the way up to his groin, occasionally pinching his scrotum, which really pissed him off. The doctor said his torn ligaments were the worst he had ever seen. He faced eight months of rehabilitation. The gaffer could barely disguise his fury when he told him he tripped on the stairs. Shaw stank of stale sweat. Showering would have been difficult with the pot on his leg so he hadn't bothered. He had been drinking since midday – quite a feat for a man also on strong codeine-based painkillers. The more he drank, the angrier he got. The cunts had crippled him. A couple of pints in Stalybridge had led to a taxi into town. He'd been joined by two freeloaders who were happy to keep going to the bar for him as long as he paid for their drinks too. Eventually there had been a row about money and he had told them to fuck off.

He noticed his sleeve was in a puddle of beer on the table. He didn't care what it looked like but the fact it made his shirt sticky annoyed him. He had no idea how many beers he had sunk. Oh well, just another fucking Christmas with no mates and no bird. Might as well keep drinking. He eased himself up on his crutches, taking his weight on his left leg. He hobbled over to the bar, swaying from side to side.

"Another Budweisha pal," he slurred at the barman, a young man with a pony tail.

"Sorry pal, we're closing."

Shaw leaned on the bar but was so drunk he couldn't tell the time from his watch.

"Yeah, but you're not closed yet. Jusht give us one beer. Al neck it quick."

"No, the bell's gone mate. Time to go home."

"Prick." Shaw belched. Then he turned and hobbled towards the door.

He didn't notice how cold it was outside until he reached the Corn Exchange and nearly slipped over on a patch of black ice. A group of girls across the road were all wearing glittery pink plastic party hats and skimpy outfits. One was getting a piggy back ride from a bigger girl. Suddenly they fell to the ground, cackling. He made his way over to them, hoping to cadge a cigarette, and noticed the bigger one had no knickers on.

"Alright darling..." he said.

She giggled as she picked herself up.

"She can't speak," slurred one her mates. "She can fuck though!" She was skinny and wore a sleeveless vest top that displayed a wonky Tweetie Pie tattoo on her arm. She exhaled a lungful of smoke. "What have you done to your leg?"

"Give us a fag," he said, swaying.

"Please."

"What?"

"Say please. Where's your manners?"

"Just fucking giz one... please," he said.

The girl, who was probably in her early twenties, reached into her bag, took a cigarette from her packet and gave it to him. He could tell he had made her wary of him.

He put the B&H in his mouth, and managed to say "light".

The girl started to say something, then stopped, and took out a lighter. Shaw couldn't keep his head still enough in front of the flame. She laughed nervously.

"What's so fucking funny?"

"Fuck you... creep," she shouted, and turned to her mates. "I give him a fag and he starts giving me shit!"

"Fuck off, knobhead," the big girl shouted, regaining the ability to speak and pushing Shaw. He swung a crutch, narrowly missing her face.

"You fookin twat," shouted one of the other girls, a redhead. She slapped Shaw's face and it stunned him. Then a handbag hit him hard on the right ear, leaving it ringing. The girls were now standing in a line, side by side like an army unit ready to do battle.

"Fuck you ugly bitches," he said, flicking the half-smoked cigarette at them. "Slags." The click clack of his crutches echoed into the night sky as he went off in the opposite direction.

"Pin dick!" He heard one shout after him.

After hobbling around for half an hour he found himself in Chinatown. His biceps and triceps were killing him. Every building, although Georgian by design, seemed to house a Chinese restaurant. Maybe I should eat, soak up the booze. A sweet and sour pork maybe. As far as he could remember he hadn't eaten anything since a bacon butty at ten o'clock that morning.

A man emerged from a red door with a huge grin on his face. He winked conspiratorially at Shaw. All thoughts of eating left him as he realised it was a brothel. What he really wanted to do was fuck. He would have to act sober. He spent a few minutes breathing in the fresh air, and finally shuffled across the street. He rang the bell beside the red door and after a few seconds a buzzer sounded. He just needed to negotiate the stone steps on his crutches and he was in.

>>>

THEY sat with their hips touching on the red couch, taking it in turns to swig from a bottle of Perrier. Victoria tingled from the back of her skull all the way down her spine to the tips of her toes. She was wearing a pair of cheap white-framed shades a friendly fellow clubber had given to her as "a Chrimbo prezzie". She leaned forward and Cal ran his fingers gently down her back. It felt amazing.

"I spose this is what they call loved up," she said.

She leaned back against his chest and it was like leaning against warm wood.

"Spose it is," replied Cal.

Her brain tingled as he ran his fingers through her hair and tapped the tips around the soft nape of her neck. She tickled his wrist in return.

"What time is it?" she asked.

Cal checked his watch, a cheap Timex he'd bought as a substitute for his Rolex. "Just gone two... How did this happen?"

"What?"

"Us."

The thought of Miles sad caused her to take a sharp breath. "What do you mean, us?"

"Have you got a boyfriend?"

She paused, deciding whether or not to come clean. "Yeah. But things haven't been good for ages. He... bores me."

"Why do you stay with him?"

Good question. "I suppose I'm afraid to leave him," was the best she could come up with. "Actually, not afraid. He can be quite nice. It's just... when I was younger I wanted someone to love me. He seemed to fit the bill. Now I seem to be stuck in a groove. Stupid eh?"

"You're obviously not stupid."

"Have you ever loved anyone?"

"How can you tell?"

"You would do anything for them."

"Like... die for them?"

"Yes. I think if you really loved someone you would die for them."

"In that case no... I never have. Not so far."

"Don't apologise. I don't think I have either." Two dozen butterflies were flapping their wings in her stomach. "Can you take me back to the hotel?"

"Sure. Big day ahead. Santa's coming." He was seeing stars even though he was in a basement.

He went to get his sheepskin jacket from behind the bar, wrapped it around her shoulders and put his arm around her. She took off the sunglasses and put them on him. They waved at Billy as they shuffled out of Reds and he gave them a thumbs-up and forced out a smile. They got upstairs to find it was snowing. The cab Cal hailed on Deansgate struggled to keep a grip on the ungritted roads but Victoria felt safe in his arms.

"Amazing," he whispered as the warehouses of Castlefield, converted into flats, clicked past in a multitude of still shots. It was as if he were looking through the viewfinder of a camera with a high-speed automatic shutter. He licked his lips.

"I need to make a confession," she said, out of the blue.

She had his attention. "Really? What is it?"

"I know you're bent."

The statement stunned him. He scratched his head, confused, and it felt pleasant on his scalp. "Bent? I'm not bent. I've been out on the piss in Canal Street a few times but... hang on. Is this a practical joke? Where's Jeremy Beadle?"

"I don't mean I think you're gay. What I mean is... I know you fix matches. I assume Nigel, and Edo, and Simon have something to do with it as well. I'm a reporter. God, what am I doing with you, here? I like you... but I can't stop probing you. I won't. It's my job and I'm bloody good at it."

His pupils were still massive and he was still rushing. "Shush, will you?" he said. He checked the cab's silence button was activated. Thankfully it was. "This isn't the time or place."

"You could just tell me to get lost you know... get him to pull over and kick me out."

"I don't want to. I know you're a reporter. Have done all night. I saw your picture on the front of the paper. You exposed that dirty rabbi fella. But I'm not as interesting as you think. I'm just an average bloke who kicks a ball around for a living."

Victoria's cheeks felt hot. "I'll be the judge of that."

A thought popped into his head. "I get it now. Your boss is a genius."

"What do you mean?"

"Ever heard the term honey trap?"

She bristled. "I'm not just some 'honey trap'. I can assure you. I'm here because I've enjoyed your company. I intended to be tucked up in bed long ago."

"The thing is, we're chalk and cheese, you and me. You're posh, I'm not. And you're telling me your boss hasn't dreamed this up? Did you spike the drinks?"

"No, and I'm not posh. I was born at Wythenshawe Hospital."

"Oh. So was I." His hair tingled as he gently rubbed it.

The taxi stopped outside the Majestic as requested. Cal paid the driver. Pleasant warmth hit them in the faces as they entered the hotel. They went straight to the lift, holding hands.

"What floor?" he asked.

"Three."

He pressed the button and scratched his chin and looked forward. Victoria gazed at the pattern on red carpet as the lift rose. When she heard the ping, she looked up. The doors opened.

"Third floor," he said.

They shuffled slowly along the dimly lit corridor until Victoria stopped at the third door on the right. "This is me..."

As she felt her pockets for her key, Cal pulled her towards him and kissed her. He held it for a few seconds, tenderly massaging her lips with his, then gently pulled away.

Cal broke the silence, his hand still on her waist. "Sorry about that. It's late. Night then, Victoria. Sorry you got spiked. It was bang out of order."

She shrugged. "It was scary at first, but it turned out to be a nice experience. I wouldn't want to have done it with anyone else."

His heart thudded as he felt euphoria rise in him again.

"Er...," she chewed her lip. "Should I invite you in?"

"You'd better not. It's late... I should say goodnight."

"You have already."

They kissed again, briefly, before he walked off down the corridor.

>>>

SHE felt an odd mix of thrilled and rejected as she undressed. As she put on the white towelling robe there was a knock at the door. She opened it and Cal burst in, grabbed her and pulled her to his chest. "I can't leave it like that," he said.

She looked into his eyes and kissed him this time. Her tongue was in his mouth and he was feeling her ribs and boobs as he pushed her towards the big bed and thrust her down. He took care not to squash her but the kiss was passionate and forthright and although his stubble felt rough against her face, she didn't mind. After a few minutes, he stopped suddenly and whispered "sorry, I need a piss" and got up.

Victoria untied the bathrobe, hung it up and lay on the bed, stark naked. She was glad she had shaved her bikini line just a few days earlier. Cal emerged from the en-suite, naked too. She admired his tanned, muscular torso and his lightly hairy chest. His cock, a good size, was pointing up and to the left, semi-hard. His breathing was heavy as he climbed on the bed beside her, slipped his hand underneath her and began stroking the insides of her thighs. "You promised to look after me," Victoria whispered.

"I will." Spooning her, he guided the tip of his erection so it just touched her lips. The fact that he couldn't wait to ravage her was exciting. Victoria got on her hands and knees and straddled him. They gasped in unison. Her hands were on his muscular chest. He ran his hands up her torso to her boobs and pinched her nipples. The exquisite pain made her tense up. Minutes passed in mutual ecstasy. His thrusts became faster.

"Slow down," she whispered, and he stopped. "I didn't mean stop," she moaned.

She moved herself forward, feeling him leave her, and rolled onto her back. He lay next to her, grinning, his erection glistening and his nipples erect. Her cheeks were flushed. He turned and began kissing her boobs. His tongue ran down her torso. She felt his chin stubble tickling her thighs. He began tonguing her, applying gentle suction to her clitoris, and then pushed a finger into her. Victoria gasped and felt she was floating on pleasure. She was so moist.

"Your turn now," she gasped, after several minutes of euphoria.

They were both hot and sweaty and, as they swapped places, a slurping noise emerged from somewhere between their bodies. Victoria stifled a laugh by biting her lip. She checked Cal was still hard with her fingertips and went down on him. He ran his hands through her brown soft hair as she sucked his cock. She toyed with his balls and felt his body tense up. She didn't want him to come outside her so she stopped. She crawled up his torso, grabbed his shoulders and slowly reversed onto him again, taking him as deep as he could go. With her knees bent, she rested her hands on his shoulders and ground her pelvis against his, picturing him inside her. She let out an involuntary yelp. She was ready to come now. He was thinking the same thing. Her shallow breathing was turning him on. She pulled him closer, her nipples rubbing against his chest, as hard as Midget Gems. He rolled them tenderly between his fingers as she repeatedly rose up and slowly lowered herself down again. Every muscle in his body tensed up and he came.

"Ooooh!" she groaned. She was out of control. She felt hot. Her body tensed up and a wave of ecstasy rushed through her. She was coming. Really coming. Her body shook like she was having a fit, the most beautiful, delicious fit ever.

They lay on the bed, covered in each other's sweat. It had not been a simultaneous orgasm but it had been close enough. Cal hugged her tightly. Every time their eyes met, she giggled. Five minutes must have passed before she was back to normal.

"That was lovely," she whispered.

"It was amazing," he agreed, then dozed off.

Victoria stared up at the ceiling rose. There they were, two heads, one pillow. Cal was a gentleman, nothing like what she had expected. He was tough, brave and strong. He had an amazing body. Miles was bulky and sluggish but Cal was built like a street fighter. He had made her come like a train. She imagined night after night straddling him, pressed up against his chiselled torso, waiting to be taken to heaven a fraction of an inch at a time. I'm in trouble here. She once thought she loved Miles. Now she realised she never had. She had liked him, occasionally a lot. That week in Tuscany for instance. But it was never love. Could this be love?

Cal was snoring now. If it had been Miles, it would have got on her nerves, but because it was Cal, it didn't. Victoria was sure Dave was right and Cal was up to something, but what if he was doing it for good reasons? Could there ever be a grey area for wrongdoing that could be covered up? If she exposed him, she could lose him forever. If she didn't, and he was exposed by someone else, her career would be over, her reputation ruined. She was in trouble.

CHRISTMAS DAY

SHE awoke lying on her front with her hair all over the place. She rolled over. Her travel clock on the bedside table said it was seven. She felt surprisingly well considering she had only had a couple of hours sleep. She wished she could just stay with Cal, dozing, making love, eating, dozing again, making more love. She leaned over to switch on the bedside lamp and kissed his head. He moaned "mmm..." as he came around. As his eyes adjusted to the light, there was Victoria, dishevelled yet still beautiful.

"Merry Christmas, Mr Murphy." She smiled. "How are you feeling this morning?"

Cal was rough. He had a hangover mixed with a comedown. He felt depressed and... paranoid. He was in bed with a reporter who probably wanted to ruin him. This was not part of the plan. "Yeah... I'm ok cheers," he mumbled, "er... Merry Christmas."

She stroked his crew cut. "Do you fancy a brew?

"No... I'm okay ta."

"Well I'm having one. Are you sure?"

"All right. Tea, please."

"Sugar?"

"Two."

"Two? Yuck." She crinkled up her nose. The expression he would have found endearing just a few hours earlier bugged him. He needed to get outside in the fresh air, do his usual training run along the Rochdale Canal, up to Newton Heath and back, sweat out the booze and try to clear the vile feeling of insecurity from his head. "Yep, always two. Thanks. I'm, er, not sweet enough."

Victoria kissed his neck and face, but he didn't kiss back. She got up, still naked, and he allowed himself to stare at her naked body. He admired the way her hips curved into her sides. Beautiful but there was something scary about her.

She put on a bathrobe, went over to the desk and flicked on the kettle. Cups clattered on saucers and the sound of the little teabag envelopes being torn went through him. As she set her brew down beside him he shuffled up and sat up. His head throbbed. She got back in and leaned against him, her hair annoyingly tickling his ear. He reached for his cup with his other hand and sipped. "Mmm. Nice one," he said.

She rested her head on his chest and started fidgeting with the duvet, trying to get comfortable. Her wriggling got on his nerves. She could feel him looking at the top of her head. "Do you want to go back to sleep?"

"Yeah, cheers." He rolled over.

She sighed and nodded off too. She woke again at twelve minutes past eight. His side of the bed was empty. She looked around in the gloom and saw him buttoning up his polo shirt. "Where are you off to?" It wasn't meant to sound demanding.

"Why do you want to know?"

He had spoken to her curtly and it stung. "I was just wondering, that's all," she said.

"Sorry," he said, realising. "Nowhere. I mean... I've got to go. I've got a big game tomorrow so I need to go for a run and clear out the cobwebs. Haven't you got somewhere to be?"

"I'm supposed to be going to my mum and dad's for Christmas dinner. Not 'til midday though."

"Right. Well, have a good time. I s'pose I'll see you around." He walked over and kissed her on the head. He thought about what he was going to say next. "Come and see me at Reds any time."

Victoria was confused. Why was he being so hostile? He was going to sneak out without saying goodbye. "Fine," she said. I'll see you... soon." It wasn't meant to sound like a threat but it did.

"Okay." He leaned down to kiss her, but this time their lips missed each other. "Sorry," he said, and left the room without looking back.

>>>

CAL and Billy were parked side by side on the top level of the long stay multi-storey at Manchester Airport. The car park was close to full of holidaymakers' cars but they had managed to find two spaces together. Billy was in his red Sierra L smoking a Craven 'A'.

His radio didn't work. Cal sat in the driving seat of his gunmetal grey Ford Sierra Sapphire RS Cosworth with the Stone Roses' *Bye Bye Badman* coming from his Blaupunkt speakers. Billy wound his window down. "What the fuck am I doing at Ringway on Christmas Day?"

Cal's window was already open. "I've got the fucking press all over me, that's what."

Billy had invested his life in making Cal a footballer. He'd decided Wythenshawe was a wasteland of prefabricated houses and social problems and Cal should've been his ticket out. He invested hour after hour training the boy on the football pitches at Wythenshawe Park. He would clear the field of dirty syringes, empty bottles, crushed cider cans and dog turds and then line up traffic cones, making the boy dribble, sprint and crawl in and out of them. He would go in goal while young Callum belted footballs at him.

"The little fucker can kick a ball harder than any of you cunts," he used to brag to his pals over Sunday lunchtime pints. Cal was right-footed so some days Billy would only allow him to shoot with his left foot. If the boy scored, Billy would give him ten pence to spend on sweets. He came on leaps and bounds until Carol decided the sweets were rotting his teeth and made him stop it. They would take turns driving him to training twice a week and every Sunday between August and May he would ferry him all over

Manchester for matches. He would bark instructions from the touchline, which Cal found embarrassing as he got older.

It was around that time that O'Donnell said he was stepping in with finance. It wasn't a selfless act. Billy had been boasting about the boy's potential and his old mate was doing well from pimping out a couple of good-looking girls. His three hundred pounds a year paid for training gear, the best boots and taxis to matches. He would have a quiet word with Billy's boss if he got annoyed about him missing work. When Cal was signed up by United, both men thought their investment was about to pay off.

"Why the fuck did we have to meet here?" Billy yelled, gesturing up at the grey, midday sky as a Boeing 737 with a Monarch livery roared overhead, probably off to Malaga or somewhere. "We could have talked over a turkey dinner at my house."

"What, a fucking heated up Birds Eye one? I wouldn't risk my life by eating summat you made. I'm being followed."

"Followed? Fuck off. Who would waste their time following you? You're not Princess Diana."

Cal scratched his chin. "A fucking blue Mazda stayed behind me all the way here from town, I'm telling you. I think it's the press. Remember that bird who was in the club last night? The posh one... fit?"

"Which one?"

"You know, the martini bird."

"The one you sneaked off with while I was cashing up?"

"Yeah. She's a reporter.

"Get to fuck."

"She came right out and told me."

Billy sighed and a cloud of tobacco smoke billowed from between his lips. "She told you she was investigating you? And you fucked her?"

"Well I like her. It was more than a fuck. It was a bit weird."

"You're a bit fuckin' weird," growled Billy, tapping his temple. "You fucked two sexy birds on two consecutive nights and you are fucking moaning? I've heard it all now. What did Miss Martini say exactly?"

"She said 'I know you're bent'."

Billy exploded with laughter and flicked the butt of his cigarette at the low wall in front of their cars. "Bent? Well you do look a bit queer."

"Shup, Bill, listen. She named Nigel, Coz and Edo. Said she'd been doing her homework on us." He bashed his steering wheel. "Fuck. I don't know what to tell the lads."

"It that it? Is that all she said?"

"Well... yeah. Summat like that."

"I think the fucking press have got better things to do on Christmas Day than investigate you to be honest."

"But what if she does know something?"

Cal knew he had made the right decision to sneak out on her but she had made him feel rotten for match fixing. There had to be a better way of making fast money.

"How could she?"

"Shaw."

"Didn't Nigel tell you Mark Shaw wouldn't be a problem anymore?"

Cal shivered at the name and cranked up the heater in his car to full. "Yeah."

"And you trust him?"

"I do."

"Then you're fucking worrying about nothing. It sounds like this journalist is just speculating, trying to get you to open your trap... letting you shag her as well! Class. What's her name anyway?"

"Victoria Heath."

"Did she take it up the arse?"

"For fuck's sake, Bill... she's not like that."

A British Airways 747 roared as it flew over their heads, much louder than the first plane.

Billy was not amused and waited for it to pass. "You've got to relax, for fuck's sake. You've got a big game tomorrow, concentrate on that. I know things haven't worked out exactly as planned so far but we can't back out now. O'Donnell will fucking kill you. And me. Now go and get your head down and forget all this fucking press nonsense."

Billy rolled his window up and drove away. Cal gazed ahead, knackered, as his electric window buzzed up and closed with a dull thud. He left unaware that the dark blue Mazda that had followed him there was parked two rows back. The driver, O'Donnell's thug Hugh, waited for him to pass the ticket barrier before driving out of the car park himself.

\>\>\>

VICTORIA was trying to get through an in-depth *Vanity Fair* article about some bastard corporation which had dumped toxic waste on a beach in Haiti. It must have been three thousand words long and she couldn't concentrate. After waking up feeling sparky at the Majestic, just hours later she felt guilty and she felt used. She felt like shit. Miles was playing loudly with her nephew, Simon, perhaps deliberately trying to annoy her. Miles had barely said a word to her since she arrived home at nine, showered and changed. She drove them in silence to her parents' house in Astley. They hadn't even exchanged Christmas presents. At least John seemed to be fine, lying snoring by the roaring fire.

  The big, soft leather armchair in which Victoria was slumped had been in the family all her life and longer. She thought about her parents in the kitchen, basting turkey, flipping pigs in blankets, roasting spuds, stewing sprouts, and having a laugh as they always did.

The guests would be seated in time for the Queen's Speech as usual. Victoria's brother Connor and his wife Deborah were upstairs getting ready, or more likely having a nap while Miles occupied Simon. Connor, a hotshot lawyer as the Americans might say, had turned up in a brand new BMW saloon which was parked on the gravel drive behind Victoria's MG.

Her nephew Simon, proudly wearing the full Batman outfit which Father Christmas had brought him, was shouting "dinna dinna dinna dinna dinna dinna dinna dinna Batman!" She grimaced as she put the magazine down and went into the kitchen to see how her parents were getting on.

Max was fifty-nine, Wendy fifty-four. They were best friends as well as husband and wife and she loved and respected them both. When she was growing up they would often have between ten and twenty people from the school community, teachers, their kids, over for Sunday feasts. Wendy was always the head chef, Max the kitchen hand. Today he stood at the cooker in his slippers, a plaid shirt and beige chinos, tasting the gravy with a wooden spoon.

Wendy had on a long, embroidered dress with a red cardigan over it. Her hair was tucked under a colourful headscarf. It surprised no-one who met her that she was an artist. She spoke in a broad east Lancashire drawl. "Max... Get your blummin' fat head out of the gravy... there'll be none left. Make yourself useful and baste the turkey."

"Again?" he sighed, and heaved the baking tray out of the Aga, set it down on the worktop and began ladling fat over the brown, sizzling bird. It was huge; plenty for the annual turkey and stuffing toasties for supper, and possibly a turkey curry on Boxing Day. Max was sweating and his combed-over hair hung down by his left cheek.

"Here she is, the intrepid reporter." Victoria's dad peered over his half-rimmed specs at her as he continued to baste. "How's life in the gutter press. Still all crime, football and showbusiness?"

"Don't start," she said.

"You're in a good mood," he said sarcastically.

"I'm knackered. It's been hard graft, always is this time of year. Too many late nights."

"Well aren't we feeling sorry for ourselves. This'll get you in the festive spirit." He picked up a Christmas cracker. "Eight in the box, seven eating, and Connor nowhere to be seen. You get to pull the spare cracker." He held it out.

"Amazing," she said drily. "I thought you were going to hand me the keys to a Mercedes. Or at least a glass of that fancy wine."

She took her end of the cracker. Max let her win and a miniature magnifying glass fell to the floor. She picked it up and tried to give it to him. "It'll help with your crosswords. With your old duffer's eyesight."

He declined it. "I'm not quite an OAP yet, Victoria. You hang on to it. It's bound to come in handy for your amateur sleuthing."

"Professional sleuthing. Get it right."

"Enough basting," ordered Wendy. "Put it back in the oven now."

"The bastard's basted," said Max, and chuckled at the joke he cracked every year. He lifted the huge bird back into the oven.

Wendy was seated on a high stool holding a large glass of the red. She looked at Victoria as though there was something she had to remember. Then out it came.

"Any plans to give me another grandchild any time soon? A little girl would be nice."

"Don't, mum. Not today. I can't take it."

"I know but look how happy Simon's made your brother. He's a changed man. If you never try, you'll never know. You know we like Miles, don't you?"

Connor? Happy? Victoria didn't think so and didn't answer.

"Can we at least expect him to make an honest woman of you any time soon?" asked Max.

Victoria put her hand to her mouth to stifle a yawn. "Sorry... I don't know. We've got our own little family already, with John, and Miles needs to finish his novel before we start thinking about marriage."

"Ah, yes, his masterpiece," said Max, checking behind him that Miles wasn't in earshot. "I never got to finish mine. Your mother distracted me."

"You'd think an English teacher would have half a clue, but bloody hell, the tripe he was writing. Some rubbish about vikings with a social conscience."

Max laughed. "We can't all make money painting pictures of vaginas."

Victoria couldn't help but crack her first smile of Christmas Day. "Can I have a drop of wine?"

"Staying over are you?" her mum asked as she passed her a wine glass.

Victoria helped herself to a good amount of the Chateauneuf du Pape. "Probably. If anything breaks, I'll call a cab."

"Victoria," said Max, "You're twenty five. You know Wendy had Connor when she was twenty four. The thing is.... we don't think you should hang around waiting for Miles to propose if you don't want to marry him. It's not fair on him and it's not fair on you. Your mother and I only care about your happiness, yours and your brother's. I know we always say it but we're so proud of you both. Miles seems a nice chap, but if he's not the one, get out now and move on. We only want what's right for you."

Wendy nodded supportively.

It wasn't Miles' face that popped into her head when her dad said that. It was Cal's.

That he had treated her like a casual one-night stand and crept out like a burglar made her ears burn. He's a cheat and a player. Callum Fucking Murphy Bastard Piece of Shit.

>>>

CAL had been for a long run around the city. He had arranged for room service to bring his Christmas Dinner at three o'clock. Prawn cocktail, turkey dinner with all the trimmings and Christmas Pudding with custard. He planned to lie on his bed watching videos on the big Sony Trinitron until then. He would have loved to block Victoria from his mind with a few festive cans of Guinness but he couldn't risk his sharpness with a match to fix the next day. He instead drank black tea and did four dozen press-ups in his underpants. It was getting dark so he pulled the heavy velvet curtains on his view of the central library in St Peter's Square. The reporter was still on his mind.

He went to the box of football videos he had in the walk-in wardrobe. Watching the masters at work was all that kept him enthusiastic about the sport these days, and it would be a nice distraction. He took down the VHS of the World Cup Quarter Final. All the talk had been about Maradona cheating England out of the tournament with his Hand of God goal, but his second was the best goal ever as far as Cal was concerned, and no one ever mentioned that.

The Little Magician picks up the ball inside his own half. Two men approach to close him down, but he beats them both with a cheeky spinning turn and nudges the ball forward. He carries it down the right flank and then drops his shoulder to trick the defender that he is going outside him before edging inside. Another defender approaches as Maradona reaches the penalty box. The Argentine drops his shoulder to fox him, too, then changes direction and passes him on the right. He is yards from the goal. Keeper Peter Shilton comes out to block. Maradona pulls back his left leg to shoot. But that's just more smoke and mirrors and he dribbles the ball around Shilts and side-foots the ball coolly into the net. Breathtaking.

Cal pressed rewind on the remote and watched it again. Maradona goes past one, two, three-four, five, six England players as if they aren't there. They look gutted. They know they are going out of the tournament. If things had gone differently, he might have been in that England squad. He pressed stop on the remote and went back to the wardrobe.

He took a tatty shoebox down from a high shelf and carried it over to the sofa. Inside were mementoes such as his Lancashire Cup winner's medals and the laces from his first football boots. There were Polaroids of him as a boy holding up trophies and kicking footballs about wearing different United kits which O'Donnell had bought him. There was one of when he had won Manager's Player of the Year for his club as a ten-year-old. The nice old man with his arm around him in the picture was called Sid, he remembered. He loved his football back then. Auntie Carol and Billy stood next to them, smiling proudly. Carol looked young and beautiful.

He came to another snap. It was a black and white image of him with Carol at an anti-nukes camp in Somerset when he was fifteen. It was his only picture of them together. Carol was saying something to him, and he looked fed up. In the background, adults with matted hair were milling around tents with washing lines tied between them.

He remembered the day. Carol was ribbing him about the attention he was getting from a girl named Sarah. Sarah was a year younger than Cal and wore a stud in her nose. She didn't have a dad either. She lived in a camper van with her mum and they travelled around a lot. Later on the day the picture was taken, the campers all ate together. After scraping up, he got his ball and went for a kick about. He was doing step-overs when Sarah shoulder-charged him. She wore her hair in two thick plaits and she had a funny accent like a farmer's daughter. He liked her big gold hoop earrings. But the best thing about her was the big tits. Most of the girls at Cal's school were yet to grow tits. He was mesmerised.

"Stop staring at my tits," she said, crossing her arms and putting her hands over them.

"Shut up," replied Cal, going bright red.

Sarah grinned. She had a nice smile that made her eyes sparkle. "Don't worry. All the boys do it." She took her hands away. "What's your name?"

"Callum. What's yours?"

"I'm Sarah. Wanna come for a walk?"

"Yeah okay," he said a bit too quickly. "You're not going to tell my auntie I was... looking are you?"

"Depends if I think you're nice. Come on... I want to walk around the campsite... come with me."

Cal picked up his ball and Sarah lit up a fag. When he told her smoking was bad for you she shrugged and said: "And?"

They walked on for a while, passing rows of tents and men and women painting banners, and passing some massive gates that led into the base where the bombs they were protesting against were thought to be stored. Sarah said she was from somewhere near Ipswich, but he didn't say anything about them having a good team. He didn't think she was bothered about football.

"Where are you from?"

"Manchester," he replied proudly.

"Oh. I went there once. My uncle moored his barge there for a bit. It rained all the time."

"You must travel a lot." His voice seemed squeakier than usual and he had butterflies in his stomach, which was weird.

"Not so much now," she said, apparently not noticing the voice. "We've been here for months. It's boring unless there's a protest. Then it's fun... the coppers start trying to arrest people and you get to swear at them, like 'fuck off pigs!'"

He laughed. There was a "pig" back home who kept confiscating the ball when him and his mates were having a kick about in the street. He was a dick. He thought of telling Sarah about him but didn't. There was a ten-second silence before he said, trying to modulate the wobble in his voice, "I like your nose stud. It looks cool."

She raised an eyebrow, something he'd been trying to learn for ages. His heart beat again.

She stood still. "Want to kiss me, do you?"

"Kind of," he admitted bashfully. "I do now you've said it."

She caught his eye and he looked away. She grabbed his hand and led him off to a nearby copse. Then she pushed him up against a tree and kissed him. He had kissed girls before, but this was different; she put her tongue in his mouth. It had the metallic taste of cigs but felt good as it wiggled around. His tongue joined in, pushing hers out, letting it in again. He soon felt dizzy with desire. His hands were on her hips, then moved up to her tits, feeling and kneading them, firm but gentle, not too hard. He didn't want to hurt her.

"Naughty boy," she said, barely understandable mid-kiss.

"Mmm," he moaned, feeling the warmth around her armpits through her cotton blouse. He wanted to touch skin. He undid one of the buttons and slid his hand inside, onto her bra. He slipped his hand inside the left cup as they continued to snog and toyed with her pointy nipple. He felt a warm rush down the back of his neck, down his spine. It felt like his legs were going to buckle.

They dropped slowly into the long grass. Sarah fiddled with his shorts and it wasn't long before their shorts were around their ankles. She gripped his cock. "It's the hardest thing I have ever felt," she whispered, which seemed a very adult thing to say. He remembered looking up through the trees, panting.

Cal lost his virginity in a matter of seconds. Sarah assured him he had done well and they walked back to the camp holding hands. He sat down crosslegged and she rested her head on his thigh. He had this daft grin on his face and couldn't stop looking at her. The grown-ups must have suspected something. Cal remembered Carol ruffling his hair and giggling as she went to get something from the tent. Sarah's mum didn't seem too happy.

Their camper van was gone when he woke up the next morning. This had become a recurring theme in his life. Women never stuck around after shagging him. They disappeared, back to their boyfriends with their sensible houses and sensible jobs, and that was that.

Since losing his virginity that day, he had shagged a further twenty-five women. He remembered the number like he remembered how many goals he had scored. He didn't feel guilty, because he had loved every single one of those girls, at least for a few hours.

Cal put the photos away. *A View To A Kill* was starting. He sat enjoying Roger Moore's performance as 007 pretending to be James St. John Smythe until some adverts came on. The Queen's speech was thirty minutes away so his chef-prepared turkey dinner would arrive soon.

>>>

CARLA Hornby lay across the hand-made three-seater sofa, still in her pyjamas and slippers despite it being well after noon. She hadn't said much that morning as Kim excitedly opened her presents. A *Challenge Anneka* Christmas Special was on in the background. A glass of vodka and orange sat on the lamp table next to her chair pretending to be orange juice. She picked it up and took a generous sip. The Christmas dinner, pre-ordered from a caterer in Marple Bridge, was sitting in the fridge in takeaway tins, ready to be heated up.

Outside the patio doors, Nigel was playing with their daughter in the big snow-covered garden. He was trying to teach her to hit an oversized golf ball with some plastic clubs from a set Father Christmas had brought her. Kim was only three and Nigel doted on her, but Carla couldn't help wondering if he wished they had a son instead.

It didn't look like they would be having any more kids. Carla felt they had been going through the motions. They argued a lot and abused each other, mentally and sometimes physically. They occasionally had sex but Carla didn't really try, she just lay there, and it was dull and she rarely came. They had a nice enough life but she just thought it would be... more satisfying. Footballers didn't earn as much as people thought. They were just getting by. It was depressing. She knew her husband had secrets but couldn't say anything as long as the wages kept going into the joint bank account.

When Nigel first joined Belle Vue, Callum Murphy would sometimes go round to theirs with fish and chip suppers or takeaway curries. The three of them came from similar backgrounds, Cal from Wythenshawe and Nigel and Carla from Hulme, and they used to have such a laugh. Cal had helped Nigel fit in to life as a footballer. It wasn't like a normal job. People would pester Nigel when they were out having a quiet drink and say things to him like "I'd fuck your missus". Supporters of rival teams would try and pick fights with him, desperate to look hard in front of their mates. One night, five drunk Oldham supporters surrounded Nigel and Cal at the Grey Horse in Portland Street. One had thrown a punch. Nigel had smashed a beer bottle over his head and they had to fight their way out of the tiny pub. Nigel was worried about getting done for ABH, or even grievous. You could get locked up for a long time for that. Cal told him not to worry, that somebody he knew would smooth it over, and thankfully the brawl was never reported to the police.

These days, Cal only went round to work out or mess about in the games room, something she was happily excluded from. She would occasionally hear muttering and whispering and see worried faces but if she asked her husband what was going on he would snap at her: "Nothing for you to worry about."

Carla believed she could depend on Nigel to provide for his family. She could only hope that whatever he was doing wasn't putting their lifestyle at risk. She wasn't just thinking of herself, she was thinking of Kim. She didn't know what she would do if they lost the cottage.

Carla's thoughts turned back to Christmas. She finally picked herself up from the comfort of the armchair and shuffled slowly into the kitchen to switch the oven on to heat up. Gas mark six should do it. Her Majesty would be on soon.

>>>

THE beautiful Dutch model Christina Kruger had risen at nine, heated up the oven for the freshly-plucked, family-sized turkey from the butcher in Didsbury village and peeled the potatoes and vegetables. Edo had promised to do it but he was still in bed asleep.

Christina had fallen for Edo De Haan when all the experts were predicting he would be Holland's next football superstar. He was a man about town but she had no doubt she was a match for him. Everyone said he would end up playing for the Netherlands, just the kind of man she was looking for. One day, he was playing for Ajax against Feyenoord in Rotterdam when an opposing defender jumped on his leg, breaking it in three places. One photograph, which Edo had ghoulishly kept a print of, but which had never been published, showed his shin bone sticking out through his sock at a jaunty angle.

Ajax stuck by their talented young midfielder during the eighteen months it took him to recover. When he eventually got fit again and played a few reserve games, whispers started circulating that his bottle had gone. Edo insisted it was bullshit, and that the rumours were started by another player who didn't want him taking his spot in the team back. The club had been doing just fine without Edo, however, and wanted him off their wage bill. Belle Vue, a small English second division club in Manchester, made him the best offer. His agent described the move as "a stepping stone" in his career. Edo hoped it might lead to interest from Manchester United or City but that hadn't happened yet.

It was nearly time to eat and Christina was back pottering in the kitchen. She was in bare feet, toenails painted purple, wearing tight low-waisted jeans, a white Yves Saint Laurent blouse and a vinyl apron with a cartoon buxom body in black lacy lingerie printed on the front. Edo had not come down yet. Simon Cosgrove sat playing *Super Soccer* on the Nintendo in the adjoining TV room. Simon's parents had gone to spend Christmas in Blackpool so Christina had told Edo to invite him over. No one should be alone at Christmas.

Christina liked Simon and thought he was a very funny guy who would one day find a nice girl and settle down. He caught her looking at him and smiled at her lingerie apron, thinking, I've seen her in the real thing. He had gone round for a Nintendo night with Edo and Christina had walked into the living room in full lacy lingerie, not knowing they had a guest. That had kept him in wanks for months.

"How's it going, Chrissy? Need a hand?"

"Nah, leave it to me. I'm enjoying myself. Just make sure you help Edo with the washing up."

"No probs," he said, focussing on his game again. "We can't have your hands getting all wrinkly."

After a beating from Brazil, he switched off the games console and went upstairs to the guest room. He wanted to have a snooze before dinner. Before long he was naked, tied to his bed by the wrists and ankles with stretched Wham! bars while Christina, wearing a Sexy Santa outfit, poured rice pudding over his cock and balls and spanked him hard with a candy cane, leaving raw gashes on his chest that oozed pink marshmallow. Then he heard Edo calling him. He sat up, a bit too quickly, unsure for a moment whether the dream was real. He rubbed his eyes.

"Coz! Dinner!" Edo shouted again.

He slowly got up from his bed. "Nice, coming," he shouted back, his duvet bunched at his feet. His semi-hard cock was resting on his soft underbelly. He quickly adjusted his dress and went downstairs. Something terrible had happened.

"You are supposed to take out the giblets from the turkey, baby," Edo was explaining to Christina as he pointed to a melted bag of guts protruding from the bird's neck.

"I know that now Edo! Is it spoiled? Oh my God, I've ruined Christmas!"

Simon grabbed the bag and yanked it out, thinking: So this is what it must be like to deliver a baby. "It'll be fine," he assured her. "Me old dear does it every other year. Mind you she's got an excuse. She's usually been on the sherry."

He nodded at Edo who nodded back appreciatively. Then he sliced off a bit of breast and took a bite. It tasted slightly plasticky but he ignored the flavour. He was starving. "Tastes fine to me. Let's eat."

It wasn't long before Simon was drunk, his alcohol levels topped up to what they had been the night before. He started on gin and tonics, then opened a bottle of Moet and Chandon which he had brought as a surprise. Edo and Christina politely had one glass each, he drank the rest. By dessert, some sort of Dutch cake with a cross between Santa and a Golliwog on top, he was back on the Stella. Unlike Cal, there was no way Simon was going to stay sober on Christmas Day.

As *News At Ten* began he decided to treat himself to a joint and a good night's sleep, his concession to the game the next day. The occasional smoke helped him relax and the spare room at Edo's had a sash window which you could open wide and blow out your smoke. "Right. I am off to bed," he declared.

After the door closed behind Simon and he could be heard padding upstairs, Edo and Christina started kissing. It was a passionate snog, one that made them both gasp for air as they groped each other's bodies like teenage lovers.

When their lips finally parted, Edo said: "Thanks for dinner, honey, it was great."

"My pleasure."

"What would you like for Christmas?"

"Your big cock, silly," she replied. "As deep as it will go."

He gulped but thankfully she didn't notice. He had never deliberately set out to cheat on Christina, it just happened. He couldn't help it if women found him irresistible, but he felt bad all the same. He was cheating on her and now he was cheating on his fans. He was being an idiot. In the New Year he would make an effort to be a little bit nicer.

"Let's go to bed," he said.

>>>

UNCLE Billy lay on a double bed at Sensations. The Caribbean Suite had a feature wall papered with a panorama of an empty white beach with a beautiful, still blue ocean lapping up onto it. Two palm trees had a hammock slung between them. The idea was that the punter felt like he was having sex on a deserted tropical island. The bed was a four poster, brown plastic posts moulded to look like coconut tree trunks. The canopy above the bed was not very skilfully woven from straw, like a shit Caribbean beach hut. Billy had spent four hours of Christmas Day at the club and had nearly polished off a full bottle of Scotch. He had also smoked two packets of Craven 'A'. His Christmas dinner, taken during a game of gin rummy, had consisted of a Ploughman's in a bag - a Laughing Cow cheese triangle, two crackers and a couple of minuscule pickled onions - followed by a small, stale ham roll.

It was seven at night now and he was just at the beginning of his second hour with the Russian. He usually only spent an hour with the girls as they were not cheap but it was Christmas and Ivanka was something else. She was twenty-eight and wearing bright red lipstick. She had a slim, toned body, B-cup breasts, and a firm arse that all the punters liked to squeeze. Her skin was so alabaster that the lightest slap left a red hand print behind. She had studied art history at university in St Petersburg but knew that in Britain she would have to use her body as an instrument to make money. She didn't mind as long as it wasn't forever. Her English needed to improve and she quite liked to fuck. She would prefer to fuck someone her age who was her boyfriend and had money and treated her like a princess but until he came along she would have to take the money of these dirty old men.

What she was about to do was one of the most satisfying parts of the job. She was naked apart from a studded leather belt buckled around her waist. Two straps were attached to it at the front, going under her crotch and fastened at the back of the belt. A pink, solid plastic, nine-inch dildo with a bulbous, bright red tip was attached to the front, pointing upwards at an angle of about fifteen degrees.

Billy was in front of her, naked, on all fours. His gut hung down and his back and shoulder blades were darkly hairy. His arse, wizened like a walnut and hairy, was sticking up in the air and Ivanka had smeared a blob of Vaseline between the cheeks. He was about to experience something completely new. Ivanka had assured him she was an expert and would be very gentle.

"Arghhh!" He shouted, biting down on the pillow as she inserted the giant dildo into his rectum. "Sweet fucking Christ. Nnnnng!"

The second hour was to be a long one.

>>>

HARRY O'Donnell sat at his desk watching grainy CCTV footage on one of the portable TV sets stacked on his desk of one of his oldest friends being fucked with a strap-on. Billy was daft as a brush, always had been, but had never meant any harm. That was why he still tolerated him. The pimp opened his desk drawer and took out a photograph of them taken alongside the donkeys by an old gipsy on Blackpool beach one hot summer's day many moons ago. It was in an ornate silver frame but hadn't been seen by anyone but him for a long, long time. It was taken in seventy-two or three, he couldn't remember which, but he knew it was around then because he had arranged for some of his cousins to come over from Ireland to break a strike.

O'Donnell used to box regularly at a gym in Burnage back then and he looked lean in his cut-off jeans and vest with sunburnt skin peeling on his shoulders. Billy was as podgy as ever, with his hair hanging long and greasy onto his shoulders, and his belly hanging over his football shorts. Carol stood between them in a sky-blue bikini, sexy as a Bond girl, with her arms around both of their shoulders. It was a travesty what happened to Carol. O'Donnell had loved her from the second he clapped eyes on her, and he always would. She was tall, slim and brown, the most beautiful girl in Manchester in O'Donnell's opinion. And she was not in the slightest bit aware of her own beauty, which made her all the more attractive.

The three of them had gone to the same school and became mates because they all used to crawl through a hole in the fence and sneak off to smoke when they should have been in lessons. After leaving school they shared a party house in Wythenshawe. It was the Swinging Sixties and it was the place to be after kicking-out time at the local pubs. Then Billy and Carol started fucking... and it wasn't long before they asked O'Donnell if he wouldn't mind moving out. Why had Carol picked Billy over him? Because he never had the bottle to tell her that he fancied her, probably. It was his greatest regret. O'Donnell had money and he was the sensible with it. Billy wasted his cash on his motorbike. If Carol hadn't died so young, maybe she would have seen the light and realised she should have chosen O'Donnell instead. He would have forgiven her in a heartbeat.

O'Donnell felt the familiar fire of anger which rose from his belly to his throat whenever he looked at the picture. It hurt, for sure, but it kept him on edge, where he needed to be, to be the person he now was. Gangster, pimp, whatever, these were all just labels. He was a businessman and a fucking good one.

The anger brought to mind Callum Murphy, a young man for whom he had bent over backwards to help, time and time again. He had financed all the boy's training and travel and without that he would never have become a professional. The football club tours to France and Holland, the top-of-the-range boots. He paid the scout from United to go and size up his potential, then paid him even more to recommend him to the manager. He had invested thousands of pounds in the boy. In return, he was supposed to make him a lot of money but the stupid little twat fucked it all up. No-one really blamed the bastard at the time, but he was the one who killed Carol.

BOXING DAY

VICTORIA peered at her bedroom ceiling through gummed-up eyes as her clock radio bleeped. Green digital numerals told her it was 08:04. She had already pressed snooze once and it was time to get up. She had a hazy head after sharing two further bottles of fine wine with her parents but her pulse quickened as she remembered what lay ahead. She was going to expose Callum Murphy and his motley crew. She was going to get her best front page yet. Her pièce de résistance.

Miles groaned and rolled over onto his other side as she got out of bed and put her feet in her slippers. She went downstairs to make herself a cup of tea and as the kettle heated up she noticed the blanket of snow which had fallen overnight, covering the back garden.

She switched on the kitchen portable and the weather was of course the top story on Sky News. Her ears started burning as a man in a thick winter coat reported that most of the day's football matches had been called off due to nationwide snowstorms. A list of cancelled fixtures popped up on the screen. As the correspondent read them out her heart sank. Coventry City versus Belle Vue of Manchester. P-P. Match postponed. Fuck. Fuck, fuck. Fuck fuck... Fuck! She slammed her hand down on the worktop. John trotted up to her, tail wagging, and started barking and jumping up at her legs, so she lifted him up and held him tightly to her chest. The hug was more for her benefit than the dog's.

Victoria's brew was half-finished as she clicked off the television set and went back to bed. The information she had gleaned so skilfully from Cosgrove was useless. Anger was boiling up inside her. She hated life. Actually she didn't, she just hated Callum Murphy. She was going to sleep all day and pretend her world hadn't come crashing down. It was supposed to be her day off any way. She had been thinking about working harder on things with Miles but she noticed herself taking care that their bodies didn't touch as she got under the sheets and buried her head under the pillows.

She had left the bedroom door open. John padded across the carpet and jumped up onto the bed. He wasn't really allowed on the bed, but that was Miles' rule, not hers. John rolled onto his back, moving up beside her so she could feel his little heart beating. Suddenly the dog sprung to his feet, pawing Miles' face. "For fuck's sake," he moaned.

She lay on her side facing away, pretending not to notice the dog. "Fuck's sake," repeated Miles. After that there was silence; thick, awkward, unruly silence that strangely brought clarity to Victoria's thoughts. For the first time, she realised that she was going to leave Miles. She didn't know when, but it was going to be soon. She rolled over, put her arm around her little dog and drifted off into a deep, satisfying sleep, a feeling of relief making her melt into the mattress.

Hours later, she woke up to her arm being roughly shoved. "I'm off to the Dog and Partridge for a session with Paul," said Miles. She rubbed her eyes and peered at the clock radio. It was two o'clock. Her boyfriend was dressed and had even shaved. He reeked of Joop. He walked out of the room without looking back and a few moments later the front door slammed. She stared up at the ceiling rose and wondered if he knew it was over too. He hadn't even said which Paul; they knew three. She assumed it was Paul Knight, a single friend from Macclesfield who played a lot of rugby and drank a lot of beer. Miles would return home late, drunk, possibly hoping to trigger a reaction about the state he was in. He would be disappointed, because she couldn't give a monkey's. She rolled over and dozed off again, the dog still snuggled up against her.

>>>

LOFTY winds carried sheets of icy rain over the snow-covered training ground from the Irish Sea coast more than fifty miles away. The footballers were soaking wet and their faces were stinging. It was two o'clock in the afternoon. The gaffer had rung them all early to say the Coventry match was off and that they would be training instead. He wanted to see his players sweating out the turkey dinners and festive booze. The groundsman, called in on his day off, had hastily shovelled the snow from the lines on the second pitch. The gaffer stood on the centre spot holding his stopwatch, ready to shout each player their time as they came in. The whole squad was in a huddle at one corner of the pitch. "READY... STEADY... GO!"

The players moved slowly along the length of the pitch to the next corner like a cycling peloton. When they got there, each pair of legs exploded into a sprint along the dead ball line to the far corner. They slowed down into a jog again, this time for both a length and a width. They could jog as slowly as they liked up to the corner; but then they had to sprint again, this time also for a length and a width. Pulses had begun racing by now, but at least there was a length, a width and a length of jogging to come in which to recover. Of course, that passed a lot sooner than expected, and it was time to sprint again, three sides of the pitch now. By this stage, the fitter lads led the pack. Nigel, who as a keeper who didn't need to be as conditioned as the outfield players, was at the back. Next up was a full lap of the pitch, all four sides, jogging, no resting. Once that lap was done, it was a full, sprinted lap. Anyone who pulled up knackered would have to do fifty press ups and start the whole exercise again.

That was the halfway point. Next up was to jog the four sides again, then sprint them. Then they would jog the three sides, then sprint them. By the time they had done that, Cal, Edo, Jed Brennan and a couple of others had opened a big gap in front of the rest. Cal's lungs were burning as he lapped Nigel. The keeper grunted "bastard" as flecks of icy mud from Cal's heels spattered on his face. There were just two sides left to cover; a width to jog and a length to sprint. As they passed the finishing line, the gaffer barked out their times. They had to write them on the blackboard in the changing room later. Forgot your time? Fifty press-ups and start again. Slower than the time you posted during pre-season training? Fifty press-ups and start again.

The gaffer was looking at his stopwatch, an old fashioned pocket one, still shouting times. "ten minutes, twenty seconds; twenty eight; thirty five..."

Cal was relieved the match had been called off as it had bought him some time. He had chatted briefly to his crew, asking them how their Christmases were, but hadn't even told Nigel about the reporter. She was probably out there right now, blowing people for information or whatever it was that she did. Simon was hung over and finished lower than half way down the pack. Nigel was last.

Second to last was young Tony Butterworth. He bent over and was sick on his boots, retching out bits of regurgitated Shreddies which melted the snow that they landed on.

The blackboard was an intimidating fixture on the wall of the tactics room. Sweaty footballers with mud splattered on their faces scrambled and pushed in for bits of chalk to scroll down their times before they forgot them. Some times were suspiciously only slightly better than the summer times entered beside them. Others were massively improved, like Cal's. Young Tony sat folded over on a gym bench, struggling for breath. He didn't look well. The gaffer came in and inspected the board.

"There's a fucking time missing here," he declared after a few seconds. "Some thick twat has forgot to put down their time... Where the fuck is TB?"

There was silence. "Sorry gaffer." Butterworth was bright red in the face and still struggling to breathe. "Give us a sec," he wheezed, taking another pull of the inhaler. "It's me asthma..."

"That's fifty press-ups," Jed piped up. "And another run round. Rules are rules."

Tony looked like death warmed up. "I c-c-c-an't breathe, Jed... Gaffer?"

Jed roughly put him in a headlock and dragged him to the floor. He rested his knee on the gasping teenager's chest. "Stop being such a poof. Fifty press-ups right, gaffer? Same rules for everyone."

The gaffer nodded. He didn't know Tony had acute asthma because it was a secret that only his family knew. It just looked like a bit of banter between his players. Jed was being a bit OTT but he was the captain and was just trying to toughen up one of the young lads. Tony wasn't moving but Jed put his foot on his back. His studs must have dug into his spine because Tony yelped. Jed snorted, then lifted up the leg of his training shorts, took out his cock and started pissing on the back of Tony's head.

Jed was cackling like the clown at Blackpool Pleasure Beach. Tony started coughing and he aimed the stream into his mouth. A few other fringe players joined in the heckling, wanting to suck up to Jed. "Ruthless," laughed one as Tony struggled to catch his breath.

"Listen to him, he sounds like Darth fucking Vader," chuckled Jed, as piss splashed onto the linoleum and a puddle grew around Tony's head.

Joking around at training was one thing but this was stone-cold bullying and Cal didn't like it. He looked at Nigel who nodded as if to say, do something.

"Pack it in, Jed," Cal said loudly.

Jed turned and looked directly in his eye and carried on pissing. "What? Are you his fucking dad or summat?"

Cal stepped forward, jabbed him on the chin and shoved his chest so he fell backwards. He crashed down onto a bench, piss trickling out of his cock and onto his training shorts and the tactics room floor.

"You're a cunt," Cal growled at him. "You're lucky I don't fill you in properly."

The jeering stopped. Jed was seething. He wanted to fight back but Cal was a better player and had the respect of more of their teammates. He shook his head, got up and walked towards the toilet door at the end of the room, his cock still out. "You'll regret that," he muttered.

A puddle of sticky, brown fluid surrounded young Tony, who was still gasping on the floor. Cal wished he had stepped in sooner. No one deserved to be pissed on. He shook his head, picked up a piece of chalk and wrote 10:20 in the gap next to the teenager's initials on the blackboard. "That was his time, gaffer," he said. "If anyone thinks it was any different send them to talk to me."

The gaffer nodded. "Okay, Cal."

Cal helped Tony to his feet and took him into the adjacent changing room, where he sat him down and put his arm round his shoulder. "Listen," he said. "Jed was just trying to make a point. What point it was, fuck knows, but it won't happen again."

Tony was snivelling. "The gaffer will never pick me now, Cal. I c-can't fucking keep up. I've got asthma."

"Don't worry about the gaffer, he knows Jed was out of order. You're a fucking good footballer, you've got some nice touches, you think before you pass the ball and you don't give it away. That's rare in a kid your age."

"But if I'm not fit enough..."

"How old are you?"

"Nineteen."

"Fucking hell, is that all? You'll be fine, believe me. Just try and pace yourself better next time. Make sure you don't come last and don't make a scene and you'll be fine. And if Jed gives you any more shit like that, let me know."

"Thanks very much," he said, wiping a dried patch of sticky piss off his face with his sleeve.

"No problem. Have a shower. Then walk out with your head held high and a grin on your face. Don't let them see you're bothered."

"I will."

Cal slapped him on the shoulder. "Nice one. I meant to ask, did you pull at Reds the other night?"

"No, we were going to chat these three girls up who were looking over at us but we got too pissed."

Cal gave him a matey punch him on the arm. "Fucking hell. That's no good is it? Go easy on the JD next time, eh?"

\>\>\>

THE voice was Irish. "Is that Mr Shaw?"
"Yes."
"This is Hugh from Sensations. You've left something here."
Shaw automatically felt for his wallet, then realised he had seen it since his visit. "Have I? What is it?"
"Never mind, just come over and get it. Today."
"I've got a fucking broken leg..."
"Yes. Just come and get it. Today." The phone clicked off.

Getting a taxi back to Chinatown with crutches had been a pain in the arse and had cost him four quid. His memory of Sensations was sketchy to say the least, but he remembered the African girl who did dirty things with him. He even knew her name was Ebony but that was because her calling card in the pocket of his jeans. She was like Whitney Houston but with big tits. He didn't know he was attracted to black girls but her scent really turned him on and he had never gone in at the tradesman's entrance before. He'd hobbled in on his crutches, shit-faced, and ordered a beer. Hugh wouldn't serve him a beer but said he would get him a coffee and some sandwiches. Maybe he could have a beer later. Shaw was a bit annoyed and was about to start arguing until he realised he was starving and the big fella seemed to be talking sense. It certainly helped him when it came to fucking Ebony.

Now he was back. Two old men were playing cards. He recognised the man behind the bar as Hugh.

"Mr Shaw," said the Irishman, drying a panel glass with a tea towel.

"I didn't know if you'd remember me."

"I know all our members."

"I'm a member? I was a bit pissed t'other night, looking back."

"You did seem a wee bit in the festive spirit but you were well behaved enough. I put you in a taxi at about four."

Shaw grinned. "Thanks for that, pal. I wondered how I got home. I slept right through Christmas."

"No worries."

"So what's this thing I've left here?"

Hugh passed him four fifty pound notes. "You left two hundred quid here."

Shaw couldn't remember having that much money on him. "I don't think I did, pal."

"You did. Put it in your pocket." Hugh wasn't taking no for an answer so Shaw did as he was told.

"The owner would like a word with you. Mr O'Donnell. If you don't mind."

Shaw racked his brains. "Did I meet him the other night too?"

"No, you didn't. But he likes his football. You could say he's a fan. I'll take you in to meet him."

He helped Shaw across the room and knocked on the panelled door of O'Donnell's office. "He's here," said Hugh, loud.

"Come in."

They went in. O'Donnell sat behind his huge desk in his giant leather chair. "Ah Mr Shaw," he said, Irish too but less strong. He pointed at the smaller chair in front of the desk, which he kept to remind visitors who was the boss. "Have a seat."

Shaw nodded and sat down, placing his crutches on the floor beside him.

"Can I bring you something to drink?" Hugh asked Shaw.

"Er, yeah, a beer please."

"Budweiser?"

"Thanks."

"Bring me a cup of tea, please Hugh," said O'Donnell.

Hugh nodded and left the room.

O'Donnell got down to business. "Sorry to drag you in here like this but I've got a business opportunity to discuss with you. A little bird tells me Nigel Hornby did that to you on the orders of Callum Murphy." He pointed at Shaw's leg.

Shaw was surprised. "Dunno what you mean," he said. Having been warned not to talk by Nigel Hornby, he had a long chat to his mother in Leeds. She said she was worried about him and wanted him home in one piece.

He would give Callum Murphy a kicking one day, but on the football pitch.

"It seems a bit over the top, smashing up a footballer's knee just because he wouldn't help you fix a match."

"Hang on. I said I don't know what you are talking about."

Hugh came back with the drinks. He was massive. He had carried Shaw down the stairs over his shoulder and put him in that taxi after his last visit. And Shaw weighed fourteen stone.

"Budweiser," he said, delicately pouring the beer from its bottle into a tall crystal glass so a light head fizzed at the brim. He took a steaming pot of tea off the tray and placed a china cup and saucer in front of his boss. He then stood by the Christmas tree with his hands clasped in front of him like a security guard.

"Save your breath, Mark," said O'Donnell. "We know what happened. Surely you want to get your own back?"

Hugh stared at Shaw, nodding at him as if to prompt him to reply.

"I just want to put all that behind me to be honest," Shaw said, unconvincingly.

"Well I need your help and I won't take no for an answer." O'Donnell opened a drawer in the desk in front of him and pulled out thick wad of ten pound notes. "There's ten grand here."

It was more cash than Shaw had ever seen. "What's that for?"

"It's for you, for your trouble."

It was a ridiculous amount of money. Shaw couldn't help but think about a five series BMW he had his eye on and Callum Murphy was a cunt. The change of heart came as quickly as it had when he decided to score the goal against West Ham. "What exactly is it you want me to do?"

"I need you to hand a tape incriminating Murphy, Nigel, Edo De Haan and Simon Cosgrove in rigging matches to a journalist who I think will be very interested."

Shaw frowned. "Why me?"

"Because you're a footballer and more importantly, a team mate of these characters. It'll carry more weight as evidence coming from you."

"What's in it for you?"

"Let's just say I'm a fan of the beautiful game who doesn't like people manipulating it to their own ends."

Shaw scratched his head. "Where's this tape?"

O'Donnell grinned. "We haven't got it yet."

FRIDAY

VICTORIA peered at her bedroom ceiling through gummed-up eyes as her clock radio bleeped. Green digital numerals told her it was 08:04. She had already pressed snooze. At least she didn't have a hangover today.

Miles had come in at around ten the night before and apologised to her for getting on her back about work. Evidently Rugby Paul had advised him over several pints. She had accepted, anything for an easy life. Miles was like a big kid, and he thought she was his teddy bear. When they started going out it was endearing. Now she found it pathetic. He rolled over in bed, put his arm around her and started fiddling with a button on her nightie. She had her back to him but their legs were entwined. Physically they were touching. Emotionally they were miles apart.

He hadn't cleaned his teeth and she could feel his stale, beery breath against her neck as they lay between the Egyptian cotton sheets. They were locked together by his arm. He was clinging to her like a piece of property. He was tall, but his body was now only average. He certainly wasn't the athletic hunk he was when they first met.

"What time is it?" He asked, half asleep.

"Only eight, Go back to sleep," she whispered.

"Mmm." He took her hand and placed it on his boxer shorts, where his cock was engorged. They had made love, or at least had sex, the night before. It was the first time they had done it in a couple of weeks. His manhood had felt tiny after her tryst with Cal. His humping went on for ages until she faked an orgasm. Cal's face popped into her head as Miles grunted and came. Now it seemed he was after morning-after-sex sex. After about ten seconds, she took her hand off his groin.

"I don't have time now, sorry," she said, trying to look upset. "I've got to get to the paper."

She went to kiss him but he moved his head slightly and it turned into a clash of teeth. She got out of bed and went into the en-suite bathroom. She turned on the shower, waiting until the water was steaming before she got under it.

Forty-five minutes later, her hair had been blow-dried straight and she was buttoning up a light blue casual blouse. She went to the window and pulled back the curtain. The snow on the street outside glistened. She pulled some tight stonewashed jeans up over her French knickers. Then she put on an oversized cream jumper with a shawl neck, slipped on black ballet flats and threw her trenchcoat on.

Miles woke again and sat up. "Coffee?"

"I've really got to go. Don't forget to walk John." She again leaned towards him for a kiss. She gave him a peck on the lips but he was frowning.

"Love you," he said. It sounded like a question.

"You too, grumpy," she said. "See you tonight."

"Yeah. At midnight, no doubt," he replied.

Victoria left the house and drove off with her window down, drinking in the cold, crisp air as she passed the Toast Rack on her way to town.

>>>

THE sky over Manchester's Heaton Park was pewter grey. Conditions were perfect for sledging and kids were flying down the snow-covered hills of the golf course, waving their arms and screaming as the icy wind froze their cheeks.

The four professional footballers jogged past an overweight dad who was pulling a sledge up an icy path towards the elevated sixteenth green. His son and daughter were tip-toeing gingerly behind him. The dad nearly fell as he tugged the rope. He grunted "fuck" and took a puff of a cigarette. Simon heard him wheezing as he overtook.

The wind jabbed into the players' ribs and steam rose from the shoulders of their tracksuits as they ran. Led by Cal, they were heading towards the Temple, a Tuscan observatory at the park's highest point. It had a breathtaking view of the city out to the

Arndale Tower and the CIS building and beyond.

Simon, naturally-gifted but definitely the least fit of the gang, had been dripping with sweat since they left the car park. "I could do without this," he moaned to Edo. "I feel like turd. My knees were killing me after the gaffer's fitness session so I went straight out for a few. Turned into a late one."

"Did you win?"

"I came out a grand up. I always win at Blackjack."

"Like fuck," Cal shouted over his shoulder as he skipped over a slushy puddle. "If you did you wouldn't be living at your mam's."

They dodged patches of grey mud on the silt path. They ran through a small copse of naked trees and bushes and around a bend in the path. Someone had spray-painted "fuck the law, smoke the draw" in foot-tall letters on the wall of an electrical substation.

Simon was puffing and blowing. "Couldn't we have just run round Whitworth Park? It's fuckin' miles up here."

"It's more secluded," Cal replied as they trotted along the deserted path to the observatory. "I don't want any cunt hearing us."

"It's secluded at Whitworth as well... if you keep away from the alkies."

The players eventually reached the Temple, an old lookout tower dating back to the city's Industrial Revolution boom. It stood at the grand old park's highest point. You could see for miles around from it and be confident no one was listening in. A walker was heading down the hill a hundred yards away but there was no-one else around. Simon stopped by a large tree, whipped out his cock and pissed against the trunk, steam rising from his urine. He then re-joined his mates by the frozen grassed area by the Temple and Cal asked him to suggest a stretch.

"Calves," he said, leaning forward with a bent left knee and pulling his toe upwards. He always called for calf stretches because they expended the least energy. Plus you didn't have to lie down and get your kit muddy.

Nigel, Edo and Cal followed suit. Then they swapped legs. The backs of their calves burned as their muscles lengthened.

"Okay," said Cal. "There's a reason I brought us here. Listen up."

"This sounds serious," said Nigel, standing up straight and putting his hands on his hips.

Cal had toyed with the idea of speaking to Nigel personally but decided it had to be as a group.

Cal continued. "As you know, the pimp went fucking ballistic when he heard we weren't going to Coventry."

"So?" said Edo. "What does he want us to do about it? We can't fucking help it if it snows."

"Fuck all mate and that's what Billy told him. But he said he keeps losing money and face and can't afford to take any more risks with us. So he's changing the deal."

Nigel spat on the snow. "We are still getting our hundred grand aren't we?"

"Yep," said Cal. "But he says we have to throw the Leeds match."

"What?" said Edo. "We don't throw games, do we?"

Cal exhaled a hot, deep breath. "He reckons we've got no chance against Leeds, regardless of what we try and do, so he wants us to make sure we lose two-one."

Edo was shaking his head. "I dunno man... Losing on purpose? That's serious."

Cal had decided honesty was the best policy. "Yep. And I'm pretty sure the press are onto us. And I mean all of us. So we'd have to be dead careful not to make it obvious."

"The press?" Edo was surprised. "Where's this come from?"

"Remember the bird from the club on Christmas Eve? The one who you'd already met, Cozzer? She told me she's a reporter for the *Chron* and says she knows what we're up to."

Simon laughed. "So that's why she went for you. She knows you're the ringleader. She was like a fly on a turd, man. I swear."

Cal shook his head. "All right... shut it will ya? She's got no proof about anything, but I still think it's still dodgy as fuck. I've got no choice but to try and throw it, O'Donnell will murder me if I don't. But you three are my mates and I need to know if you're with me. Nige? You've got a bit put away. You've got a daughter to think of. Surely you don't want to risk that?"

"You'd have no chance without a keeper, though."

"I know, but... put your family first for a minute. This is big time."

You didn't shit on your best mate. Yes, he had a daughter, but he needed money to bring her up, especially the way the missus spent it. He wasn't a Belle Vue fan, he just worked there. He grinned. "I always put my family first."

Cal breathed a sigh of relief. "Does that mean you're in?"

He sighed. "Yeah man. Fuck it. Count me in."

"That's two of us. Cozzer?"

He shrugged. "Whatever, Cal. I'll do what you do."

"No way, man. Not this time. Make your own fucking mind up for a change."

"Do you think it's worth the risk for twenty five grand?" Simon's hands had moved behind his head and he was leaning backwards, stretching his stomach muscles. Light flakes of snow were landing on his face and melting.

"Like I said, mate. I've got to do it. It was me who got us into this and if you want to pull out now, I get it. You're young, you've still got a good career ahead of you if you look after yourself. You know, early nights, eating right, boozing less, taking care of yourself. Not many people have a left foot like yours. You've got talent."

Simon thought for a moment, shrugged and laughed. "I'm only two years younger than you, knobhead. Anyway, it's only a game and I want the dosh. I'm in as well."

"All right. Ed?"

Edo stood with his arms folded. He was the closest thing Belle Vue had to a superstar and was paid more money than any of them. But like Nigel's wife Carla, Christina certainly knew how to spend it. The house in Didsbury, the designer clothes, the Porsche, she insisted they had it all.

"You didn't force any of us into this," he said. "We're all men here. And what am I going to do? Shit on my mates? I'm in too. But no fuck-ups eh?"

He directed this at Simon, who flicked the Vs at him.

"Sound," said Cal. "We need a plan. We've got work to do."

He took a deep breath, turned around and looked over the rooftops of north Manchester to the CIS office building dominating the city centre skyline. He realised he hadn't actually taken in the beauty of where he lived for a long time.

"We drink to us tonight," he said.

\>\>\>

THE reporters had been for delicious tapas at El Rincon and were sitting in Victoria's MG in the car park on St Mary's Parsonage. They had been given a free bottle of Rioja by Rafa, the owner, whom Kerry knew. Victoria could taste anchovies and garlic and curled a stick of Doublemint into her mouth. "You ready? I want to go and see what Murphy's up to."

"I bet you fucking do... you want to see him back between your legs."

Victoria wasn't going to tell Kerry about her and Murphy on Christmas Eve but had confided in her after a second glass of red. Like most reporters, she wasn't very good at keeping things to herself. "No, I'm not doing that again. He's a dick. It's just work. "

Kerry put on her best flasher-in-a-mac pervert voice. "Dirty work."

They got out and walked up the alley to Reds. It was dark, smoky and hot inside and Victoria couldn't see much apart from flashing lights. The place was packed and a sea of hands was reaching for the lasers as a heavy drum beat boomed out and shook the floor. It was *Rhythm Is A Mystery* by K-Klass. A saxophone solo gave way to deep vocals.

"Drink?" Kerry shouted in Victoria's ear.

"Coke." Victoria replied, scanning nearby faces. "I've had two already."

"Fuck driving... Stay at mine. We'll cab it."

It had been a dull, pedestrian day at the paper. Victoria had turned up to the morning news conference with nothing on her pad, so Waters told her to speak to a group of pensioners in Audenshaw who claimed there was lead in the tap water. Charles Reynolds, a ninety-four-year-old veteran of not just one but both world wars, was their spokesman. She went to his house to interview him and it stank of cats despite there being no evidence that a cat lived there. She had declined his offer of a cup of tea, just in case. She had gone back to the office and phoned North West Water to get their side of the story. The spokesman promised to arrange for water samples to be sent for even more tests. He made it obvious the company had been pestered by these oldies before, but she still arranged for a photographer to go and take a picture of ten old farts standing around Charlie's sink holding glasses of water.

She was enjoying Kerry's company but wondered if she should go home. She had spent the evening worrying about whether Miles was looking after John properly. She kept trying to convince herself that he loved the dog just as much as she did, but the thought kept niggling her. What if he had gone out on the lash again? There was nothing she could do now, she supposed. She shrugged. "Surprise me," she said.

Kerry chuckled. "That's the spirit."

A minute or two later Kerry handed her a high-ball glass of bright red liquid garnished with two cherries and a wedge of pineapple on a tiny plastic sword.

Victoria was impressed. "Singapore Slings?"

"Nice guess, piss head," laughed Kerry.

"How did you get that miserable old fart to make you these?"

Kerry just shrugged. "Billy? He's a big softy. You just have to know how to handle him."

Victoria shook her head, impressed. Kerry seemed to have a contact in every bar in town. She sucked a slurp through the straw and took a sharp intake of breath. "That really is the spirit. There must be a triple gin in there. Any sign of Murphy?

Kerry shook her head negative. "Fuck me, listen to you. Don't worry, loverboy will be here somewhere. Let's go and have a dance."

>>>

CAL was in fact just twenty feet away from Victoria. His stood with his elbow resting on his beloved Russian maple bar alongside Nigel, Edo and Simon. He was holding a bottle of Beck's, chuckling about Billy and the Russian whore who had serviced him on Christmas Day. Nigel drained his can of Colt 45, crushed it and held it up in the air. Billy was serving someone else but noticed him and raised a thumb. After taking the customer's money, he prepared a new round of drinks for Cal's gang.

A blonde in a figure-hugging silver dress sitting on a stool at one of the high tables over near the front door caught Simon's eye. She was about five foot two, and beautiful in a Salford sort of way. Her silver dress was short and low-cut, lifting her impressive tits up towards her chin. She was smoking a cigarette and looking bored.

"I need to meet that," he said to no one in particular as he set off towards her. He wasn't going to let Cal steam in ahead of him this time. He had his hands in his back pockets, swaying his shoulders. If he thought it looked cool, it didn't.

Cal saw him approach the girl. She pulled on her fag, blew out a massive cloud of smoke and shook her head. She was laughing at him rather than with him and was hugging her elbows defensively. Simon looked like he was shitting himself. Twenty seconds later he was back at the bar with a face on. "Stuck up bitch," he said.

"What happened mate?" asked Cal.

"She knocked me back, what do you think happened?"

Cal could tell he was hurt. The girl and her friends were all laughing together, probably at Simon's bungled approach. She had amazing, thin legs. Her blonde hair cascaded over her shoulders.

"She's fit, man. What did you say?"

"I asked if I could give her a Christmas kiss."

"What did she say?"

"She said... you can kiss my arse."

Cal chuckled. "She's just having a laugh. Anyway, it's not fucking Christmas any more. Go and tell her you got your dates mixed up." He slapped his shoulder. "Or try it on with her mate, she'll be well confused."

"What? The fat one sat to her left? She's clinically a beast."

"It's obese, knobhead. Look, I saw her smiling, waiting for you to say something else, chat her up more, you know. You don't ask girls like that for a kiss, you just give 'em one. Why do you think she's dressed like that? Not to get pissed, have a kebab and get a taxi home on her own. Go back over and stick your tongue in her mouth. It's got to be worth a slap."

"I can't. She thinks I'm a dick now."

Cal shook his head. "Fucking hell. Wait here."

"What do you mean? Hang on a sec..." said Simon, but Cal was already going over. "Fuck, man."

Cal approached the girl from behind and tapped her on the shoulder. She turned around quickly, startled, and a huge grin appeared on her red lips. She fluttered her eyelashes. She had lovely big blue eyes, caked in dark mascara. "Callum Murphy," she said confidently.

"That's me. Er, sorry to mither you, but I was just wondering, what did you say to my mate?" He nodded his head towards where Simon and Nigel were standing.

"The little one who just came over? I can't remember. A drink might refresh my memory."

She was flirting with him. He was clean through on goal. He just needed to dribble the ball around the goalkeeper and roll it into the empty net. But he could see a team mate, one he knew was struggling with his form, and who needed a boost in confidence, waiting in the middle, pleading for a pass and a share of the glory. Simon was that man.

"That's my pal Simon. Don't you fancy him?"

She looked at the group again. Simon was watching them and smiled. "He is sort of cute but he seemed a bit shy when he came over... he was physically shaking. I'm not really into the nervous type."

Cal smiled. "He's not shy when you get to know him. He's a top lad. One of my best mates. He's piss funny when he gets comfortable with you. He's also loaded and generous to a fault. And he thinks you're mint. What's your name?"

The girl dropped her cigarette on the floor. "Charlotte. Charlie."

"Charlie. Nice. I want you to make this the best night of his life. Get off with him."

She looked at her empty glass. "Piss off. What if I'm waiting for someone else?"

"Bollocks to someone else. He'll buy you all the drinks you want, all night... in fact, any night."

"That's really appealing," she said. "But we were going to go up to the Hacienda soon."

"You don't wanna go there tonight. There's no one good on, it'll be dead. Look, you don't have to shag him. Just let him feel your tits. You'll probably want to suck his knob. But that's between you two."

She laughed. "Don't take this the wrong way, but you're an arsehole."

"I won't."

"My dad says you should be playing for England."

He gestured around. "I got all this instead. Listen, I'd love to stand here chatting all night but Simon is waiting. Do we have a deal or what?"

"I'll talk to him... but I'm not promising anything."

"Cheers, er, what's your name again?"

She rolled her eyes. "Charlotte."

"Charlotte. Nice name."

Within ten minutes, Simon had his tongue in Charlotte's mouth on the couch in the chill-out area.

>>>

CAL was thinking about the reporter again. She had been on his mind all day. She had got him to like her, but wasn't that how these journalists operated? Get your trust and then turn on you? She said that wasn't her intention but she was pilled up at that point. How could he trust her? He was brought back to himself by a surge of punters towards the dancefloor. He turned to the bar. "What the fuck's going on, Bill?"

"Caz is here," said Billy. "She's dancing. She gave me a little wink when she came in."

"She gave you a little wink?"

"Is there a fucking parrot in here?"

"Why didn't you tell me?"

"You were talking to Cozzer's bird. I don't even know if Sweet Caroline's still talking to you. I can't fucking keep up with all your fanny."

Sweet Caroline. She was the girl of his dreams. Not Victoria. It was too difficult with Victoria. Caroline knew what he was like. She was his best bet. He turned quickly and barged through the crowd, saying "scuse pal, sorry... cheers, scuse" as he went.

Caroline and a blonde writhed around in the centre of the floor, hands all over each other with eyes closed as the sax solo in *Rhythm is a Mystery* boomed from the speakers. They swayed their hips and raised their hands in the air. Both were tanned and wore big sunglasses with fluorescent frames. The blonde wore a tie-die skirt that clung tightly to her arse and a tight, bottle green cropped t-shirt cut down the front with scissors, showing off her cleavage. Caroline had her hair up and wore a baggy, fluorescent yellow string vest. Underneath was a black lacy bra. Her camouflage combat pants hugged her arse tightly and were rolled up at the ankles to show off a new pair of white, pink and black Nike Air Max.

Cal stood nearby, swaying to the music. Caroline saw him and took his hand. Her friend pretended to be upset she had been snubbed but carried on moving to the music. A muscular, tanned lad in a baggy vest with blonde highlights in his hair danced up to her.

"Fancy seeing you here," shouted Caroline.

"Welcome to Reds." Cal said. "What do you reckon?"

She smiled. "It's a bit... derelict."

"It's supposed to be like Berlin."

Caroline pointed at the old black and white televisions with static flickering on their screens in the chill-out area. "You could have got some tellies that worked."

"They're just for effect. Part of the theme."

She punched his arm. "I know, I'm taking the piss. Listen, I need that favour." Her lips brushed against his ear as she whispered: "Can you get me some coke?"

Cal let go of her hand and stepped back. "Do I look like a fucking dealer?"

Caroline's hands went to her hips. "No, but I'm desperate and you owe me."

"I'm a professional athlete, for fuck's sake... I can't be scoring gear for every Tom, Dick and Harry."

She stood in front of him, arms folded, biting her lip. "I'm not a Tom, Dick or Harry."

Victoria's face popped into his head, a serious look, frowning, telling him not to do it. His cock twitched inside his jeans. He put the thought to one side and sighed. Caroline was the one, it was already decided. "I'll see what I can do."

"I need seven grams... if it's no problem."

He nearly dropped his beer. "Seven grams? I'm not fucking Keith Richards, you know."

"I know you're not fucking him, he's way too sexy for you." She smiled at him. "Please, Cal."

He blew out, shaking his head dramatically. "Jesus. I'll see what I can do. Meet me outside in twenty minutes."

The Shamen's *Move Any Mountain* dropped to whoops and cheers.

>>>

KERRY whooped and started pushing sweaty men out of the way to form a small circle for them to shuffle their feet in. Victoria had a head rush from drinking her cocktail at Kerry-speed. Now they were raving.

A scrawny thirty-something geezer in a pink Global Hypercolor T-shirt and green army surplus pants danced up to them, arms and legs all over the place.

"All right, darlin'?" He was sweating profusely, had a fag hanging from his lips and he was obviously on something. Victoria reckoned ecstasy, which suddenly brought her back to thoughts of Cal. Why did he bother being so nice to her if all he wanted was sex? He took care of her all night and listened to her and was gentle and she felt safe in his arms. She really thought there was a spark between them. She caught herself frowning again.

The scrawny man shuffled his feet backwards and forwards and bent his knees alternately to the beat. Kerry didn't seem to care that he was wasted. She nodded and moved closer to him. The three of them danced for a while.

"Hey look!" he shouted. "You dance like me!" He was joking. "So... what about you two giving each other a snog?"

"Only if you and your mate snog too." Kerry pointed at another lad with a step haircut, who was squinting and clinging to a crumpled can of Stella.

"I'll ask him but I don't like your chances, love. He's off on one."

"That's a massive shame," she said sarcastically. "What's your name?"

"Baz. What's yours?"

"Dirty Diana to you."

Baz laughed. "I'm just going to ask him for that kiss. Stay there."

He turned around and went over to his mate. They started talking.

As the song reached a crescendo with Colin Angus' gruff rapping, Kerry yelled: "He's fit as fuck."

"Who? The singer?"

"No, that lad, Baz."

Victoria scowled. "What? He's a dick. Did you hear him? Asking us to snog... wanker."

"He's only having a laugh. Fuck, you haven't half got one on you all of a sudden. Have I missed summat?"

Victoria took a deep breath as she checked her attitude. "Sorry... you're right. I feel a bit crammed in here. My round. I'll be back."

"Nice one, I'll stay around here," shouted Kerry. "Try and find your boy. That'll cheer you up."

>>>

CIGARETTE smoke, cannabis fumes and dry ice made Victoria's eyes itch and she almost brought up vomit. She hadn't been home since she left for work and was tired. A Coke would spark her up, she thought, but she needed some fresh air first. She swallowed hard and went upstairs and through the outer door.

As she enjoyed the cold night air, she heard a blood-curdling cry from a narrow service alley which ran alongside the building that housed the club.

Victoria, naturally, wanted to see what the commotion was but couldn't without making it obvious. She waited a moment and casually walked past the opening, glancing to her right as she did so. She just had time to register Cal punching a man hard in the stomach. She took cover in a dark fire escape entrance which had a view of the alley.

Cal threw the man on the floor as hard as he could and his skull whacked against the cobbles with a sickening thud. "Not so fucking hard now, are ya?"

Someone laughed deeply. It was Hornby, looking on with his fists clenched.

"Give us a break," groaned the man on the ground. Blood was trickling from his nose and onto his beige Stone Island jacket. "We were only trying to shift a few grams. I'm a Belle Vue fan."

"I couldn't give a fuck who you support," said Cal, kicking him hard in the ribs.

The dull thud made Victoria's stomach churn.

"No one sells fucking gear in my club," said Cal.

Hard, dirty snow had piled up by the side of the club's overflowing metal bins and a fourth man stood beside them, smoking. His name was Tom. "Are you fucking joking? Loads of people do, you just don't know about it," he said. He flicked his butt on the floor. "Listen man, it's Christmas. Just give us the fucking coke back. It's not even ours."

Cal hoped it wasn't some Moss Side psycho's drugs he was taxing. The last thing he wanted was the Gooch crew turning up with guns blazing. "Whose is it then?"

"A mate's. I don't want to name names but she's connected, man."

She. Cal was relieved. It was unlikely 'she' was a gangster. "Well so am I. You can tell her to forget about her gear. And you two are banned for life."

Tom snorted. "As if we give a fuck about being banned from this shithole. You think you're it, don't you?"

The man lying on the floor, Mick, groaned again, clutching his side. Tom moved towards him but Nigel stepped in his way.

Tom suddenly sprung forward aggressively. "Raaaaarrr!!!" he yelled, windmilling his arms.

Nigel calmly took a step backwards and held him out of range with his massive left hand on his chest. He then planted his right fist square on his nose. Tom staggered backwards, hit the wall and slid down it. He ended up in a seated position with his head lolling to one side.

For no apparent reason, Cal booted the other man, Mick, in the mouth. "Do not fuck with us," he growled, as blood dripped on the cobbles.

Victoria could understand that drug dealers needed to be dealt with but couldn't see why such extreme violence was necessary. Dealing was a crime, a police matter. A chill ran down her spine and she moved back into the darkness, feeling the rivets of the fire door through her shawl neck sweater.

Cal and Hornby dragged Mick and Tom past and down towards Deansgate by their coats. She now had a great view of them and wished she had her camera with her.

Five minutes later, Cal and Hornby walked back up the alley, the bigger man rubbing his knuckles. He went back into Reds but Cal kept walking on towards St Mary's Parsonage. Victoria followed him, staying back to ensure her presence wasn't noticed. As the narrow alley opened out onto the square she saw Cal on a bench beside a woman. She casually strolled in the shadows in front of the shops, staying out of sight, and eventually reached the car park. She quietly got in her MGB and reached behind the passenger seat for her camera. She had a great vantage point and zoomed in on the bench. The woman was pretty but looked slutty in some kind of see-through string vest.

She also had a shiny forehead which had a few zits on it.

CAL passed Caroline the plastic bag. She was surprised by the size of it and raised her eyebrows. She dipped the tip of her front door key in the white powder and sniffed a bit up. "Wow... that's good shit Cal," she said, her eyes lighting up. "Here, try a bit."

He had been offered cocaine many times over the years but had always avoided it. No one gave a fuck about weed but coke was different. A drugs ban would fuck up his football career but he knew Caroline wouldn't grass. The reporter would probably be disgusted with him if she knew... Caroline was more edgy. More his type. His best bet. He looked around. "Go on then... just a bit, though."

Caroline giggled as she held out her key. He coughed after sniffing it. His nostril started stinging and his eyes started to water.

"That's a sign that it's good," she said.

"It's the best I could do at short notice."

There was nearly ten grams in the bag. The prostitute Melanie, who knew Tom and Mick from school, had taken it from Rabbi Yehudi's coffee table.

"Nice one, you've really done the business," said Caroline, putting the bag in her handbag. She then took out a joint, lit it, had a large drag and offered it to him.

Cal's heart was beating ten to the dozen and he hoped a smoke would calm him down. He had a drag. Moments passed, during which thick vapour came from his mouth in quick and constant puffs, which blew back into his face.

"So, are you all right?" she asked.

"My heart's beating like fuck."

"I meant after the other night. After us."

It was the perfect moment to tell her how he felt but something bland came out. "Oh, you know me. Fine."

"Just fine, eh? Me too, thanks for asking."

"No worries." He coughed again.

"Fancy a blowback?"

He laughed, wired on the drugs. "I'll take a blow job."

She smiled. "In your dreams, mister."

She leaned in very close and blew smoke into his mouth.

Victoria was watching through the viewfinder, shocked. Cal was a drug dealer now? The slut leaned in to him and snogged him. That was what it looked like from where she was sitting. She imagined their tongues going into each other's mouths. It felt like she was being knifed in the heart but she managed to keep holding the camera steady and pressing the shutter button. Click. Click.

>>>

"THIS is top," declared Caroline, looking around wide-eyed.

"Thanks. It's no Hacienda, I know, but we're getting there."

She frowned. "Not Reds... I meant Manchester, with the snow and the hot wine stand outside Yates' and stuff." She noticed he was hurt. "Sorry... I'm talking shit."

Cal wanted to ask her how she felt about sleeping with him but couldn't think how to bring it up again. He felt wasted.

"Speaking of the Hac, are you coming tonight? Graeme Park's doing an extended set."

"I can't, I promised Billy I'd stick around here tonight. And I've got a game tomorrow."

"Come on, that's never stopped you before. It'll be fun." She smiled wickedly.

"Stay here with me," he said, pretty pathetically.

"I can't, I'm meeting people. Friends of Sal, my mate I was dancing with before. That's what the coke's for."

In the car, tears were causing condensation on Victoria's SLR viewfinder. She was relieved when the slut stood up and walked away. She had a good figure. Victoria slammed the shutter button on the camera down. Click. Click.

>>>

IT was two in the morning at Charlotte's house in Burnage and Simon couldn't remember her name. Cal said it when he introduced them but it had left him in a flash and no matter how hard he racked his brains it wouldn't come back to him. He couldn't ask now, he'd left it too long.

"Thanks for bringing me home, Simon," she said, and hiccupped. "You're my knight in shining armour." She inched up to him on the baggy old couch, their thighs touching. She put her arm around him and kissed him deeply. His heart skipped when her hand moved to his groin and she ran her fingers along the outline of his already-erect cock. The kiss lingered on for a few seconds before she stopped and sat back. The silver dress was riding up, revealing pink and yellow knickers with an embroidered image of a teddy bear on the front.

She took his hand and stood up, sticking out her bum as she pulled him up with her. She led him upstairs to her bedroom, a double that overlooked a small back garden.

She closed the door and Simon pushed her up against the wall and started feeling her tits and her sides and her arse. She suddenly pulled out of the kiss. "Wait," she whispered. "Let's get in bed."

"O... Okay." He always got nervous before a big game and this was no different. He was shaking again. Charlotte moved away from him, smiling, and unzipped her dress. She took it off and chucked it in the corner of the room.

"Get undressed," she whispered.

"What are you whispering for?" asked Simon, as he pulled off his jumper and t-shirt, then his trainers, socks and jeans. He left his boxers on, paranoid she might think he had a small cock.

"It's sexier. Shh." She wagged a finger at him. She was now down to a lacy pink bra and the teddy knickers, nothing else. Simon's boxers were blue and white-striped like a butcher's apron.

"Sorry," he said.

They lay on the bed together and started kissing again. Simon was running his hands over her body with uncertainty. He might have been lying skin-on-skin with a gorgeous bird. And she might have told him to take his clothes off and got undressed herself. But it had been so long that he still wasn't absolutely sure he was going to get his end away. He tried feeling her arse harder and was slightly surprised to get away with it. He decided to unhook her bra. They were kissing still, he was multi-tasking well, but the fucking bra clasp wouldn't come undone. He pulled the elastic out but it slipped from between his sweaty fingers and snapped back against her skin. "Ow!" she exclaimed, their lips still touching.

"Soz."

"Stop apologising. Relax." She sat up, smiled, and unfastened the bra herself. He could almost hear the satin sliding down her tits as her nipples came into view. She was completely un-self-conscious, even with the lights on. She had every right to be, her body was fantastic. He could hear imaginary fans singing here we go, here we go, here we go. He felt like a centre forward who hadn't scored for ages and was being trusted to take a late penalty in the FA Cup final.

They got under the continental quilt, kissing again, and Simon wanted to find out what was going on in her knickers. He played with the waistband a bit, slipping his fingers underneath. Eventually he took the plunge and put his whole hand down. The fabric was wet and no wonder. She was soaking wet. He rubbed where he thought her clitoris might be.

"Ahh," she moaned, biting her lip, eyes closed. She didn't appear to be faking. That boosted his confidence, so he pulled her knickers down. She put her hand on his cock, which was aching. She took his boxer shorts off.

"Lie back. I'm going on top," she told him.

Simon's cock was still as hard as a stick of Blackpool Rock. She took a condom from a drawer by the bed, ripped it open and rolled it down his shaft before climbing on top of him.

His breaths shortened as she enclosed him. The heat of her radiated through his groin. He was going to come already. She was oblivious, bouncing up and down. No! He started off by counting backwards from ten. That he managed, but his balls still wanted to erupt. Don't come, don't come, don't come! Charlotte was propping herself up with her arms, head thrown back, nipples pointing up at the ceiling. The quilt had fallen on the floor. She was getting hotter, Simon could feel it. The feeling was sensational. He started trying to think of City's starting eleven in the seventy-six League Cup final. He had got to number seven, Peter Barnes, without coming, which was some achievement, when she let out a couple of strange squeaks.

"Mmmmmm," he moaned, feeling a rush of euphoria from his balls up his spine and into the pleasure vortex of his brain as he climaxed too.

After a few moments, Charlotte got off him and rolled on her back. He would be ready to go again soon. Just having her by his side, their bare, sweaty skin touching, was making him hard again. She might even get a third one later in the night if she was lucky. The hat-trick! But she said: "You've got to go. I'm going to visit my mum in Bolton in the morning. I need some sleep."

"I can drive you there," he said hopefully.

"And how are you going do that? You haven't got a car here."

"We can get a cab to mine first."

"No."

He felt his confidence draining away again. "Can't I just leave when you leave?" he whinged.

"No. And don't sound so desperate. It's unattractive." She grabbed a lipstick. "Roll onto your front."

"Why?"

"Because I said."

He did as he was told and she wrote on his back: 437 5579 Charlie X. "Write it down before you have a shower, or you'll never see me again. And don't wait too long to phone me or I'll come and find you and kill you."

She smiled at him and he smiled back. He kissed her again, his tongue going back into her mouth. He was getting hard again and he put his hand on her tit. "Time to go," she whispered.

Simon got dressed. Undies, jeans, T-shirt, trainers. His Rossignol ski jacket was in the lounge. He kissed her goodbye, got his coat and set off running. Burnage wasn't that far and he felt like getting fit again. It wouldn't take that long. All the way home, sleeves pulled down over his hands, he was grinning so much his cheeks ached. He couldn't wait to find out what her name was.

SATURDAY

SHAW stared out of the passenger-side window at the Cosgroves' council house. "It's not proper football if you can use your hands."

"Fucking bollocks," said Hugh. "You can use your hands in American Football and Australian Rules football, so you can."

"Yeah, but there is only one pure form of the game, and that's Association Football, where you only use your feet."

"What about fucking headers then? Why don't they call yours headball?"

"You're the fucking head-the-ball. I'm telling you it's..."

The Irishman leaned across and grabbed Shaw's coat. "You don't fucking tell me nothing," he said, with a chilling look in his eye.

"Okay, it's fucking football. Whatever. You crazy bastard."

Hugh let go of Shaw's coat, and sat back in the driver's seat. Anglo-Irish relations had been going on in this basic fashion throughout the half-hour drive from town. Shaw straightened himself up and then stuffed his hands down his trousers to give his balls a good, satisfying scratch. The pot on his leg made them itch like a leper colony.

Shaw had got Simon's address from Jed Brennan. He'd phoned the captain for a chat about his damaged knee. O'Donnell and

Hugh had listened in as Brennan recommended a good physio on Shudehill. He was from New Zealand. A few Belle Vue players had used him when they were injured. Cozzer had probably had the best results, when he was out for three months with ankle ligament damage. Really? I might give Cozzer a shout. Do you know where he lives?

"Burnage."

"Bloody hell, my auntie lives there."

"Small world."

"Innit? Don't suppose you know what street?"

Hugh had parked across the road from the only two houses that didn't obviously have kids living in them. It was a dull morning and a light had gone on and off a couple of times in the left house.

"Are you going in or what?" asked Shaw.

Hugh's hand rested on the gearstick. His watch said it was nine. "Yep," he said. He got out, went round to the boot of the car and took out a black briefcase. He crossed the road and walked through the gate and up the front path of the left house.

He rang the bell and a stooped old man came to the door, squinting over a pair of Jack Duckworth-style NHS bifocals. "Yes?"

"Season's greetings, old fella. Is Simon in?"

"You've got the wrong house. The boy lives next door, number thirteen." The old man was barely able to move his head to motion which side he meant.

"Sorry about that, my mistake," said Hugh. "Are the rest of the family at home, do you know?"

"Eh?" The man twiddled a knob on his hearing aid.

"I said: 'Are the rest of the family at home, do you know?'"

"No need to shout, I'm not that deaf. I just needed to turn her up. They've gone to Blackpool. Simon's on his own, if he's in. He comes and goes."

"Blackpool?"

"Eh?"

"Blackpool?"

"Aye, they go and stay at the same hotel every year. Christ knows why."

"Not going to the seaside yourself then?"

"Fat chance of that. I can't afford to go shopping. Did you know the council put the rent up again this year? Call themselves Labour. Rubbish, they've never got their hands out of my pocket."

"Bastards. I bet you fought for this country as well."

"I bloody well did, son. Morocco. Shrapnel in me knee since forty-two. No bugger gives a monkey's these days."

"Sorry to hear that," said Hugh. "All the best for nineteen-ninety. Have a Happy New Year."

"Aye. And you." The old man shut the door in his face.

>>>

"I'M very sorry," said the vet, who was about the same age as Victoria. "The internal bleeding is too serious. The only thing I can do is put him to sleep."

Victoria dabbed her eyes with a tissue. She had left Kerry's at seven, just as the day was breaking. She thought about Miles as the cab carried her along a deserted Mancunian Way through Moss Side. He was dull and couldn't satisfy her, but he was a safe bet and maybe that was all she needed. When she got out of the taxi, he came out, put his arms around her and told her John had got out and been run over.

"I must have left the back gate open," he said. "I'm so sorry, Victoria. I forgot I'd let him out. A young girl found him by the side of Barlow Moor Road. The bastard driver didn't even stop. His back legs have... they've been flattened." He sobbed. "I'm so sorry."

Now they were at the vet's. John was lying on his side on a stainless steel table, a plastic sheet covering his hind legs. A tube fed into his mouth and his tongue lolled out. His eyes were open, but it was a battle for him and the lids kept fluttering.

"I'll give you a few minutes with him." The vet looked almost fox-like, the sort of person who never wore make-up.

Miles placed his head on the dog's ribcage. "I'm so sorry," he whispered, his voice cracking.

Victoria sniffed up. "I can't believe this is happening."

Miles stood up and moved back, not replying. Victoria leaned down and kissed John on the nose. She heard him take a raspy breath as he licked her top lip. "It's okay, little one," she said. "You won't feel any more pain soon. Remember I love you. You're the best dog ever. And the best guard dog anyone could ever hope for."

She kept her hand on him, feeling his ribcage weakly inflate and deflate. After a few minutes, the vet came back in with a large syringe. "Are you ready?" she asked.

Victoria blinked but said nothing and sat down. The vet took John's paw and stuck a long needle between the claws. "Don't worry, he won't feel anything," she said. "He'll just slip gently away."

A big, round tear rolled down Victoria's cheek as John died. Miles had killed him. She needed to be away from Miles. She needed to be at the paper, thinking about something else. She knew very well who she needed to be thinking about.

>>>

HUGH put his briefcase down on the back step and pulled a small aluminium glass cutter from his pocket. A dart sucker from a child's toy gun was attached to it by a few of inches of string. He licked the sucker and stuck it on the corner of the glass panel closest to the back door's lock. He then quickly cut a circle in the glass and tapped it with the cutter and the piece fell through. He'd kept hold of the string so it didn't fall and make a noise. He reached through the hole and unlocked the door.

He tiptoed through the kitchen and quietly made his way up the stairs. He pushed the door of the back room ajar and there lay the footballer in a double bed. He was snoring loudly. A ragged-edged Duran Duran *Rio* poster was pinned to the wall above him.

Hugh took a deep breath. "Mr Cosgrove," he shouted. "Wake the fuck up!"

Simon suddenly sprung up in bed, shocked. "Eh! What?" he said, still half asleep. "Fuck... Fire? Eh? Who the fuck..." His arms were flailing.

Hugh punched him in the face and he fell back on his pillow. Blood dripped from his left nostril. "Don't get up," he said.

He went to the wardrobe and took out four brightly-coloured kipper ties. Simon tried to get up again but Hugh cracked him on the jaw. He then bound his wrists and ankles to the frame of the bed. Simon, still just coming to, felt a cold rush of fear course through him. Debbie from next door was away, there was only old Brian on the other side. In desperation, he shouted "Brian!"

"I take it Brian's your man next door." Hugh calmly pulled a knot tight. "He's deaf as a nail. I'd save your breath."

"What do you want?"

"I represent your employer, Mr Benny O'Donnell. I hear some cheating has been going on. And Mr O'Donnell doesn't like cheating."

Simon decided to play dumb. "Who? Mr O'Donnell? I've never heard of any O'Donnell. My employer? I play for Belle Vue, that's my employer."

Hugh opened his briefcase and took out a small video camera with the words Sony Handicam written on the side. He set it up on the bedside table so it pointed at Simon. He took a sheet of paper from his pocket and unfolded it. Words were scrawled on the lined A4 in black felt tip pen. He held it up in front of Simon's face. "I'm going to need you to read this out now."

"Fuck off."

"You don't want me to hurt you, Mr Cosgrove."

Simon strained against his bonds. "What? What the fuck are you on about? I'm not reading anything. Let me go. When Cal finds out about this he'll fucking kill you."

"If you can take comfort in that... that's fine. I can't do anything about that. But it's confession time. And you will confess." He rolled up Simon's pyjama leg. "I am certain you will."

Simon strained and wriggled frantically but Hugh had done some sailing when he wasn't involved in thuggery and his knots were good and true. Hugh bent over the briefcase again. When he straightened up he was holding an axe in one hand and a portable blowtorch with a propane gas canister attached to it in the other. The blade of the axe gleamed. Written on the side of the blowtorch were the words Black & Decker.

"What the fuck!" Simon shouted, his mind suddenly consumed by panic. "What are you doing? It's only a game!"

"Are you going to read the statement then?" said Hugh.

"Fuck you," said Simon defiantly. Horrific torture surely only happened in books and films, not real life. Hugh slid his right hand down the handle of the axe, almost down to the blade. His left held the handle farther up and spread his legs like a logger. Suddenly, the professional footballer wasn't so sure about his horrific torture theory.

"Don't fuck about, mate," he whimpered. "I've got a game this afternoon."

"I don't think you'll be playing," Hugh replied, absent-mindedly.

The axe came down hard and fast and buried its head in Simon's right leg just above the ankle. Pain exploded up his body in a gigantic bolt. Dark red blood splattered across Hugh's face. The blade squealed against the bone as he wrenched it free. Simon's bed was turning red. He saw his toes wriggling. Then he saw Hugh raising the dripping axe again, a wicked smile on his face.

He tried to pull back in spite of the pain in his leg and knee and realised that his leg was moving but his foot wasn't. All he was doing was widening the axe tear, making it open like a clown's mouth. He had only just realised that his foot was only connected to his leg by the fat, muscle and sinew of his calf when the axe came down again with a shlock.

Hugh pulled the bloody tool away and tossed it aside. He looked at the stump of Simon's leg as a stream of blood jetted from it and pulled a lighter from his pocket. He then picked up the blowtorch.

"Now, you know how serious I am," he said menacingly. "If you don't tell us about the match fixing, you'll bleed to death. It will be slow and the agonising pain you are experiencing is only going to get worse."

"Jesus," cried Simon, "I don't want to die..."

"Then do as you are fucking told and read." He held the paper up again. It was wet and red with Simon's blood.

Simon looked at his stump, blood still flowing from it. "You bastard..." Blood loss was weakening him. He was crying like a child. He had no choice.

"My name is Simon Cosgrove. I was born on the sixth of June nineteen sixty-six... I am a professional footballer for Belle Vue FC... I am part of a match-fixing ring... we have fixed the scores of at least... fifteen... football matches in the last two years... we have made... thousands of pounds by betting on ourselves... the names of the people also involved are... my teammates..." He winced. Hugh waved him on. "...Nigel Hornby... Callum Murphy... Edo De Haan..." He gulped. "The score of today's game against Leeds United will be... a two-one defeat..."

Simon gulped again. Hugh nodded like a workman admiring his own skills. He twisted the valve on the side of the blowtorch. It hissed. Blood continued to pour from Simon's leg. Hugh clipped the top of the Zippo open, brushed the ignition wheel in one smooth movement and held the flame under the nozzle of the blowtorch. There was a whoosh and a long yellow flame appeared. Hugh adjusted it to a wicked-looking blue flame.

The more blood Simon lost, the less lucid he became, drifting in and out of consciousness.

"I'm going to cauterize the wound now," said Hugh. "If I don't you'll bleed to death. It'll only hurt for a... well, quite a long time probably."

"P-p-p-please. Get me an ambulance..."

Hugh was in some kind of trance. He leaned forward. Simon screamed as intense heat washed over the raw, bleeding stump. Smoke drifted up. It smelled sweet. Simon had been to a village fête once where they had a pig on a spit. It smelled the same as when they carved the pig's belly open. He was still screaming. The bed sheet caught fire and the stump was as black as the pig's skin had ended up. Everyone at the fête had a bit, everyone loved crackling. The bottom of Simon's leg was essentially pork crackling. He was screaming silently to himself. Hugh's eyes were wide. He flicked the off switch on the blowtorch.

"There," he said, putting the torch down.

He picked up Simon's bloody foot and examined it.

>>>

A RADIO blared out the BBC hourly news as the double doors of the newsroom swung shut behind Victoria. She grabbed a paper from a pile sitting on a table. CHURCH SLAMS TRAMS PLAN was the headline. She nodded hello to the sports editor, Roger Gorman, and went to the drinks machine for a cup of Nescafé. At her desk, she sipped the bitter concoction and grimaced at the gloom outside as her Apple Macintosh warmed up.

Most offices are quiet over the festive period but not a newsroom. There was a cacophony of ringing phones and journalists conducting interviews.

She noticed the envelope of photographs next to her spike. They were the pictures from Nigel Hornby's house, taken what seemed like ages ago when investigating Cal was just work. But by using her, he had made it personal. She wished she had lied to him that night, offered him a ridiculous sum of money to throw a game and then taped his answer. Acted like she worked for the *News Of The World*. If he sued her, surely a judge would agree she acted in the public interest.

She thought about what her next move would be. She could try to trick Cosgrove again. Or throw herself at De Haan or Hornby. Why don't you just go down to the training ground and get your tits out until one of them tells you what's going on? She snatched up the envelope angrily and pulled out the contents. She wanted to see that smug face again.

There were twenty four and in the dozen or so that weren't spoiled by glare, Cal didn't look smug at all. In one, he had his arm around Cosgrove like a younger brother. In another, he appeared to be in a serious conversation with Edo De Haan. In a third, he was blowing into a mug of hot tea. The footballers were in some kind of games room and there was a dartboard partially visible beside Cal's left shoulder. Something caught her eye.

There was something pinned to the dartboard that she hadn't noticed before. She squinted at it. She couldn't make out the face. It was too small. But something was written on the person's forehead. She reached for her brown leather handbag and delved into it, scratching around among fluff-covered Polos and copper coins until she felt the miniature magnifying glass from her Christmas cracker. She took it out and held it over the photo.

The picture appeared to have been torn from a copy of *Shoot* or *Match*. It was riddled with dart holes but she could clearly see it was of a man in his mid-twenties with a crew cut. He was wearing a football shirt but the head of a snake was visible on his neck, a tattoo. The snake looked like it had slithered up from his torso. Someone had scribbled CUNT across his forehead in capitals.

She stood up and hurried over to Gorman, who was typing away. She needed to be careful here. She didn't want him asking questions she didn't want to answer. She decided to make out she was really busy but wanted him to see something silly. "Hey Roger," she said. "Have you seen the state of this?"

He stopped bashing away at his keyboard and looked at the photo she handed him. "What have you got here?"

"Just a picture my mate gave me. It's hilarious. Look what they've written on that man's head!"

She gave him the magnifying glass and he peered through it. "Oh, that's Mark Shaw from Belle Vue. He's a proper head-the-ball. Who gave you this?"

She didn't want to reveal too much. "Oh, just a source. How was your Christmas?"

"Oh, you know. I was in here for most of it. At least they've given me New Year's Eve off. How was yours?"

"Same really." She took back the photograph. "Well, no rest for the wicked. If I don't see you, have a lovely night."

"You too." He watched her go back to her desk and started typing again.

She leaned back in her chair, took a deep breath and exhaled slowly. She finished the coffee, which was already lukewarm. She needed to find Shaw.

She went down to the library to pull out the cuts on him. There was a story from the summer about him joining Belle Vue. It discussed his disciplinary record and his record for attacking people. There was a cut-out of a *Daily Mirror* article headlined MARK OF A THUG. She grabbed the previous week's papers and sat cross-legged on the floor, leafing through them. It didn't take her long to discover that Shaw had been back in the headlines. His knee injury had warranted a page lead inside. He had damaged his cruciate ligament, one of the worst injuries in sport. Apparently he had fallen at home, but a columnist mused how rare it was for such an injury to occur somewhere other than the pitch. Something was rotten in the state of Denmark. Why would Cal be throwing darts at him? She needed Shaw's address and telephone number. She needed to talk to Granada Dave.

She went back to the newsroom and was just about to pick up the phone on her desk when it began to ring. She lifted the receiver.

"Newsroom. Victoria Heath," she said robotically, looking again at the photograph.

"Victoria, it's Michelle on the switchboard. I've got a call for you."

"I'm a bit busy at the mo... did you get a name?"

"Mark Shaw. He says it's important."

>>>

IT was throwing it down, turning snow into slush at the roadside. Her heart raced as the taxi passed the smoking chimneys of Boddingtons Brewery heading towards Cheetham Hill with its wipers on full. The observation tower at Strangeways loomed on her left. She was defying Walters again, going to meet some nutter all by herself, but she already had the front page she had pictured in her head. FOOTBALL STARS IN MATCH FIXING SCANDAL seemed to cover all the angles. Callum Murphy would live to regret the night he seduced Victoria Heath and crept away like a thief in the morning.

The driver pulled up outside the Marble Arch. Victoria asked him to wait. She hadn't had time to do much research on Shaw but thought it best to have a getaway car ready. The pub had a sloped tiled floor and Simply Red's *A New Flame* played on the jukebox. She made her way to the bar and ordered a Bloody Mary for herself and a pint of Stella for Shaw. She noticed a couple standing up and putting their coats on and barged over to the table they were vacating. Victoria spent the next fifteen minutes flicking through her notepad, deciphering scribbled shorthand from her initial meeting with Granada Dave, the excursion out past Disley with Kerry in the car, the Cosgrove betting slip incident and the night Callum Murphy had his wicked way with her.

At a quarter past four, Shaw hobbled up to her table on crutches. He was tall and had closely-cropped hair. A plaster cast covered his right leg from the toes to the hip. He wore a wet black blazer and wet chinos with wet brown slip-ons.

"Are you Victoria?"

"Yep. Mark, I take it?" She stood up, shook the hand he had extended and sat down again. "Er, I got you a pint. Is Stella okay?" She beckoned at a short bar stool beside her.

"Wife beater? Thanks. Sorry I'm late. The leg doesn't hurt that much thanks to the codeine but it's a right pain in the arse." He smiled, sat down and put his crutches on the floor. "I've hobbled over from Cheetham Hill."

He blew hot air into cupped hands. Suddenly there was a shriek as a woman in heels slipped on the tiles. A stranger caught her before she hit the floor. She started laughing and gave her saviour a kiss. "Bit daft wearing high heels in this weather..." said Shaw, trailing off as he noticed her boots. They were black patent leather with high heels.

He looked embarrassed so she said: "Best watch my step, eh?"

He took a swig of his pint. "I suppose you want this tape then?"

"Yes... but tell me what happened first, chapter and verse. I need to take notes."

He breathed in. "Okay, but don't you make anything up or fuck me over."

"I won't."

"I joined Belle Vue at the start of the season after being stitched up by the press."

"So I've read," she said. "Sorry about that."

He looked sad and she felt a bit sorry for him. He seemed troubled but not what she expected. "In the first game, I am straight into the team." Victoria scribbled this down in shorthand in her notepad. "I had a few decent games... We kept two clean sheets and won the third two-one. The other team's centre forward was a tricky bastard but I had him in my pocket. He was mouthing off, giving me shit, stuff about my mum, the usual. But I just ignored him and got on with the game. Anyway, the goalie Nigel Hornby, takes a shine to me after this. Starts offering me lifts to training and matches. He got this new Range Rover. Nice motor."

"Right."

"So about a month ago, he invites me out for a beer, as mates like. We go to the... I can't remember off the top of my head. Some boozer in Sale. Does it matter?"

Victoria shook her head. "Not at the moment... keep going."

"After a couple of pints he starts saying he knows I'm not on much money because of my track record... and then he asks if I'd be up for earning a few extra quid. Well obviously I'm interested. He's right after all, my contract's worth peanuts."

"Hmm."

"So he says, 'it involves rigging games'."

Victoria was scribbling furiously. "I can quote you on all this?"

"Sure. That's why I've come to you. I want it all to come out in the paper. I heard about that paedo rabbi you caught in the act. Nice one."

"He wasn't a paedo, he just liked young lads... but thanks."

"Fair enough. Whatever you say. Anyway. 'We're not throwing games', Hornby tells me.

'We're just trying to fix the scores when we win so people can bet on us.'"

"Who's we?"

Shaw paused, knowing this was the point where he became a grass. "Him, Cal Murphy, Simon Cosgrove and Edo De Haan."

Victoria took the time to write out the names in full and in capital letters. "Hmm... What did you say?"

"Well obviously, I tell him to go and fuck himself. Well not in so many words, I don't want to fall out with him because he's really my only mate over here. I'm from Leeds, you know? But I tell him I'm not interested. There's no way I'm getting involved in match fixing, or rigging, or whatever he called it."

"Then what happens?"

"Right... yeah. A few games pass, nothing happens. I steer clear of him. Then one morning last week, he turns up at mine at the crack of dawn. I don't trust him but I invite him in for a brew. He's my teammate after all, and a senior player, so what can you do?"

"So he's your only mate, but you don't trust him," she mumbled, writing. "Not really a mate is he?"

"Spose not. So he says, 'look Mark, you've got to request a transfer.' Cal's not happy about you being around'. I say no, I'm enjoying my footy, the boss rates me, I'm not doing it. I say, if it's that match-rigging thing, don't worry, I won't say owt."

"Then what happens?"

"He flips, pins me up against the wall in my own home and jabs me with a needle he had on him. Pumps me full of drugs."

Victoria shook her head and exhaled sharply as she carried on writing. She had seen what Hornby was capable of with her own two eyes, in the service alley outside Reds. Could he have drugged her?

Shaw went on: "Then I wake up gagged with my own filthy sock and tied up with my own washing line."

"Really?"

Shaw winced. "Yep. Then, without saying a word, the bastard does an elbow drop on my knee. He must be about sixteen stone. I felt all the bones snapping inside. It felt like someone had set my leg on fire. The doctors say it's a right mess."

"What happened next?"

"Well he goes all calm but with a mental look in his eyes – he's like that, it's like there are two different Nigels. And this is the nice one. He's all apologetic... He unties me and carries me to the settee and gently lies me down... I was still pretty doped up to be honest... It was like a dream. I couldn't ring anyone up for a couple of hours." He nodded at the cast on his leg. "And here we are. I'll probably never play football again."

"Did you call the police after it happened?"

"No. I rang up the club doctor," he replied. "I told him I'd fallen over."

"Why didn't you report him? You'd been assaulted. It looks like grievous bodily harm to me."

He scratched his head. "He threatened to kill me if I did. Anyway, it's only my word against his. Who are they going to believe? Nigel's a family man, he's been playing football for years and has never even been sent off. And who am I? That thug who got kicked out of Leeds for battering someone. Which was in self-defence anyway."

She nodded. "What's made you change your mind?"

He reached into his pocket and pulled out the Sony Handicam. "This. People will believe me when they see this."

"And where did you get the tape?"

"That I can't tell you, Victoria."

"And how much do you want for it?"

"I don't want money for it. I just want to do what's right."

>>>

WATERS sat ominously in his big leather chair peering at a blown-up Xerox copy of the dartboard photograph. He was wearing loose-fitting stonewashed jeans and deck shoes. A purple cardigan covered his white shirt. Victoria and Kerry sat before him, waiting for him to erupt. They had called him in on a rare day off. Victoria decided to break the silence.

"Remember you told me no more secrets, John?"

He put the sheet of paper down in front of him. "I do. I suppose that is why you two have dragged me away from my brother in law's. Speak."

"It all started when a contact got in touch about his suspicions that some footballers are fixing matches and betting on themselves."

Waters' interest was piqued. "Hmm. Who's the source?"

"A mate of mine at Granada. He's very credible... I mean it."

"Who are the players he suspects are rigging games?"

"Callum Murphy, Nigel Hornby, Edo De Haan and Simon Cosgrove."

"They all play for Belle Vue."

"Yes."

"Did you know that my mate Dave Chandler is the chairman?"

"No." She was annoyed with herself. She knew Waters didn't like it when his reporters hadn't done their research.

"Well, he is. And he's not going to like having his club's good name dragged through the muck. What sort of evidence have we got against these players apart from a blurred picture of someone with cunt written in his head? I take it you do have some evidence? You have investigated this thoroughly?"

"Yes," said Victoria. "I've found out some very explosive stuff. It's massive. I'm no fan of football. But hundreds of thousands of men in this the country, and even some women, think there's nothing more important. Some of them spend half their wages on season tickets to watch these clowns perform. If Callum Murphy and Nigel Hornby and their mates aren't throwing straight dice, people have got a right to know. They've probably been mixed up in this silly game since they were kids and made a damn good living out of it."

"Ahem," coughed Kerry.

"Sorry... I mean we... we have some very explosive evidence."

"What's she got to do with this?"

"Remember you said I shouldn't go out investigating things on my own? Actually, it was more of an order, wasn't it?"

"I do, but I meant..."

"Well I've done what you said. Ordered. I've been investigating with Kerry."

"That wasn't what I meant... I decide who works with whom at this paper." He took a deep breath. "Never mind. What's this evidence?"

The editor fiddled with his glasses as Victoria told him about her initial meeting with Granada Dave and how Hornby seemed gutted when his team snatched a result from the jaws of defeat. She recalled how she and Kerry went on an apparent wild goose chase to Nigel Hornby's cottage in the Peak District, and how that had since borne fruit with the discovery of the picture of Shaw's head on their dartboard. She described how she had learned Shaw, who had scored the goal that so disappointed the goalkeeper, had ended up crippled just days after. She spoke of liaising with the sports desk, and how she tracked him down. She didn't say he had phoned her.

"She's been undercover," grinned Kerry. "Taking it deep."

Victoria glared at her. "We have a video tape of Cosgrove, admitting the whole thing."

"What?"

"We have a video tape. Of Simon Cosgrove."

"Yes, I heard you the first time."

Kerry butted in. "We have a tape of Cosgrove admitting the four of them have been fixing matches for money. He says what the result of today's game at Leeds will be. We need to get this on page one of the late final today so people can read it on their way home from football. That's why we got you out of bed or wherever you were. Boss."

Waters stood up. "Watch it. You two bright sparks expect me to take a perfectly good story off today's front page just because you may or may not have a scoop? Why does it have to be run today? What if it turns out to be bollocks?"

"We only have the exclusive today," said Victoria. "The person we got it off says he will give it the *Mail*. And they will scoop us in the morning. You know it."

"Yes, but they'll be privy to the actual final score of the match. Who is the whistleblower?

If I am even going to consider this... pissing off one of my friends..."

"Mark Shaw," said Victoria. "The lad on the dartboard. He told me Hornby jumped on his knee because he threatened to expose the gang. That's GBH."

"Yes, but what evidence have we got? This Shaw could have an axe to grind. What if he just got pissed at the Christmas party and fell over. What if he's blackmailing Chandler for compensation?"

"Well, Cosgrove is saying what they plan the scoreline to be," said Kerry. "But we won't know for sure until today's match ends."

"So you are asking me to publish a libellous story about four wealthy footballers calling them match-fixers on the off chance their match today ends five-nil?"

"Two-one," said Victoria. "They're going to throw it. I'm telling you John, it's going to happen."

"What if it doesn't?"

Victoria pondered. "If it doesn't, you can tell everyone I tricked the printers into stopping the presses and put it on myself. I'd put my whole career on the line for this. I'm that sure."

Waters tapped his nose with his Parker ballpen. "If you're wrong," he said, "you'll never work on a newspaper again. And nor will I. Fucking hell." He ran his fingers through his hair, dandruff falling on his shoulders like a snow storm. "But it'll be your name at the top of the article."

"Ahem," coughed Kerry. " Mine too. We want a joint byline."

"So you believe this too?"

"I've seen these idiots together. I know it's happening."

Waters took his glasses off and started wiping the lenses with his tie. Then he put them back on. "Let's see this bloody tape then."

>>>

"JESUS Christ," said Waters, eyes wide as the screen on the television in his office went black. "That was like a video nasty. It looks like he's had that confession kicked out of him along with seven bells of shit."

"Does it matter?"

He exhaled. "I suppose not, but it's still a massive gamble. I should give Dave Chandler a ring about this."

Kerry ejected the VHS cassette from the Ferguson Videostar. "You can't. What if he blows the whistle on us? Murphy and his gang will have got away with it."

"I need to think. He might play along... if we make him the hero. If it means the ring gets smashed and his club's reputation is saved."

"Maybe... but maybe not. His club's reputation is intact. I've already written the story, the pictures are ready to go and we've got the video to present to the police. How well do you know him?"

"We went to school together. How would it look if they went there and beat Leeds?"

"I thought you had a pair of balls," said Kerry.

"Do you like working here?"

"You wouldn't dare to sack me. I bring in too many exclusives."

"Don't test me, Kerry. You're good at finding out gossip but this is proper news we're dealing with. Now get out of my office, while I have a think, the pair of you. Count yourselves lucky I can't fucking stand my brother-in-law."

>>>

IT was the Saturday after Christmas and no-one at the Elland Road football ground in Leeds knew that Simon Cosgrove was lying on his bed at home with a foot missing. There was only half an hour to go until kick off.

"We can't wait for him any longer," said the Gaffer, looking at his watch. He was fuming. "I bet the little shit's hung over somewhere... Tony, you're number eleven. I'm starting you on the left side of midfield."

Butterworth looked nervous. "Th... th... thanks Gaff..."

"Don't start fucking gasping again for crying out loud. That's the last thing I need."

Butterworth pulled the number fifteen shirt he was wearing over his head and slipped on the shirt the Gaffer had thrown to him.

Cal couldn't believe Simon had let them down. He had tried ringing him but there was no answer. Usually on away days the squad would all travel together on a coach. But Leeds was only a short distance from Manchester and the gaffer had given them permission to make their own way. "Where's Cozzer?" he had asked Cal, getting out of his Jag with a hot cup of tea in his hand.

Cal had shrugged, pretending not to be too concerned. "Your guess is as good as mine, gaffer." He hadn't seen Simon since he left Reds with Charlotte the night before. But as they were supposed to be under a strict pre-match curfew, he couldn't tell McNeill that.

>>>

JED Brennan won the toss and elected to kick off. Cal's hamstrings were burning thanks to the Deep Heat he had applied to his legs. Icy Yorkshire air stung his lungs as he breathed in deeply. He was standing by the centre spot, nervous. All around him was green and lush. You would not know any snow had fallen thanks to Elland Road's advanced underpitch heating system.

The plan had to go ahead, Simon or no Simon. Nigel and Edo had agreed. But they knew they faced a near impossible task.

Howard Wilkinson's Leeds United were favourites to win the second division title so the most difficult thing would probably be restricting them to two goals. Then there was the matter of actually scoring against them.

Chanting, cursing and shouting rang around the football ground. More than thirty thousand people were at the match. A young Yorkshireman shouted that he had fucked Cal's mum the night before. A song about the Munich air disaster rang out from the South Stand. Cal was a former United player and they wanted to get under his skin. He instead focussed his attention on *Fools Gold* by The Stone Roses, a song he adored which was blaring from the public address system.

The players jogged to their positions around the pitch. Some bent down, stretching their muscles as they waited for the match to start. Edo danced on his tiptoes, breathing into his hands to warm them. Cal faintly heard the clacking of Nigel's studs against his goalpost.

The plan was to allow Leeds to go two-nil up for a while and rally for a consolation goal. Cal hoped he could provide one. Down the field were the Leeds players, all in position too and waiting for the referee to blow his whistle. He checked the goalkeepers and linesmen were ready and put the whistle between his lips. He started his stopwatch as he blew hard.

>>>

CAL received the ball early and knocked it to Edo, who nudged it to Butterworth on the left wing. Cal jogged up front and took position beside the Leeds centre half Chris Fairclough as the Belle Vue back line passed the ball around between them. He knew he was in for a rough ride; Fairclough was tough. But Cal took heart in a passage from a training manual Billy once brought home. A striker can make any number of mistakes as long as he works hard to win the ball back. One mistake by a defender and a striker can punish him immediately.

Jed played a short pass to Cal who used his upper body to shield the ball from Fairclough. He felt a fist punch him in his ribs. He pretended not to notice as he took a touch and nudged it back to Jed. The midfielder Gordon Strachan, who Cal half-knew from his United days, stood a couple of yards away. Strachan was a good guy but he ignored Cal. It was funny how people changed when they crossed the line onto the pitch.

The next time the ball came, Fairclough stamped heavily on Cal's toes. It was a good area to win a free kick so he fell to the ground clutching his foot. Fairclough leaned over him and said in a deep voice: "Welcome to Leeds."

The referee blew his whistle, called Fairclough over and bollocked him. Cal decided a blast of Tommy the physio's freeze spray was the last thing he needed in the cold weather, so he got up, wiping icy mud off his knees.

The next ten minutes of the game passed by in a blur. Possession was constantly turned over between the two teams. Leeds' central midfielder Vinnie Jones was booked for a late, heavy challenge on Edo, who was left limping. Cal had hardly touched the ball. Victoria. He felt odd. Should he have phoned her, just to say... well, anything? He hadn't had the time. Should he have made time? She could have called him...

Cal was brought down to Earth when Edo passed the ball to his feet and Fairclough clattered into the back of him. His forearm connected with Cal's nose as they hit the turf. The referee sprinted over from twenty five yards away, whistling for a free kick.

"One more and you're going in the book," he said to Fairclough.

The ref placed the ball not far from the edge of the penalty box; maybe twenty yards from goal. Jed stood over it, but he wasn't known for his shooting. Cal wiped his nose, and realised his eyes were full of tears. "Tony!" he shouted to Butterworth, misty-eyed. "You take it."

Jed looked at him, about to argue, but shrugged and ran off towards the far post. He was wary of Cal after the training ground incident and any illusion that they were somehow mates had been shattered.

Butterworth was thrilled to get the chance to have a shot.

Five Leeds players stood together in a defensive wall as their goalkeeper Mervyn Day yelled: "Left, left, one more step... stop, hold it there!"

"Come on ref!" shouted Jed. "That's never ten yards."

The official nodded and walked up to the ball. He then strode between it and the wall, reaching it in eight paces. He took two further strides past where the defenders were positioned. "Back here please," he shouted. There were grumbles from the Leeds players but they eventually moved back.

Butterworth stood four paces behind the ball. Cal joined the end of the wall, and Fairclough grabbed his sleeve. Normally he would growl get your fucking hands off me, but not today. The whistle went. Butterworth approached the ball and swung his right leg. He used his instep the give the shot minimum backlift so it would hopefully dip after going over the wall. It was something he had been practising. But there were two elements in the equation; the defenders might jump up and head the ball away or the goalkeeper might scamper across his goal and save it.

Butterworth caught the ball sweetly. The Leeds right back jumped up but it was already over his head. The wall broke apart and they all turned to see Day flying through the air. But he could only get his fingertips to it and it bulged the top corner of the net. He landed in the dirt. Goal!

All eyes were on Butterworth as he ran towards the Belle Vue fans, punching the air. Cal knew there were no TV cameras on the game and took his chance to deliver a swift uppercut to Fairclough's jaw. The defender's eyes were blazing as he spat blood on the pitch. "Nice to be here," Cal told him, grinning.

Day rushed out of his goalmouth and shoved Cal in the back. He swivelled around all tensed up, the muscles in his neck like steel cable.

"Fuck off, Day, you cunt," he snarled, saliva flying out of his mouth. The referee marched over, aware of something going on. Cal didn't reckon he had seen anything but realised it might be an idea to stop rubbing his sore knuckles.

"Nothing going on here, ref." He patted Fairclough on the back. Fairclough grunted.

Cal then put his arm around the referee but he shrugged it off. He was well aware that some dark arts were being employed behind his back. Cal caught Nigel's eye down at the far end of the pitch. The giant keeper was keeping a straight face.

>>>

THE game got under way again. The Leeds fans had found their voices again and were roaring Cal's favourite song who are ya, who are ya, who are ya, who are ya? He would love to meet the genius who came up with that one. He was soon back in the game, running around snarling and tackling and demanding the ball, bringing his teammates in to play. His biggest concern now was that Butterworth was having the game of his life. He was literally running rings around the Leeds right back Mel Sterland. In the time it took for the hands of the big Elland Road clock to move from twenty-past to half-past three, he had dispossessed Sterland twice. If his crosses had been better, Cal might have needed to deliberately miss a good chance. For all he knew, O'Donnell could have a carload of thugs tooled up with shotguns waiting for him, Edo and Nigel outside. Hello Mr Murphy, I have a message from Mr O'Donnell. Then BOOM as the other two try to dive for cover. Old ladies and autograph hunters peppered with shotgun pellets. It didn't look pretty. Fucking Simon. Cal decided that the less Tony saw of the ball on the left the better. The referee finally blew up for half time at three forty-six.

>>>

TOM Semple, who had just turned ten, was sitting with his mother among the away supporters. She didn't usually take her son to football matches - that was his dad's thing.

But it was his birthday and she didn't want to explain that his dad was in Manchester Royal Infirmary with miniature scaffolding holding his jaw together after a beating in town. So here she was, pretending to enjoy herself. At least she hadn't had to pay for the tickets.

"Mam?"

"What?"

"I'm hungry... Please can I have a pie? Dad always lets me go and get them."

She smiled. She quite fancied a pie herself. "That sounds nice," she said, taking out her purse. "I'll have one too."

They went down into the belly of the away supporters' stand. Trisha Smith was touched by the way the men and a couple of ladies shepherded her son to the front of the queue and stood back while he ordered the pies. Some of them seemed to know her son and ruffled his hair. She took a tissue out of her handbag and blew her nose. She was proud when he walked back to her with a pie in each hand, oblivious to the fact that for a few minutes he was part of the day's entertainment. He was growing up so fast. He was getting to be good at football too.

Tom pulled a face when she tried to help him get his pie out of the paper bag and told her he didn't need any help. He'd got that off his dad. Too clever by half, her other half. Maybe he would learn now. He had come home with a few black eyes and cuts and grazes over the years but this time someone had kicked the crap out of him. He couldn't even move his jaw. She was relieved they didn't find drugs on him in the ambulance. He was clean when they picked him up off Deansgate, apart from all the blood on his shirt.

"Mmm," she said to her son, "this is nice..." she wasn't lying, she was surprised at the quality of the football pie. "Meat and potato?"

Tom nodded, too polite to speak with his mouth full.

Trisha was twenty-eight and she was a looker. She was nineteen when Tom's dad Tom got her pregnant, but she thought she loved him. Actually she did love him... she just wished he would calm down. Bloody men... like big kids. She blamed that arsehole Mick he hung around with, a gobshite of the highest order. It was probably him that had talked them into the beating. Thick as thieves they were, had known each other since school. Mick always had some get-rich-quick scheme, usually involving dealing or petty theft. He had got away with a fractured right leg and a bit of blood in his piss but they were side by side on the ward. Idiots.

The pie was a Hollands. She made a note to pick some up from Iceland. It would make a great easy tea, a pie with a couple of potato waffles, some frozen peas and a bit of Bisto. She finished hers off and watched Tom as he ended up with filling and gravy across his cheeks. She took out the tissue she had been wiping her nose with to clean the boy's face.

"What's happened to Simon Cosgrove?" Tom asked his mum.

Trisha looked baffled. "I wouldn't know Simon Cosgrove if he came up here and planted a kiss on me," she admitted.

She noticed a fella standing beside them reading a match programme had overheard her. He was about thirty with designer stubble, and wore a leather bomber jacket and fairly tight jeans. He had a nice arse. She liked to see that, all the blokes these days seemed to wear baggy jeans. Didn't they realise women liked to look at their arses just the same as they liked to look at women's arses? Their eyes met and she smiled. "Er, scuse me, do you know what's happened to..." she looked down at Tom. "What's-his-name?"

"Simon Cosgrove," said Tom, shyly. "Cozzer."

The handsome man shrugged. "Dunno mate. His name's down on the teamsheet in the programme... I thought he'd be playing too. Apparently he likes a drink, so..." He shrugged.

Tom was gutted. He'd heard about drunks from his dad. Watch out for beer monsters, his dad had warned him. Maybe he should think about having someone else as his favourite player. Someone like Tony Butterworth. He could run nearly as fast as Cozzer. He had a really hard shot too, the goalie had no chance when he scored that amazing free kick.

"Don't worry," the man said to him. "Cozzer'll be back. He always turns up... he's like a bad penny." He winked at Trisha.

>>>

"YOU'VE got to ask him to help us," said the goalkeeper to the striker. "If he scores again, that's it."

Nigel and Cal were standing in the corridor outside the away dressing room talking about Tony Butterworth. The gaffer was still giving his team talk inside but Nigel had whipped out a stud from his Adidas boots and had been excused to go and ask the Leeds staff if there were any spares knocking about. Cal just got up and went with him.

"I know, but..."

"Well... why aren't you talking to him then? What the fuck's up with you? We're lucky to even still be in with a shout of getting through this. My life is on the line here, so is yours, so is Ed's and so is Simon's, even if he's not turned up. Don't go soft on us, mate. Not now."

"Easy pal..."

"I'm not kidding."

Jed stuck his head out of the changing room. "What are you two faggots whispering about? Let's get back out there, eh? Finish off these sheep-shagging fuckers..."

Nigel shook his head and exhaled. He said: "Dick. So are you with us or what, Cal? Forty-five minutes and we can put all this shit behind us. Just have a word with Tony... We can give him some of Simon's share."

Nigel was right, what was forty five minutes? Nothing. Then it would all be over. Leeds could easily get back into this if Butterworth went off the boil. The ref appeared and nodded at them. He rapped on the door with his pencil and said loudly "Second half please, gentlemen."

The rest of the Belle Vue players filed out. Butterworth was second to last in the line. Cal put his arm around his shoulder and held him back. He whispered: "I need a favour."

Butterworth was surprised. "Sure Cal, anything."

They followed their teammates out on the pitch. The crowd was so loud he virtually had to shout in Tony's ear. "Here it is pal... Please don't ask any questions because I can't answer them at the moment... Now, that lad you are marking, Sterland. You've got to let him score. And stop playing so well. I'm going to be honest with you here, we need to lose this match two-one, or I am dead. I'll be murdered by a gangster. Honest. Do you get me?"

Butterworth looked at Cal like he had a screw loose. "But..."

"No questions mate, remember... please..." Cal was begging now. "I'll never ask you anything like this ever again, I swear it. I've been such a cunt... I mean, I can't even tell you what a cunt I've been. And because of it I need us to lose this game two-one. I swear it'll never come back on you. Please."

Butterworth thought for a moment and shrugged. The bitter taste of Jed's piss sometimes came back to his mouth. It would no doubt menace him for life. "Don't worry, Cal. Everything will be fine."

>>>

THE second half kicked off. Cal was determined to finish what he had started. He knew young Tony was nothing like Mark Shaw; the kid could be trusted. Not that he deserved it. He also knew he was in for a kicking from his opposite number, Fairclough. That he could handle.

After ten minutes the Leeds full backs were making progress. Butterworth was doing a sterling job of going off the boil. He was diving into tackles; sliding in on his opponent but completely missing the ball, and taking longer than usual to get up. He would have to be substituted at this rate. Cal was impressed.

Sterland received the ball out by the right touchline. Butterworth was doing what he had been trained to do – show him down the line, opening up the possibility of making a tackle or even booting the ball into touch. But instead of biding his time, he put in a clumsy, right-footed effort at a challenge that Sterland saw coming a mile off. He cut inside, weighing up whether to attack Nigel's goal himself. Darren Richards, another Belle Vue youngster who was playing instead of Shaw, took a step towards him but changed his mind. That gave Sterland a couple of seconds to hook his right foot around the ball.

The cross was good. It was driven in with pace and it rocketed through the air. Cal knew Nigel would normally come and punch it away or even catch it, but not this time. He remained rooted to his goal line. Lee Chapman, the prolific Leeds striker who had been lurking around the penalty spot, threw himself headlong towards the ball at the near post. His forehead connected with it and it smashed into the net with such force that Nigel would have stood no chance anyway. Goal! The ground erupted. Chapman sprinted away, kissing the badge on his shirt. Nigel picked the ball out of the net and booted it back upfield. It was one-one with twenty-five minutes to go.

Leeds could see all three points dangling tantalisingly in front of their faces. Chapman was a big presence up front, and was brilliant at holding up the ball. Richards was being totally outclassed. Butterworth received a simple sideways pass from Edo but it got tangled up in his feet. Cal could not tell if he had miscontrolled on purpose or made a genuine error. It didn't matter because Leeds'

David Batty swiped the ball from his toes. He drove forward, pushing into a large gap Edo had left, and drilled it hard to Chapman's feet. The striker's first touch was sublime and his right footed shot from the edge of the box flew into the bottom corner of the net before Nigel could even react. Goal! The scoreline was now perfect. Two-one.

The gaffer was up off the bench and jumping up and down on the touchline, shouting at Butterworth. Butterworth was bent over with his hands on his knees, coughing and spluttering. Cal went over and put his hand on his shoulder.

"Are you all right, Tony?"

"Asthma, he said. He winked. "Can't breathe... Inhaler..."

Cal signalled for Butterworth's inhaler but the gaffer didn't notice. His plan had gone awry and Butterworth was to blame. He shouted over to the bench and Robbie Billington, a mate of Brennan's who was sub most weeks, quickly took his tracksuit off and jogged to the touchline. Butterworth was being dragged, which wasn't part of the plan.

>>>

THE fightback had fatigued the Leeds players and with just five minutes left many were huffing and puffing. Jed stuck a toe out and gained possession of the ball. He played a smart one-two with Richards and as he pressed into the Leeds half they backed off. Suddenly, he was through to the defence with two midfielders trailing in his wake. Jesus no.. he couldn't score could he? Jed hadn't scored since Cal joined the club.

"Jed!" Cal called, peering across the line of defence so it appeared he was trying to stay onside. He was relieved that the linesman seemed desperate to put his flag up. He only managed to get half a yard offside before Jed toe poked the ball into the space in front of him... there was no one between Cal and the keeper, it was one-on-one.

Surely the flag would go up soon, put the fucking flag up.... Jesus, he wasn't going to flag. The gaffer had once called Cal the king of one-on-ones. He would already be celebrating in his mind. Cal would have to be artful to miss this chance. Within a split-second, the Leeds goalkeeper Day was in front of him, eyes blazing. He was still wound up from the first half. A bit too wound up. Cal poked the ball towards him, a terrible touch that Day would have cleared under normal circumstances... but not this time. Day jumped at him, both sets of studs catching him below the right knee. Cal tried to keep his feet so he could fluff the shot but there was no chance, he was going down. The ref had blown for the penalty before his arse hit the turf.

The Leeds players were furious at Day. With all the pushing and shoving going on, it took a while for anyone to realise Cal was still on the ground. He glanced at his knee and saw the skin had opened up like an eye, a two-inch gash exposing his snow-white kneecap. His stomach did a somersault and there was a ringing in his ears as fresh, purple blood began to ooze out. Edo took a look at the gaping wound and waved to the bench for Tommy the physio. Nigel, who had run the length of the pitch to get stuck into the fight, turned and saw Cal on the ground. His face went white as a sheet.

"That's gonna need stitches," the physio diagnosed. "You'll have to come off."

"Fuck that, bandage me up. I've got a penalty to take."

"Don't worry, Jed will slot it in," he said cheerfully.

Cal liked Tommy, a harmless old duffer who had been at the club for years, but it was time for stern words. "I said put a fucking Band-Aid on it."

"It needs more than a Band-Aid, Cal." He unzipped his kit bag and dressed the wound. Cal felt like screaming and had to bite his lip as he dabbed TCP on it. He then placed a square of gauze on the gash and wrapped a bandage tightly around it. Admiring his handiwork he added: "You'll need stitches later though, I'm not kidding Cal. It'll never heal otherwise."

Cal nodded and stood up. He was in agony but he couldn't let it show as he walked over to Jed, gritting his teeth. "Jed, give us the ball."

"Look at your fucking leg. You can't even bend it. I'll take it."

"I said give us the fucking ball," Cal growled. "I take the penalties round here." He grabbed the size five Mitre Delta.

"You'd better not miss," Jed muttered.

"I never miss."

It was twelve minutes to five, according to the big clock. The only singing was coming from the Belle Vue fans at the other end of the pitch. Cal placed the ball on the spot. The Leeds players were jeering, trying to put him off.

"He always goes left, Merv!"

"It's going over the bar. He can hardly stand up."

"He's shitting himself! Biggest game of his career, this."

Then Cal heard a shout from the crowd, from a Leeds supporter with a radio held to his ear. He sounded like Geoffrey Boycott. "Don't worry Mervyn. He's going to miss on purpose. I'd bet my house on it."

The whistle went and Cal's stomach went watery as he jogged up to the ball. He's going miss on purpose? A jolt of pain burst through his gashed standing leg as he swung his right boot at the ball. He looked at Day and he had moved first... he was going left... normally Cal would slot it in the right hand corner... not this time though... I'd bet my house on it? Cal pulled back, side footing the ball to the left. Day dived low and pushed it away. Sterland cleared it and it rolled off the pitch.

"Fuck!" Cal shouted theatrically, booting a sod of turf in front of him. A bolt of pain shot through his knee.

Edo patted him on the back. "Unlucky, Cal. Good effort."

Jed overheard him as he ran back. "Good effort? He could hardly walk up to the fucking ball. I should have taken it!"

Cal held his palms out. "Sorry mate... I thought I'd score."

Cal looked at Nigel, who was just shaking his head. The gaffer stood by the dugout in a cloud of Rothmans smoke with a blank look on his face. The Leeds fan with the radio shouted: "He missed it on purpose! He's a match fixer!"

As the final whistle went, the BBC's radio stations were already reporting on the *Chronicle*'s front page story.

FOOTBALL STAR IN MATCH FIXING SCANDAL Exclusive by Victoria Heath and Kerry Winters

Belle Vue star Callum Murphy agreed to fix the results of football matches for £100,000 in bribes.

An anonymous tip-off to the Manchester Chronicle included allegations that the team would lose today's match at Leeds United 2-1.

The paper has passed to police a tape recording of a source close to the striker saying Murphy has been paid to fix the results of at least 15 recent matches.

The tape also implicates the striker, 25, in plotting to fix last week's league match at West Ham and a match the club was due to play against Coventry.

A Greater Manchester police spokeswoman said officers would tonight be working to substantiate the claims of corruption.

She said: "Preliminary inquiries are being conducted but it has not been established if there is any basis for a formal investigation. This matter remains under consideration."

A spokesman for the Football League said the organisation would be launching its own investigation into the claims. He said: "We take allegations of this nature very seriously indeed."

The claims of corruption will dent football's reputation just months from the start of the World Cup finals in Italy.

Murphy, who has scored 17 league goals this season, is considered an outside chance to be selected in the England squad. He laughed off rumours he had been involved in match-fixing when confronted last week.

A Football Association spokesman declined to comment.

>>>

CAL was last into the dressing room and as he walked through the door and looked around, the gaffer kicked it shut and shoved him up against the wall. He grabbed him by the throat. He was well past retirement age but he was still strong. Cal had never seen him so angry.

"What's all this about fixing matches, eh?" he spat. His eyes were wide and the whites were closer to red. He gripped Cal's throat tighter. "Eh?" Cal was struggling to breathe.

"What do you mean, gaffer?" Deny, deny, deny. She had no proof.

"It's all over the fucking radio! The *Chronicle* is reporting that you fixed this match. They knew the scoreline."

"We lost because they were better than us. How could I have fixed the match? You've just watched it with your own eyes. You can't believe everything you read in the papers! It's fucking slander. The *Chronicle*? I wouldn't even wipe my arse with it. I shagged that reporter and she's got the hump and is out for revenge."

The Gaffer loosened his grip. He took a breath and then shook his head. "You shagged who?"

"Victoria Heath. She's got it in for me... I'm telling you. Good shag but... she's been following me around like that bird in *Fatal*

Attraction. It's a good job I've got no pet rabbits or she'd have boiled 'em."

"You missed that penalty. We could have got a point!" Cal felt specks of the Gaffer's spit land on his cheek. He could have easily wrestled out of his grip but he decided not to.

"I'm gutted about that. I fucking hate Leeds. Why would I want us to lose to them? They were singing Munich songs at me today. I've got a fucking massive gash on my knee, that's why I missed it."

Jed kicked a plastic chair. He sneered at Cal and said: "I told you I'd put it away."

"No offence cuntox, but when did you last notch? You couldn't score in a brothel."

The dressing room was quiet. All his teammates were listening. Nigel nodded at him slowly. Butterworth was already showered and dressed and was quietly wiping mud off his boots with a sock. Edo didn't look at him. He dropped his jockstrap to his ankles, stepped out of it and headed for the showers.

Cal racked his brains. Only they, Billy and O'Donnell knew the planned score, and none of them could have grassed. They wouldn't have sold him out to the press. The only other person who knew was Simon. Who was AWOL.

"Fucking hell," said the gaffer. "It's a right mess all this. I don't know what to say." He just shook his head. He was calming down.

"You've got to let me go, gaffer. Give me a chance to sort this out. I've got to go and see that reporter."

"What? Now? Go where?"

"Back to Manchester. This place is going to be crawling with press, TV reporters, you name it. Making out that I'm some sort of cheating cunt."

The gaffer let go of his throat. "Maybe you should face up to them. Tell the truth."

"What I should do is get the best solicitor in town and get over to the *Chronicle* to stop these lies being printed about me. I need to do it now. Have I ever let you down?"

The gaffer took another deep breath. "No. That's why I'm going to give you a chance. Listen. Some copper came over at the end of the game and asked the chairman if they could talk to you somewhere private after the match. They'll be looking for you."

Jed frowned suddenly. "Gaffer..."

"Jed, I made you captain because you're disciplined and well-organised. It doesn't mean that I like you, so shut the fuck up. We're a team. We stick together."

The old man in the grey overcoat sitting in the security box at the exit from the player's car park was just learning of the allegations on his little radio when Cal rapidly backed his Cosworth out of the parking space and spun the wheels as he put his foot down. He was doing nearly fifty miles an hour when he smashed through the wooden barrier.

>>>

HIS knee screamed as the bandage rubbed on the gash as he climbed over the garden wall. He noticed the broken pane in the back door of the Cosgroves' house and tried the handle. As he opened the door, a vile stench like rotting pork filled his nostrils. He kicked the cat's bowl as he tried to find a light switch and flicked it on.

"Mrs Cosgrove? Mr Cosgrove? Anyone here? Simon?" he shouted into the kitchen. "Coz, you here?"

He heard a low but blood-curdling sound.

"Cozzer! That you?"

He heard the same noise again. It was like a cross between a scream and a shout. The second time it was louder, from upstairs. Cal ran up and pushed open the door to the back bedroom. He switched on the light and there was his friend Simon, lying on his bed, the usual sparkle in his eyes gone. He was shivering. His continental quilt was pushed to one side and there was a hole burned in the mattress. Over it was a blackened stump where his left foot used to be. Fabric from his pyjamas was burned into the flesh. Cal retched, took an already-used tissue from his tracksuit top and held it over his nose and mouth as he pulled his friend's quilt over him. He retched again but swallowed it back down.

"Fucking hell, Cozzer. What the fuck happened here?"

"Jeff the kit man'll go mad when he realises your shirt's missing," croaked Simon, smiling thinly and then coughing.

"Easy mate. Fuck me." He looked again at the stump and quickly looked away. "Who the fuck did this?"

Simon struggled to get his words out, almost whispering. "O'Donnell... sent some Irish nutter round."

"O'Donnell? What the fuck? Did this bloke say anything? About the rigging?"

Simon was drifting in and out of consciousness but suddenly opened his eyes wide. "He kept saying we were taking the piss. He just kept hitting me. He went fucking mental. Psycho, man. I couldn't help it. He made me read out all our names and all about the plan and videotaped it."

"Jesus."

Simon's voice was now a barely-audible whisper. "How's my leg? I can't feel it."

Cal gulped. "Don't you worry pal. You're gonna be okay. I'll call you an ambulance and wait with you. But I won't be able to stick around and talk to them. The press are onto us and probably the dibble too. I've got to find Billy and get in touch with Nigel and Edo. Don't say anything to anyone at the hospital. You're BUPA aren't you?"

Simon nodded.

"Good. Tell them no press."

>>>

THE tyres of the Cosworth screeched as Cal took the corner at the narrow intersection of two streets in Chinatown way too fast. The car's back end slipped out and narrowly missed knocking over a parking warden who stood next to a Transit van parked on double yellow lines. Cal fought with the steering wheel and just managed to get the car under control before bumping it up on the kerb outside Sensations. Snow was coming down heavily, almost a blizzard.

The warden approached him as he got out. "You can't leave that there, sir. If you haven't moved it within five minutes you'll get a ticket. If it's still there in twenty minutes, I'll notify head office and it will be towed away."

"Fuck off mate," said Cal. He went to push the buzzer but the door opened before he could do so. His heart missed a beat when Victoria stepped out.

"Cal," she said, shocked. "What are you doing here?"

His eyes were blazing. "What the fuck are you doing here, you mean." He grabbed the lapels of her coat and shook her roughly.

She was too stunned to reply.

"I said, what the fuck are you doing here, Victoria?"

Suddenly the depth of the situation hit her. She avoided his eyes, looking down at his legs, still with his Adidas World Cup boots and shinpads on, and the big bandage on his knee. She was scared, and blurted out what her racing heart was feeling. "You never rang me after we... you know. You could have fucking rung."

He shook her again, raging. "So you decided to write all that shit about me? You stupid cow... do you know what you've done?" Some spit went in her eye, which she blinked away with the start of tears which were quickly forming. He wanted to feel bad about scaring her but couldn't help but feel glad.

He suddenly felt a skinny arm around his neck tugging him backwards. He let go of Victoria and quickly stepped backwards into his assailant. It made the parking warden, who was no fighter, release him from the headlock and Cal shoved him over.

"Leave her alone, you," gulped the man, "you fucking twat." He got to his feet gingerly, rubbing his elbow. He was skinny, not athletic in the slightest. The collar of his shirt was a couple of inches too big for his neck.

"Listen pal, this is none of your business. Do one." Cal clenched his fist ready to throw a punch, but it didn't seem like a fair fight so he let his hand drop to his side.

"I know who you are," said the warden. "And if you don't leave her alone I'm calling the police."

"Call 'em. I've got nothing else to lose."

"You think you're the dog's bollocks," said the warden, nervously. "You've always thought your shit smelt better than everyone else's. I'm not just gonna leave you to hit your girlfriend. No chance."

"We're not. I'm not...." said Victoria. "He just... never mind. Thanks for your help but I'll be okay."

"Are you sure? I know what he's like. He's a dirty bastard. He thinks he can get away with owt."

His words cut into Cal, who had been calming down. "Who the fuck's this arsehole? Go and get on with your shitty job."

"My name's Jimmy and I'm a football fan. And you're anti-football. You have been for years. No wonder the Reds gave you the boot. You've got all that skill... but mostly just go round kicking people. You're a thug."

"United wanted me to toughen up. What do you know about anything? Dick." He took a deep breath and turned to Victoria. "I'm sorry for grabbing you. Are you all right? I'm sorry. I should have rung you. I'm not... I'm not who you think I am."

This annoyed her. "Really? Who is it you think that I think you are?"

"I don't know."

"I was only doing my job. I never lied to you. But you lied to me. I know you haven't got a brother. I know you're an orphan. I haven't got time for this. I have to go. I just... I just have to go." She wouldn't look him in the face and edged past him before running away down the street.

"I... wait." She had turned the corner. The parking warden was writing him out a ticket. Cal ignored him and went into the building that housed Sensations.

>>>

HUGH let him into to the club. The door to O'Donnell's office was open. Shaw was there, propped up on his crutches. What the fuck is that cunt doing here? Cal wondered.

"Mr Murphy," said O'Donnell. "I've been expecting you. We don't usually allow people wearing sportswear in Sensations but in your case I'll make an exception."

"What the fuck have you done, you old cunt?" He moved towards O'Donnell, but Hugh stood in his way. "You've fucked up the plan..."

"I might have fucked up your plan. My plan went perfectly."

"What do you mean?"

"I mean, it's about time you started paying for your mistakes."

"What mistakes? What the fuck are you on about?"

"United... Carol."

"United wasn't my... hang on. Carol? What about Auntie Carol?"

"You killed her. The worst thing she and Billy ever did was take you into their hearts, you delinquent little bastard. It's your fault she's dead."

"I can't believe what I'm hearing... What the fuck is it to you? And what the fuck did you chop Simon's foot off for? He did nothing wrong."

"I apologise about Mr Cosgrove. Hugh got a bit carried away but I see it as collateral damage. Your mate made a full confession and all the dirty details of your little scheme is in the paper for all the world to see."

"I'll give you collateral damage, you old cunt." He again tried to reach the desk but Hugh grabbed him. Cal tried but failed to break free. "Call your fucking dog off, Harry. Me and Billy trusted you."

"Ah yes... Billy. Hugh, bring Miss Rebrova and her... client in here." He nodded at his thug.

Hugh let go of Cal's arms, went to the door and gestured at someone. A stunning brunette in a mini dress and high heels entered the room. With her arm around Billy, who was unshaven and looked like he hadn't slept. Cal realised he was a just sad old man.

"Billy, glad you could join us," said O'Donnell.

Billy spoke to Cal. "I'm sorry, Cal. I had no choice. You were supposed to be a top player, make us all rich. Now look at me. No wife, festering in that fucking council house, paying whores to fuck me, no, not just that, to keep me company. What kind of a life. Then I met Ivanka."

His moaning flicked a switch in Cal's head and a red mist descended. He automatically stepped forward and punched him. It was only a light, swift jab in the eye but Billy was stunned and grasped his face. The whore stepped forward and slapped Cal hard around the ear. "Fucker," she said. Cal stepped forward towards her, fists raised, a ringing in his ear, but she had retreated behind Hugh and was hugging Billy.

"Relax, Mr Murphy," said O'Donnell. There's no need for violence... Billy's right. You were meant to play hundreds of games for United, and maybe England. We teed it all up for you. You were supposed to sign contracts worth hundreds of thousands of pounds, you could have married a beautiful woman and had beautiful children, settled down in Bramhall or Lymm. You were supposed to be a millionaire. But you were too much of a clever shite. Filled your head with all this nightclub bollocks. Meanwhile my investment has paid fuck-all in dividends. So I came up with this little match-fixing plan. I knew you'd fuck it up. You fuck everything up. I knew I'd end up with Reds."

Cal couldn't believe his ears. "What do you want with my club?"

O'Donnell fanned his face theatrically with several sheets of thick, pink paper. "It's not your club. It's mine. Listen to this. This is to certify that Harold Paul O'Donnell is now registered as the absolute proprietor of the property 14b Back Bridge Street, Manchester, M3 4AP subject to the entries in the register relating to overriding interests set out in... you get the idea. A planning application went in last week to build a massive office and retail area called Spinningfields and the developers are paying a lot of money for buildings around there. And you... well you're going to Strangeways. It couldn't have worked out any better. You even fucked that reporter after Billy slipped you both the ecstasy. She was here a minute a go by the way, shouting the odds. I told her you spiked her. She is not a happy camper."

Cal suddenly recognised the bit of paper the gangster was waving. "Billy? That autograph at golf... you cunt."

"You cheated me," said Billy quietly. "I saw you kick your ball onto the fairway... And he said..."

Cal was wide-eyed with rage now. "You spiked me as well? Where did you get the pills?"

"Off Hugh."

"I could have been drug-tested... and banned. It would have ended my career."

"What fucking career?"

O'Donnell laughed again. "This is priceless."

Shaw was standing the closest, grinning, so Cal lamped him, knocking him off his crutches. It was a lovely, sweet, crisp, satisfying punch. There was a crunching, squelching sound as his two front teeth broke and sunk into the inside of his lip. "You fucking cunts," Cal screamed.

Hugh grabbed his top and tried to hold him up against the wood-panelled wall. Cal pummelled his ribs as hard as he possibly could. He might have thrown up, had Cal not then planted an uppercut under his chin, bashing his teeth together and causing him to bite off the tip of his tongue. He staggered backwards, blood running down his chin.

Billy was holding Ivanka, who was stroking his hair. O'Donnell giggled, nervously now. Cal stepped back, thinking of Simon lying in bed with his foot chopped off. As if he was attacking a loose ball in a penalty box, he booted Hugh in the bollocks. He caught him sweeter than any penalty he'd ever taken. He doubled over and Cal kneed him in the face. He recoiled backwards into O'Donnell's desk, cracking his head open on the corner of it. Computer monitors crashed down on his head, which had blood pouring from it. The stock trading screen fizzled and popped on the rug.

"Cunts," roared Cal. O'Donnell now looked frightened, something not many people got to see.

"Now Callum, don't do anything silly..." Cal smashed him in the mouth. The punch was so hard it hurt Cal too, compressing the knuckle of his index finger. O'Donnell's head lolled backwards in his executive chair.

Cal stood still for a moment and surveyed the wreckage of the office. O'Donnell, Hugh and Shaw were all knocked out. He shook his head at Billy and Ivanka as he zipped up his tracksuit top, which had come undone at some point, and straightened the mucky bandage on his knee. Billy opened his mouth to speak but Cal raised a hand and said: "We're finished, me and you. I'm off."

Cal left the building, shaking his head, wondering where the fuck he was off to.

APRIL FOOLS' DAY, 1990

EDO turned the jet ski's throttle to full and almost managed to get air as he skimmed over a large wave. Christina, who loved going fast, clung tightly to his waist. "Woo," she screamed. "That was amazing, Edo. We nearly took off."

"It was a Mexican Wave!" He turned and kissed her cheek. "I love you so much. No one gets me like you do."

She had heard the joke before but smiled. "I understand. I love you too."

"Exactly baby. You're the one who understands."

He was low on fuel so he rode back to the secluded beach where they lived in a little hut with a thatched roof. Edo and Nigel had also been implicated in match-fixing in the papers in the days that followed the Leeds game. Edo and Christina had fled the UK to the Hook of Holland and caught an overnight flight from Schipol to Merida. From there they had headed to the coast, where they had stayed. Life in Mexico wasn't so bad; you could live like a king for about ten pounds a day. When he started to miss football he headed up to the town beach and joined in a game with the locals. He had considered starting a coaching school but no-one had any money to pay him.

Christina had convinced him to run rather than face the music. What's the point of going to jail when we can disappear and live out our lives in the sunshine? she had argued. Edo doubted the British authorities would waste resources trying to track down a washed-up Dutch footballer with a dodgy knee who had been convicted of corruption in his absence. Their families knew where they were within a couple of hundred kilometre radius, but they would never be able to afford to come and visit. He had spoken to Simon on the telephone a couple of times since everything blew up. He had not been charged with anything, but having just one foot made it difficult to travel. Still, he promised, he would come and see them in paradise some day. He missed Simon, Cal and Nigel. He liked going out for beers with the lads. He would do the same with some of the guys here when he learned to speak Mexican.

Christina let go of him and jumped off the Sea Doo. He pulled it up on to the shore and chained it to the nearest palm tree. If he didn't the local kids would probably take it for a joyride again when he was sleeping. The beach house they were renting was just yards away. They could even afford a place with air conditioning, which was great. Edo hadn't saved much from his wages and he had never seen any of the money he was promised by Cal but he was philosophical about it. He would just have to remember not to be so trusting of people in future.

He checked his Rolex. It was noon. The sun was beating down and he was already starting to sweat. "What shall we do with the rest of the day, baby?"

Christina shrugged, her slim, tanned body glowing in the sunshine in a skimpy electric blue two-piece bikini. It was a shame that there was hardly ever anyone around to admire her. She still put in a lot of hard work maintaining her figure, taking lots of long swims in the ocean as well as daily yoga sessions. She believed it was important to maintain her good looks. "I'm going to have a read for a while," she said. "The latest *Cosmo* arrived this morning. What are you going to do, my man?"

Edo had a secret thing going with a local girl, Claudia. She was nineteen and very shy but that was one of the things that attracted him to her. She was not as tall as Christina but she had bigger boobs and a rounder bottom. He thought Christina looked a bit skinny these days. He had met Claudia not long after they arrived in town. She was working in her mother and father's general store. One of the guys who played football on the beach told him the father, Miguel, stored weapons that belonged to a local drug cartel but Edo doubted that could be true. He seemed such a nice, friendly, cheerful guy when they went to buy groceries. The shop closed in the afternoons so Claudia would be knocking around with her friends somewhere. He was being careful not to get her pregnant.

"Maybe I'll ride up to town on the scooter and check if anyone is hanging out at the bar," he told Christina. "Maybe some of the kids will be up for a kick around."

"Okay," she said, expertly climbing into a hammock slung between two palm trees. "See you tonight baby. Miguel sold me a nice catfish. I'll make us some tacos for dinner."

She settled back with her magazine and waited for him to leave. Once she had heard the Vespa's engine fade in the distance, she took the single, one-way train ticket from between the pages and began gazing at it again. Surely she would find modelling work in Mexico City, where eight million people lived.

>>>

THE centre forward spent his days trying to look on the bright side. Less talented footballers had been picked for teams he should have been playing in and that had annoyed him. That was why he did what he did. He might have even stood a chance of going to Italy for the World Cup had he been playing for a Division One team instead of Belle Vue. Reds had been fun while it lasted.

Cal's solicitor had reckoned the evidence against him was flimsy at best but twelve good men and women at Minshull Street Crown Court had disagreed and found him guilty of two counts of conspiracy to corrupt.

Obviously, legal aid didn't buy the best solicitors. He was a month into a two-year stretch in Strangeways.

If you believed the press, Manchester was the music centre of the world and people were arriving from its four corners just to experience an acid house night. The Hacienda would be their number one destination but Cal knew many would be turned away and end up in Reds, which was still there, down the back alley near Kendals. Only now it was called Soviet. He knew this because Caroline had been to visit him. Billy was running the bar while Hugh handled security. O'Donnell was raking in a fortune selling shots of flavoured vodka at six for a fiver. It had been fully re-decorated and carpeted. There were podiums for girls to dance on. The bar was brand new with chrome rails around it. Cal's Russian Maple bar had been chopped up and burned in a tin barrel by the workmen doing the renovations. Soviet sounded fucking awful to Cal.

Edo and Christina had fled to Mexico after the news came out. Simon had been in touch with them but Edo was afraid to say exactly where he was hiding out. Simon had been to visit Cal in jail, in his wheelchair. He was moments from death when the ambulance arrived and was grateful Cal had stayed with him. Cal felt like shit about what happened to him. He felt he hadn't done enough to protect him. Charlotte was still on the scene, apparently they had a good thing going. His doctors reckoned they could fit him with a false foot and have him up and walking again within a couple of years. The police nagged him for ages to say who had maimed him but he wouldn't talk. It was probably wise, given O'Donnell's reputation. Cal was still a bit worried what comeback he would get for lamping him but at least he was safe in here.

Tony Butterworth was the talk of the back pages. He had started Belle Vue's last four games and scored three goals. McNeill had told a reporter he was World Cup material. The *Chronicle* had reported that United were interested. The *Granada Soccer Night* pundits were raving about him, Simon reported bitterly. Shaw was still a Belle Vue player but would be on the treatment table for a long time yet. He hadn't heard about Brennan but assumed he was still getting on everyone's tits.

Nigel got a two-stretch for conspiracy to corrupt just like Cal. He still had plenty of cash when it all blew up though. His lawyer had somehow managed to get him a bed at HMP Kirkham, an open prison near Blackpool which compared to Strangeways was like a holiday camp with a fence around it. He still had the Disley cottage and the Range Rover and Carla was waiting to continue her life with him.

Cal was an inmate of D wing. Strangeways was built in Victorian times for a thousand inmates. There were about sixteen hundred crammed in now. The observation tower might have looked impressive but the jail itself was far from it. There were no toilets in the cells. The inmates were locked up most of the day, twenty hours at a time, and when allowed out to stretch their legs they were herded to the sewers to empty buckets of their own faeces which had been festering in the corner for hours. That was four men's shite in some cases. The whole nick reeked of shit. It was disgusting. This upset people and often made them behave violently towards each other.

Cal had to count himself lucky. There were only two of them in his cell. He bunked with Rab, a Glaswegian in for robbing an off licence. Relative luxury. He even had enough space to do press-ups and sit-ups. He did five hundred of each a day. He kept his body strong in case he was attacked. There were some nasty people on D wing. Rapists, murderers and armed robbers. He'd heard other lags – one Scouser in particular – moaning to the screws that he was getting special treatment because he was a footballer, so he stayed alert. He steered clear of troublemakers. There were people inside with nothing to lose.

Even the national papers like *The Sun* and the *Daily Mirror* covered his court case. He finally knew what it was like to be famous – or infamous. There were many City fans in

Strangeways and many United. There were quite a few Scousers too, and Leeds, and some Belle Vue. They might have supported different teams but they were football fans and in their eyes Callum Murphy had given the beautiful game of football a bad name, then shat on it, and was a cunt. Cal had always prided himself on his ability to get on people's good side, but had quickly learned that most lags don't have one.

Cal just wanted to keep his head down and do his time. He had his whole life ahead of him. In the meantime, he was expecting a visitor. A journalist who wanted to write an article about how someone goes from being a promising Manchester United player to a penniless jailbird.

>>>

THE reporter signed the visitor's book at the gatehouse at Her Majesty's Prison, Strangeways, and underlined her autograph with a flourish. She had been using the signature since she was ten, having spent hours perfecting it ready for book signings when she was a famous author.

Victoria had deliberately not mentioned the drugs in her story about Cal and the decision was about to pay off. She had been commissioned by *The Face* to report his story in depth.

As with the rabbi, there was no proof it was actually cocaine, but the pictures were pretty damning. However, Cal was clearly no Mr Big and she couldn't bring herself to ruin him completely. She still had the photographs, of course. They were stashed in a shoebox in the wardrobe of the room she had slept in since she was a little girl.

She was enjoying living back at her Mum and Dad's. Now she was older they were more like friends and didn't nag her when she came and went as she pleased. She was learning to cook, too. She could now make delicious shepherd's pies, Pad Thai and Jambalaya. When she left Miles' house with the last of her things and took a deep breath, the air somehow seemed purer, more giving. It was like a weight had been lifted off her shoulders.

Paul Knight, AKA Rugby Paul, told her Miles was still living alone, miserable she had left him. Paul's opinion was that Miles needed to get off the weed, a false friend, and get his dynamism back. Victoria had learned this during pillow talk after she and Paul had slept together a month ago. She had literally bumped into him at the Press Club and one thing had led to another. She didn't know council workers were allowed in the Press Club. It wasn't as good as the sex with Cal but Paul was surprisingly gentle for a rugby player. He was a big softy and said he felt rotten for shagging his mate's ex. Victoria felt no guilt. She was finally having the range of experiences that being with Miles had denied her.

The gatehouse guard, a ginger-haired man in his mid-twenties, looked her in the eye. He looked a bit like Mark Shaw, but obviously it wasn't him. "In you go, Miss Heath," he said. It wasn't the first time she had been to the jail, but it was the first time she had been to visit Cal.

She drove the MGB slowly along the short road to the visitors' car park and pulled it into a space alongside a red Ford Escort. New Order's *Blue Monday* was playing on the stereo. It was a bright, sunny day, but there were a few grey clouds lurking over the Pennines. There was always a chance of rain in Manchester.

Victoria leaned back in the driver's seat, relaxed about the visit. She had brought him magazines: The latest issue of *Select* and that week's *NME*. She took a deep breath. She had read his letter about a hundred times. He didn't mean to neglect her feelings. It wasn't him that spiked her but it was more than his life was worth to reveal who it was. He had an amazing story to tell. Please would she come and listen? Of course she would. Although they had only met once, they had been as close as two people could get. She thought of Cal often.

She unfastened her seatbelt. As she leant forward, the sun shone in her eyes from the direction of Stretford. Suddenly a noisy siren fixed to the wall went off and the man in the gatehouse jogged towards her, shouting into his walkie talkie. As he stood there panting she wound down the window.

"Sorry, Miss Heath... but I have to advise you to leave."

"Why, what's going on?"

He shook his head, urgently looking up at the building. "Some of the inmates are kicking off. Throwing things out of the windows and stuff. Visiting time is cancelled."

Victoria looked up at the roof and saw a shirtless thuggish-looking man with his tattooed arms outstretched, taunting the guards in the yard below. It seemed she had stumbled on a story. "Looks like you've got a troublemaker on your hands," she said. "What if I want to stay and report it?"

"I'm locking the gates in two minutes, and if you haven't gone, you'll be stuck here with the rest of us for as long as it takes to sort out. I'd do one if I was you."

His walkie-talkie crackled and she heard a panicked voice shouting that they had lost the canteen. Victoria toyed with her key in the ignition, then took her hand away and picked up her new cellular phone, a heavy block of plastic the size of her hardback copy of *Pride and Prejudice*. It had a long rubber aerial sticking out of the top and the word Motorola written on the side.

"I think I'll stick around actually," she told the guard. "I've got work to do."

Philip Fielding is an author and journalist. He was born in Manchester, studied in Australia and lives in the Peak District.

Printed in Great Britain
by Amazon